SABOTAGE

BOOKS BY JODY CALKINS

THE HEXON CODE

Taken (A Short Story Prequel)

Shattered

Redeemed

Blackout

Outcast

No Way Out

Breakout

Sabotage

Outrage *

All the Strings *

Tainted

Platform 273

Bought

Charged

*Titles available soon!

SABOTAGE

JODY CALKINS

EMERY ROAD
PUBLICATIONS

SABOTAGE

Published by:
Emery Road Publications
https://emeryroad.com

ISBN: 978-1-954708-10-5

First Edition: July 2021

10 9 8 7 6 5 4 3 2 1

CHAPTER 1

WHAT IS THE MEANING of life when someone else controls you? When you're not able to make your own decisions, when someone tells you what to do and when to eat? When he rules over you because he can? Because the rules have changed?

Somedays I didn't know if I could keep going on. Somedays were harder than others. What was the point of my life when my function had been reduced to the basic things a woman could provide: her body and her cooking skills.

"Someday, I'm gettin' the hell out of this mother effin' place," Liana said, her voice low as she glanced over at me and scrubbed the cook pot. "Go somewhere I'm respected."

"What're you talking about?" a male voice asked behind us, his footsteps approaching.

I jerked my head and saw Hector walking into the kitchen.

"Respect?" he asked, spitting out the word.

Liana and I exchanged a quick glance. Her face was flushed, and she looked scared.

"We respect you," he said, his voice softening as he set his hand on her hip.

When he bowed his head to her shoulder, she sucked in a breath.

"For your services," he added.

She sighed. "That's not what I mean. No one seemed to like the stew I made yesterday."

I knew that was a lie. She hadn't been referring to her cooking skills.

"Oh." He ran his hand over her bare thigh.

Quickly, I looked away, bowing my head and clamping my eyes shut so I wouldn't have to witness the way her body responded to his touch. Not that looking away helped keep the images out of my head.

She sucked in a quicker breath and then moaned.

"Well," he said, his voice low, "it needed more salt."

"No one said anything."

I squeezed my eyes tighter at the breathless quality of her voice and tried not to imagine his fingers between her thighs.

"I could have added more."

"We all know what you're skilled in, darlin'. It's no big deal."

As he spoke, she moaned again.

When he laughed, I bit my trembling lip harder. He seemed to love to torment her.

"And what's the matter with you?"

It took me a second to realize he was talking to me. Swallowing hard, I opened my eyes and met his gaze for a brief moment before bowing my head again. "Um," I stammered. "I'm not feeling well. My stomach hurts."

That was true. My stomach had tied into a tight knot. It always did.

Hector pulled away from Liana as he said, "I'll give you something to help you relax."

I grimaced. I hadn't expected him to come up with a solution. And I didn't need anything that would make me feel numb.

While he was gone, Liana leaned closer, grasped my arm, and whispered, "Whatever he gives you, take it, but throw it back up."

I didn't think I could make myself throw up, but I nodded anyway. She was wiser and older. By a few years. More life experience in her to make more calculated decisions.

When Hector came back, he took my hand and set two pills on my palm.

I blinked at them for a few seconds. Finally, I lifted my head and looked him in the eye. "What are these?"

"Muscle relaxers," he replied.

I repeated the words, too stunned to accept them.

"Are you daft? You need something for that, too?"

Quickly, I shook my head.

"I think what she's getting at," Liana said, "is that she doesn't understand why she needs muscle relaxers for an upset stomach."

Hector turned his head and stared at her. "If that's what she means, she should speak up."

"I'm sorry," I said, my voice trembling. "Thank you."

He retrieved a glass from the cupboard over my head and then filled it with water from the faucet. Then he placed it in my hand, curling my fingers around it. "Here you go, darlin'. Drink up. Henry will be back soon."

I looked down at the two pills. I honestly didn't know if they were what he said they were. He wasn't exactly the most honest individual I had ever met. Not that that was saying much. The last time I had met anyone outside of the gang was three years ago.

"Come on now. You don't want to disappoint him again." He raised his hand and traced the dark bruise on my cheek with his fingertips.

Blinking back tears, I bit my trembling lip.

"Do you?" he whispered, leaning closer.

Quickly, I shook my head. "These will make my stomach feel better?"

"Sure."

I wasn't stupid. I knew he wasn't a doctor. Muscle relaxers would loosen the knot in my stomach, I knew that, but they'd also make me weak. But he was standing there waiting for me to take them. "Can I take one now and see if I need more?"

He sighed as he glanced at Liana. "Sure, whatever, Kallis. I'm just trying to help you."

"I know," I said quickly. "I didn't mean to upset you."

He reached out and picked up one of the pills with his thumb and forefinger. "You're such a lightweight anyway," he said with a shrug. "Two might knock you out."

Before I could talk myself out of it and before I got a slap in the face for arguing, I washed the pill down with water.

"Good girl," he said, taking the glass from my hand and setting it down on the counter behind me. "So, what's for dinner tonight?"

While he leaned over the pot and breathed in the savory steam, Liana cast me a worried look over his head. I tried to give her a weak smile.

"It smells good," he added.

Finally, she said, "It's a creamy tomato and rabbit soup. Remember the rabbits you butchered a couple months ago? I slow-cooked one today and added the shreds to the soup."

He picked up the spoon, dipped it into the liquid, and then tasted it. Then he hummed. "I guess you *can* cook."

Liana closed her eyes like she was channeling a silent rage.

After he set the glass lid back on the cook pot, he hooked an arm around her waist and placed his other hand at the small of my back and guided us out of the kitchen and down the hallway toward the bedrooms.

At the door to Henry's room, he said, "Wait here."

There wasn't any point to nodding agreement. We did this every day. And for some reason, he felt the need to tell me what to do. I stepped inside and sat down on the neatly made bed, the bed I had made earlier after Henry had left for work.

A few minutes later, I finally remembered what Liana had said about throwing up the pills. Quickly, I rose to my feet to run to the bathroom, but then I heard footsteps from down the hall.

My pulse quickened as I sat back down. I never knew what kind of mood Henry would be in whenever he got back. But this time, when he walked in, he actually smiled at me. Which was rare.

I tried to smile back. "Hi," I said, rising to my feet and meeting him at the dresser. I reached out to help him undress, but he lifted me and set me on the top of the dresser instead. I bit my lip and clasped my trembling hands in my lap as I watched him remove his T-shirt. His muscles flexed and his skin glistened with sweat, making my throat go dry.

If it wasn't for his usually abrasive personality, and the way he treated me, I might have actually wanted him. He was physically attractive. Capable. Strong. Smart.

He eyed me as he unbuttoned his jeans. "You look tired." His first words.

"I do?" I asked, starting to panic.

His lips jutted out a little as he nodded slightly, his eyes raking over me.

"Um." I cleared my throat. "I, um. My stomach hurt. So, Hector gave me something for it. A muscle relaxer, he said."

His eyebrows lifted.

My panic intensified and I tried to smooth it over. "I only took one."

"Feel better?"

Quickly, I nodded. That wasn't a lie. The knot in my stomach *had* loosened.

"From now on, don't listen to Hector. And don't ever take what he gives you."

I swallowed hard as I searched his eyes. "Why?" I whispered.

"He's not trying to help you. I'm actually surprised he didn't give you Rohypnol."

I didn't know what that was, but judging by Henry's reaction, it must have been bad. "I was afraid," I said, looking away and then glancing down at my hands, "of what he would do if I refused."

He huffed. "What have I told you about our arrangement?" he asked. "*I* tell you what you can do."

CHAPTER 2

WHEN A TEAR SLIPPED down my face, I quickly brushed it away but then cried out when the pads of my fingers rubbed over the bruise. The bruise Henry had given me. And then more tears flooded my eyes.

"Hmm?"

I sniffled. "I'm afraid of you, and he said—"

"Am I as unkind as your previous owners?"

I let out a helpless breath. He always brought that up to compare himself to all of the men before him.

"Am I?" he asked again.

"No," I croaked, shaking my head.

He hummed. "I didn't think so."

That didn't change the fact that he scared me, but he seemed to think it mattered.

"I've kept you for over a year. Have you realized that?"

More tears slipped down my face. Sniffling, I tried to wipe my face dry. "I didn't realize it's been that long."

He hooked a finger under my chin and tilted my head back. "I like you."

That wasn't enough for him to stop cutting me down whenever it suited him.

"I don't mind that you'll never bear a child."

A small sob escaped my trembling lips as my face flushed.

He searched my eyes. I knew he was expecting me to thank him.

I grasped his wrist and closed my eyes as I tilted my head. I sniffled again and wet my bottom lip with the tip of my tongue. "I'm sorry. I appreciate all that you do for me."

"You do?"

Opening my eyes, I nodded. "Thank you."

"You're welcome." He moved his hand to the side of my neck and rubbed his thumb firmly over my throat.

Warmth flooded inside my stomach.

Then he lifted me off the dresser and set me back on my feet. "Go start my shower. I'll be there in a minute."

With a quick nod, I stumbled into the bathroom. The cool tile floor did little to wake me up. I braced a hand on the counter as I made my way to the shower stall. With a trembling hand, I turned the knobs and then turned my palm up to the water, waiting for it to heat up. I let my hand fall to my side as I rested my head against the wall and then closed my eyes.

When a hand slid across my hip, I gasped, startled.

"Were you thinking of me today?" Henry whispered against my ear.

I swallowed hard. "I always do." That was true, but never in a good way unless I was trying to justify his behavior. Sometimes I did, trying to find hope that maybe someday he would see me the way I had read that God sees me.

"This was all I could think about," he said, gliding his hand up the front of my thigh underneath the hem of my nightgown.

When his lips grazed my earlobe, I clamped my eyes shut.

"I should take you with me tomorrow. That way I don't have to wait. I can do this whenever I want."

I couldn't imagine spending all day with him while he worked. What on earth would I be doing? Sitting around while he did who knew what. "What would I be doing?"

"Looking pretty," he said, nudging me into the shower stall and under the shower head. "It's what you do best."

I moved my head out from under the hot stream as I blew out a slow breath, sputtering water. More at his comment than the hot water plastering my long hair to my head and the nightgown to my skin.

"I don't know, Kallis. Use your imagination. If you have one."

"I have one," I said, my voice so quiet I could barely hear it. I wiped the water from my eyes.

"What was that?" he asked.

Keeping my eyes downcast, I turned my head to the side. "I have an imagination."

He hummed. "Maybe you could use it more. Like right now."

"What?" I whispered, lifting my chin and catching his eye.

He huffed. "Sometimes you are so naïve. That alone is almost enough to get me hard."

I blinked back tears as I let my gaze drift from his.

"Ah, fuck," he said, sounding annoyed. "What did I tell you about crying?"

"I'm sorry," I croaked, covering my face with a hand.

He turned me around and then pressed my back to the cold shower tiles.

I sucked in a breath.

He bent down and then lifted me, forcing me to straddle his hips. He thrust himself inside me, making me cry out. With one hand supporting my weight and the other circling my neck, he thrust his hips hard against me.

I gripped his arm as I searched his eyes. There wasn't any point to fighting him. He had never squeezed hard enough to make me pass out. If there was any area with which I could trust him, it was in that. He was rough, as usual. Rougher than the others had ever been.

When he was done, he pressed his forehead to mine, his heavy breath blowing in my face. His hand around my throat loosened and his thumb started to make firm swirls on my neck. Despite myself, my muscles clenched and pulsed, making me moan.

He hummed. "I know you like it rough," he whispered, lowering his hand and splaying it over my heaving chest, warming it. "You always do, don't you?"

He always said it like it was a bad thing. Like I shouldn't find pleasure in it. I didn't want to. I wanted him to be gentle, to show that he actually loved me or at least cared about me, but he never did. I guessed the fact that he hadn't sold me to someone else was supposed to be enough.

"You can't deny it, can you?"

"No," I said quietly, knowing no other response would satisfy him.

"*Now* do you feel like crying?"

I shook my head. That was another lie. But it didn't matter anyway. He wouldn't change his behavior and give me what I wanted. Instead, he would do everything in his power to make sure I didn't get it.

"Good." He set my feet back on the floor. Then he handed me the bath sponge.

Keeping my eyes downcast, I took the sponge and then squeezed out some body wash from the soap bottle. When he turned his back to me, I pressed the sponge to his shoulder and massaged it over his bare skin.

We did this every day. Liana and I cooked their meals, cleaned the apartment, offered our bodies to them, bathed them, and shared their beds. It could have been worse. Henry could have offered me to other men. That's what Carl had done.

I had never understood why he did that. Men weren't supposed to behave that way. But ever since the people had overthrown the Detroit city government, the rules had changed. The nine gangs ruled the city now. And each gang controlled its own area of the city. Detroit had fallen, and this was a woman's fate now. At least in the Creekside district. I had no idea what it was like in the other districts.

When I was done lathering Henry with the soap, he rinsed off and then turned to me. "Make yourself some tea," he said. "I want you wide awake tonight."

Quickly, I nodded.

He regarded me a moment longer and then stepped out of the shower and dried off with a towel.

When he walked naked out of the bathroom, I lowered myself to the bench seat, wrapping my arms around my chest as I leaned my head against the tile wall. I stifled a sob with my hand and then clamped my mouth shut. If he heard me, he'd be back and who knew what he would do.

After a moment, after my breathing had calmed, I blew out a slow breath. Then I pried off the soaked nightgown and showered, washing away the tears.

If only I could wash away my shitty life, too.

CHAPTER 3

AFTER I DRESSED in a clean nightgown and towel-dried my hair, I padded out to the kitchen to make the tea.

Liana was standing barefoot at the stove, stirring the soup. Her hair was damp, and she was wearing a long sweater over a clean nightgown. When I approached, she gave me a weak smile.

"Do we have any tea?" I asked, opening the cupboard door where we usually stocked teas and other packaged beverages.

"What kind?" she asked, her voice quiet.

"Henry wants me wide awake."

She stared at me for a moment and then she shook her head like she was clearing away her thoughts. Clearing her throat, she reached up and grabbed a box of tea from the cupboard. "Try this one. It's peppermint."

"Thanks," I said.

"Everything okay?" she whispered.

I nodded and then filled the kettle with water from the faucet.

"Can you get me the cayenne pepper?"

I pulled out the drawer filled with the herbs and spices and then handed her the jar. Then I watched her sprinkle it into the cook pot.

Some of the women in our district raised rabbits for slaughter and sold them live at our market. I had never been outside. Not since the gangs took over the city and I was taken from my family by one of the leaders when I was sixteen. I stuck my head out the window whenever I got the chance to breathe in the fresh air, but as for walking outside on the streets below, it had been years.

"Will you take out the bowls?"

I jerked my head and saw Liana glancing my way. With a nod, I retrieved four bowls and spoons from the cupboard and then took them to the dining table. By the time I was done setting the four places, the kettle was whistling.

Liana turned off the burner and moved the kettle to a hot pad on the counter. She opened the box of tea packets and then dropped a packet into a mug and poured the hot water over it.

"Thanks," I said, coming up beside her and staring down into the peppermint-scented steam.

"Will you go tell them dinner is ready?" She carried the pot of soup to the table and began ladling it out into the bowls.

I wandered down the hallway and found Henry and Hector talking in the far room, the one they always kept padlocked. I wasn't allowed inside. I wasn't even allowed to peer inside it. Keeping my head down, I knocked lightly on the door.

When Henry appeared at the door, I cleared my throat and said, "Liana asked me to tell you dinner is ready."

"Give us a minute," he replied.

I nodded and backed away. When I returned to the kitchen, Liana had finished dishing the bowls. She stood at the sink, washing the cook pot with dish soap. When she set it aside, I rinsed it under hot water and laid it on a towel to dry.

"What's taking them so long?" she asked.

I shrugged. "Henry said a minute."

"The food is going to get cold."

I heard her let out an irritated sigh as I took out the tray of dinner rolls that I had baked earlier from the refrigerator. I set them inside the oven to warm.

When I leaned back against the counter to wait, she set her hand on my shoulder and leaned in close. "Are you okay?" she whispered.

My throat tightened. I shrugged my shoulder. I really didn't know what to say. I felt empty and I didn't think that would ever change. My life didn't have meaning beyond answering to someone else.

She gave me a comforting smile and then pulled me into her arms. "Someday, we're going to get free."

I nodded against her shoulder.

Finally, we heard footsteps approaching. Quickly, we broke apart and busied ourselves with cleaning the counters.

The men appeared and headed to the table. If they glanced our way, I didn't notice. I was too focused on scrubbing a section of counter. But when I heard the scrape of a chair leg, I looked up and caught Henry eyeing me.

"Get in here," he said.

I dropped the cloth in the sink and then took my place beside him at the table. I folded my hands in my lap and stared down at my bowl.

Hector made a loud slurping sound from across the table.

I silently prayed the food was still hot. They had taken much longer than a minute.

"The food is cold," Hector said, looking up at Liana.

"I'm sorry," she replied, standing up and reaching for his bowl. "I can reheat it."

Before she could touch the bowl, he grasped her wrist, making her cry out like she was in pain.

"You do that," he said.

Her throat bobbed as she shifted her gaze across the table. "Henry, do you want your soup reheated?"

"It's fine," Henry said gruffly.

I bowed my head, trying to make myself invisible.

"Please, Hector," she said, her voice trembling. "You're hurting my wrist."

"This is nothing compared to what I'd like to do to you."

"I'm sorry."

"Hector, that's enough," Henry said, his voice firm.

Hector cocked his head as he turned his attention to Henry. "Just giving her the treatment she deserves."

I clamped my eyes shut. How could he treat her that way? What made him so much better that he could treat her like she was so far beneath him? It wasn't fair.

"Come on. Let her go."

I heard the scrape of the bottom of the bowl on the tabletop. And then a hand grasped my upper arm. Gasping, I opened my eyes and stared at Henry.

"Go help her," he said.

Looking away, I nodded and then rose to my feet. I hadn't tasted the soup, but since Hector had said it was cold, it was probably at least lukewarm. He tended to be overly dramatic. When I leaned closer and cupped Henry's bowl in my hands, I could feel Hector's eyes on me, like he was waiting for something bad to happen. With a pause, I glanced at Henry and asked, "Can I take it?"

Henry leaned back in his chair and folded his arms over his chest as he said, "Fine."

I picked up his bowl and then carried it into the kitchen, careful not to slosh the liquid over the rim. I set it on the baking sheet that Liana had placed in the oven along with Hector's bowl.

I could tell she was struggling to keep calm, and I knew she wanted to fight back.

But there was no winning.

If she managed to get outside the apartment, one of the other men would stop her. And that would be worse. I had seen it happen when I was with Kent, one of the other gang members. It was never a good thing to step foot outside the apartment, unless you had an escort.

"You should take them your rolls," Liana said, gesturing toward the baking sheet of bread sitting on the glass top of the oven. "They're warm."

I nodded and then took the warmed dinner rolls to the table. As I set down the baking sheet between the men, I said, "I made bread today."

I was about to head back into the kitchen when Henry grabbed my arm and pulled me down onto his lap. He wrapped his arm around my waist, trapping me against him, with my back to his chest. His hand cupped my cheek and then made a slow progression down my neck and between my breasts while Hector watched.

Bowing my head, I tried to ignore his stare. He seemed to be enjoying the show as he chewed the bread with an open mouth.

When Henry trailed his hand up my leg and settled it at the apex of my thighs, I gasped. I couldn't do anything. I couldn't push his hand away. If I struggled, he'd make me regret it. And if I cried, he'd make me regret that, too. I was at his mercy. As Liana was at Hector's.

"Tell Hector how much you enjoy this," Henry whispered in my ear, his warm breath sending shivers down my spine as his fingertips grazing sensitive flesh made me suck in a quiet breath.

"She doesn't have to say a word," Hector replied with a laugh. "I can tell by her face."

I blinked back tears as I bit down hard on my trembling lip. I wanted to push his hand away. I wanted to get off his lap.

"Well?" Henry asked, his lips brushing gently over my earlobe.

"Henry, please," I pleaded. I was afraid of what he would do to me for pleading with him to stop, but I hoped he would finally show mercy. Just this once.

"All right," Liana said, walking back into the dining room.

Henry removed his hand and then gripped my hips and lifted me off his lap, shoving me toward my chair.

I stumbled, catching myself against the edge of the table. But he didn't seem to care. I sat down in my chair beside his before my trembling legs gave out on me.

Liana glanced my way as she set Hector's bowl in front of him. "Be careful. The bowls are hot."

He picked up his spoon and stirred the soup as steam rose from the bowl. Before he had a chance to reply—although it was unlikely that he would—she turned back to the kitchen and retrieved Henry's bowl.

"Thank you, Liana. You didn't have to do that," Henry said when she set his bowl in front of him.

"You're welcome."

To an untrained ear, his tone would have sounded genuine, but I knew he was just doing it to irritate Hector. And I was pretty sure she knew it, too. She was better at pretending than I was. And she apologized less.

Liana and I sat there in silence, waiting for them to give us permission to eat. I sipped my tea, careful not to make the slightest slurping sound.

Finally as Henry rose from his chair, he glanced my way and said, "Eat."

"Thank you," I said quietly, picking up my spoon. My food was almost always cold by the time I got to eat it. He took the joy out of eating, like a soul-sucking evil force. He *was* an evil force. Or at least he was controlled by one. Why else would he treat me like I was so far beneath him?

Back before the gangs overthrew the government, people still believed women were valuable members of society. And they held important roles. My mother was a researcher at the lab. And my older sister had been studying to be a doctor.

I didn't know if I would ever be able to work toward a career. If I escaped, maybe I would have a chance.

But I had no idea how I would accomplish that. There was always someone hanging out in one of the other apartments or in the hallway. They wouldn't let me leave.

And going through the window was out of the question since we were on the third floor. Too high to jump and still survive. And even if I did actually survive the fall, I'd no doubt break a bone. Or several. And then what would happen to me? Probably something far worse.

CHAPTER 4

WHILE LIANA AND I ate our cold dinner, the guys left the apartment without saying where they were going or what they were doing. It didn't matter. And I never bothered to ask.

Liana was quiet, and I didn't feel like talking either.

Finally, she said, "We should do something. Who knows when they'll be back."

I nodded, but I had no idea what we would do.

"I could do your Tarot reading. We haven't done that in a while. I need the practice."

I almost cringed at the idea. I had to admit it was fun, so long as it didn't involve questions about my past. I dreamed about my future often, that someday things would be different, that I would be able to choose for myself what my future held. And my Tarot readings had all been encouraging. It was just I had come to realize that nothing good would ever come out of them.

But she seemed so excited, I couldn't say no.

While I rinsed our bowls in the sink and set them in the dishwasher, she hurried off to her room to retrieve the deck of cards. Cards she had stashed in her drawer so she could keep them from Hector.

When she walked back into the main living area, she asked, "Do you have a specific question you want an answer to?"

I shook my head. What on earth would I want to ask anyway? When I was going to be free? When the country government was going to swoop back in, wipe out the gangs, and reclaim the city? Those were all questions I was curious about, but what was the point now?

She shrugged on her way to the living room. "We'll ask for general guidance then. What message the cards have for you tonight."

I joined her on the couch and watched as she shuffled the cards.

"Cut the deck," she said, setting the stack of cards down.

After I picked up about a quarter of the cards and set them beside the main stack, she combined the two stacks and fanned them out on the couch. Then she moved her hand slowly over the cards.

The first time we had done this, she explained that when she moved her hand over the cards, she would feel a sensation in her finger, signaling for her to pull whichever card her finger had hovered over. I didn't know how that was possible. But she knew more than I did. I didn't question it.

What was odd though was that the cards always seemed so relevant to my life. Which was one of the reasons I hadn't wanted a Tarot reading in the first place.

She hummed as she finished laying out the cards.

I held my breath and waited for her to process the layout and give me my reading.

She frowned, but when she shook her head slightly, her expression brightened like she had chased away bad thoughts.

"It's bad, isn't it?" I asked, afraid of her answer.

"Not exactly. Maybe just a little strange."

"Oh."

"Cards can be that way," she said with a shrug. "Let's see what the booklet says."

As she began to read the meaning of each card, I couldn't help seeing their relevance and how they fit into my life. A major change in my past. A loss of trust in my surroundings. What other things about my life would the cards reveal? Did I really want to know?

When she started to explain what the King of Swords meant, I closed my eyes. The protective nature of this entity in my future meant my life would have to change. I didn't see how that was possible. The gangs ruled the city now. How was my life going to change? Who was going to swoop in and change my life forever? It wasn't possible. It would never work.

Liana seemed as perplexed as I felt. "But things are going to change for you," she said, sounding encouraging. "I just know it."

I stared at the cards, but I wasn't really seeing them for their true meanings. My current life clouded what the spread was supposed to represent.

"I know it doesn't make sense," she said. "But maybe someday it will."

Slowly, I nodded. Maybe if I believed it, too, it would be true. It *could* be true.

"It's so strange to me," she said, sounding thoughtful. "I can't picture Henry in the way he is."

I swallowed hard. "What do you mean?"

She turned her head to the side as she furrowed her brows and closed her eyes.

I held my breath as I waited it out.

Finally, she shook her head slightly. "I don't know, but I don't sense that he is as what he seems."

The thought sickened me. How could Henry not be as he seemed? How could he do the things he did without seeming to be the person he was?

"I'm sorry," she said, giving me an apologetic look. "I can't explain it."

"What if it's someone else?" I asked. Because surely the cards must have meant someone else. Anyone else.

She shrugged. "It's possible."

"But things are going to change?" I asked, sort of hesitantly.

She smiled as she reached out and grasped my hand. "I just know it will. For you."

The thought did bring a small smile to my face. Someday, things would change. Somehow, some way, I had a light at the end of my long, dark tunnel. Just thinking about the possibilities in my future brought tears to my eyes. I wouldn't have to answer to someone else. I could make my own decisions. Do the things I wanted.

I was so lost in my thoughts I didn't notice the door opening. But suddenly Hector appeared in the doorway. I stared wide-eyed as he stormed across the floor and grabbed Liana by the arm, yanking her off the couch and to her feet.

"You and your filthy cards," he seethed.

"Hector, please," she pleaded, grasping his arm. "We were just having fun."

"Fun?" he asked, his eyebrows lifting. "Since when is it okay for you to have fun?"

"I'm sorry," she said, sounding desperate.

As I began sweeping the cards from the spread into a pile, Henry strode across the living room rug and grasped my wrist, stopping me. With his warm fingers pressed firmly against my veins and pinching my skin, I could feel the thump of my pulse, of my racing heartbeat. I thought I could even hear it.

He reached out his other hand and slid a card from underneath the others.

When I saw the card was the King of Swords, I closed my eyes and silently prayed he wouldn't ask about it. The card reflected so much I didn't want to think about.

"What does this card mean?"

Quickly, I shook my head. "It's nothing."

"Kallis."

My whole body trembled, and my face flushed with heat as fresh tears welled up in my eyes. I didn't know what to say. But even if I could figure it out, I wouldn't be able to bring myself to say the words.

He sighed as he released my wrist. And then the couch cushion shifted.

Sniffling, I wiped at my eyes. I bit my lip and tried to focus on steadying my breathing. I thought I heard the riffling of paper. When I opened my eyes, I saw him fanning the pages of the little booklet that explained the interpretation of each card.

His gaze shifted toward the card he had picked up and then he turned back to the booklet. Finally, he stopped, like he was reading the description.

Looking away, I held my breath and waited for him to speak. When he sighed heavily, sounding annoyed or upset, I flinched. I could feel his gaze on me. He was probably trying to figure out what it all meant.

Finally, he set the card and booklet down. "Put these away. It's time for bed."

Swallowing hard and keeping my eyes downcast, I nodded. With trembling hands, I gathered up the cards and shoved them back inside their box.

While he locked the apartment door, I hurried out of the living room and down the hall. I couldn't take the cards back to Liana—Hector had already closed their bedroom door and I could hear her crying through the thin walls. So, I opened my dresser drawer. As I was shoving the box in under my socks, Henry walked in, closing the door behind him.

The way he was watching me, it made me feel like he was catching me doing something wrong. He stepped closer and pushed the drawer closed with one hand as he reached out and brushed my sweater off my shoulder. The strap of my nightgown went with it, drawing the silky fabric down and exposing the swell of my breast.

I sucked in a breath as he stepped closer. He loomed over me. I wanted to take a step back—he intimidated me—but I didn't dare move. The one and only time I had backed away from him, he had reached out, his fingers clamping tightly around my arm. His words still brought chills. In a tone so low, he had said, "Don't ever do that again."

Staring up at him, I stood still. My pulse thumped gently against the side of my neck.

When he lifted his other hand and shoved my sweater over my right shoulder, the strap slipped down, taking the top of the gown with it. His palm glided over my shoulder and then his fingers curled around my arm.

With a small gasp, I bowed my head and pulled up the fabric, covering my bared breasts.

He let out a short hum. "You have nothing to hide."

Keeping my head down, I nodded. "I'm sorry."

"What for?"

"What?" I asked, sounding breathless. I glanced up at him only for a second; his intense stare unsettled me.

"You say you're sorry all the time. Do you honestly think you have something to apologize for?"

I hugged my arms tighter to my chest.

"Well?"

"Don't I?"

"So, you think you do?"

What did he want me to say? I couldn't figure out what he wanted.

With a sigh, he released my arm. "Get ready for bed."

My face flushed with heat. Quickly, I bowed my head and stepped away. Pulling the sweater back up my shoulders and wrapping it tightly around my chest, I hurried to the bathroom to floss and brush my teeth.

I tried not to think about what he had said. Or about the card that had suggested I had a protective entity in my current life. How could that be true? How could Henry count as that? The cards had been wrong. Or maybe Liana had interpreted them incorrectly.

When I came out, after I was done, I found him standing near the bathroom door. Startled, I sucked in a short breath as I paused.

He eyed me a moment, his gaze boring into mine. Had he heard me sniffling in the bathroom? Had he noticed my red eyes? Would he say something? Anything?

But when I blinked, he looked away, turning toward the door.

I folded my arms over my chest, cupping my elbows with my palms, as I watched him disappear inside the bathroom. I wanted to ask him how he thought I couldn't be sorry. I was sorry for everything. Or so it seemed.

I draped my sweater over the foot of the bed and then crawled under the covers and curled onto my side as I pulled the covers partway over my head. Maybe I could pretend to be asleep when he crawled in beside me.

He seemed to take forever in the bathroom. I could never fall asleep without him in the bed with me. Except in the mornings after he had left for work.

But when I turned my head and peered over the edge of the comforter, he was already turning off the bathroom light and walking through the doorway. He looked in my direction as I turned my head to press my face into the pillow.

My heart pounded. It was like I could feel him getting closer. The bedside lamp clicked off and then the mattress shifted with his weight. I tried to scoot closer to the edge of the bed without him noticing, but he hooked his arm around my waist and pulled me against him to the middle of the mattress.

He sighed, his warm breath blowing through my hair and against my scalp.

I forced my body to relax against his chest. I expected him to use me again—why else had he wanted me wide awake?—but he fell asleep within minutes.

I lay there listening to his steady breathing. How could he be a jerk one minute and then cuddle up with me the next like nothing had happened? Did he not realize all that he did to me? Was this how he normally was, even outside of our relationship—whatever this was? Or was it part of some plan?

Exhausted from an endless stream of thoughts, I finally fell asleep.

CHAPTER 5

IN THE MORNING, I was awakened to Henry throwing off the covers. The chilled air swept over me, making goosebumps rise on my bare flesh. I groaned as I blinked against the faint light coming in through the window behind him.

"Get up. You're coming with me today." He grasped my ankle with his warm hand and started to pull me toward the edge of the bed and away from the warm section of bedsheets.

"What?" I asked, confused and groggy from sleep. "Why?"

His hands glided over my legs and hips and he pulled me closer, not seeming to care that my nightgown was gathering up around my waist. But I was kidding myself if I thought any semblance of modesty remained. That had all changed three years ago. At least in the last year, Henry was the only one who had seen me naked. That was a small comfort.

"Henry," I said, my voice sounding more desperate than I had intended. I scrunched up my face, worried what he would do to me for complaining.

"You're such a whiner in the mornings. Did you know that? I see now I should have made sure you were out of bed every morning before I left for work." He sounded serious, but he seemed to be enjoying himself. With a slight smirk, he grabbed my arm and pulled me up and off the bed.

The sudden movements sent my head whirling, making me groan. Bracing myself with my hands on his chest, I tilted my head back and squinted up at him as I tried to nod.

His free hand settled at my back and lingered as his dark eyes searched mine. I thought he would push me back onto the bed—it looked like he wanted to—but he nudged me toward the dresser instead. "Get dressed."

Clearly, he intended to ignore my questions.

I forced my legs to carry me across the room. When I heard the sounds of rustling fabric, I looked over my shoulder and saw Henry making the bed. I stopped and watched him, puzzled by his behavior.

His gaze lifted to mine and he gave me a questioning look.

Bowing my head, I turned back to the dresser. Since he was taking me outside in the cold, I wasn't sure if he meant in a clean nightgown like I always wore per his directive or an actual outfit like jeans and a sweater. It had been so long since I had worn much more than sheer silk.

As I pulled open the top drawer, he came up behind me and pulled out another silk gown. "Wear this."

Casting him a quick glance, I took it from him.

His fingers rubbed over my thighs and then he was lifting my nightgown. I raised my arms over my head, letting him remove the silk. He dropped it to the floor at our feet as his gaze raked over me. When I bowed my head, my long hair slipped around my shoulder.

He reached out and grasped my chin with his thumb and forefinger and forced my head back so I could look at him again.

I held my breath as I blinked at him.

"Get ready," he said, his voice hoarse, as he lowered his hand. "We're leaving in five minutes."

With a slight nod, I looked away and then stepped back. I fumbled with the clean gown and slipped it over my head. As I smoothed it down with my hands, I walked to the bathroom. I glanced at myself in the mirror for the briefest of seconds and then picked up my brush to run it through my hair.

"Put it up," Henry called after me.

Glancing over my shoulder, I tried to give him a small smile as I nodded slightly. It seemed I could never make a choice on my own. He was always telling me what to wear and how to style my hair. When to eat. What to do.

After I was done in the bathroom, with my hair bound in a hair-tie high at the back of my head, the way he liked it, I headed for the dresser again to retrieve my socks and knee-high boots.

"Leave the shoes," he said, reaching for me. He grasped my wrist and tugged me against him. He wrapped his arm around my waist. His hold was so tight I was afraid I wouldn't be able to breathe. "I want you barefoot."

I closed my eyes. "Henry, there's snow on the ground." I tried not to sound too argumentative, but I definitely sounded desperate again.

"You're arguing with me?"

"Please." It should have maddened me that I had to plead with him to wear shoes in the middle of September. But it just highlighted how utterly helpless I was. Answering to someone else who enjoyed ruling over me.

"When was the last time you looked out the window?"

I took a moment to think about it, but I honestly couldn't think of when. Finally, I just shrugged.

He hooked a finger under my chin and tilted my head back.

Taking that as my cue, I blinked my eyes open and stared up at him.

He was frowning, the furrow between his brows deep. "The snow melted two days ago."

"Oh," I said, turning my head away. I hadn't expected that. There hadn't been anything to look at, not through the window, and it just served as a reminder that another year had slipped by.

"I need to take you out more. You're wasting away in here. Doing God knows what all day."

That was odd, considering the cameras he had installed in the apartment. Did he not use them to keep tabs on me while he was away? I had always thought that was his intention.

But even if the snow had melted, it was still cold outside. Too cold for bare feet. "Shoes?" I asked, my voice weak.

He sighed. "Fine. You can put them on when we get downstairs."

"Okay," I said. That was better than nothing. "Can I wear a sweater?"

"You can wear my work shirt when I get too hot."

I tried not to cringe. I had to shiver to death for hours before he finally let me wear his sweaty work shirt? "Henry, please," I said.

He sighed again as he released his hold on me. "Fine. If you must."

I tried to ignore his disappointed tone. He had a way of making me feel guilty about everything. I pulled open the drawer again and took out a pair of high socks and my thickest long sweater. While he stuffed my socks and boots into his bag, I put on the sweater and then wrapped the edges tight and hugged my arms to my chest.

When he looked up at me, he sighed once more and reached out, grasped my wrists, and pulled my arms down. Then he opened the sweater and ran his hands down my sides. "Leave it open. I want to show you off today."

I blinked at him, not sure how to respond. Who was he trying to impress? I had already been owned by five other guys before he "came to my rescue." Those were his words, not mine. And it's not like my body had changed. I looked the same at nineteen as I had at sixteen. And I didn't think my confidence level had improved. I was still the same little girl as I had been. But maybe a bit more cynical. About life and men.

I kept expecting him to make some snide comment about me and my past, but then his fingers were circling my wrist and he was pulling me out the door.

Liana looked my way, clearly taking in my attire, and then gave me a sad smile.

I mouthed 'bye' to her and padded after Henry into the main hallway of the building. There were several guys loitering in the hallway, two of them my previous owners.

"Damn," Carl said, walking toward us.

I tried to stay behind Henry, but Carl kept walking, sidestepping him and wrapping his arm around my waist. I didn't really expect Henry to step in. I mean, why would he? When he released my wrist, Carl pulled me against his chest.

"I forgot how hot and little you are." He turned to Henry and asked, "She worth the price you paid?"

"Worth enough."

Carl pursed his lips, looking thoughtful. "When you tire of her, I'll buy her back. Still got my cut from your purchase last year."

"I'll remember that," Henry said, stuffing his hands in his pockets.

The thought of going back to Carl scared me. I hated him the most.

He turned back to me and studied my face.

I held my breath as I stared up at him, my heart racing inside my chest.

Brushing the pad of his thumb gently over my cheek, he glanced at Henry and said, "Nice work. I bet she deserved it."

My throat tightened as my face grew hot.

"She did." His flat tone and lack of explanation were a small blessing. He clearly didn't intend to draw out the joke Carl was wanting.

Carl chuckled. "Good." He released me, giving me a little push.

I stumbled and fell to my hands and knees on the grungy carpet.

"Get up," Henry ordered. He made no attempt to help.

Slowly, I got to my feet as I ignored everyone's jokes and laughter about me being on my knees. I steadied myself with a hand on the wall. And then I hugged my arms to my chest and started to walk toward the stairwell.

As we walked down the stairs to the main level, Henry glanced at me. "Feeling grateful yet?"

"What?" I asked out of breath as I turned to look at him. Did he really just say what I thought he said?

"Maybe I should sell you to him," he said with a shrug. "I should have asked him how much he was willing to pay."

I hugged my arms tighter to my chest as I hung my head. How could he be so cruel? What had I done to him, or anyone for that matter, to deserve the awful treatment I received? Women were supposed to be protected, not exploited.

"Oh, lighten up. You think I'd actually sell you back to *that* asshole?"

I lifted my head as a tear slipped down my cheek. "Wouldn't you?"

"Nah, I'm not that desperate for the money. Not yet anyway."

My chin quivered and more tears slipped out when I closed my eyes. I gripped the handrail tighter in case my weak legs gave out from underneath me and sent me tumbling down the concrete staircase. It was hard pretending to be someone else, the person I thought I deserved to be. They kept tearing me down, stripping me of my self-worth. And I didn't understand why.

"Come on," Henry said, grabbing me by the arm and pulling me down the rest of the stairs. "I want to get started with work."

When we got outside, after he let me put on my socks and boots, I shielded my eyes against the bright sunlight. He had been right. All of the snow I had seen from the window the other day had melted. The parking lot and streets weren't even wet.

With his hand gripping my arm, he led me to the driver's side of a silver truck. Finally, he let go of me and then leaned in and lifted the back of the middle seat which served as the center console.

I looked around the parking lot and watched other guys pile into trucks and drive away. I wondered where they were all going.

"Did you hear me?"

"What?" I asked, my voice quiet as I turned back to blink up at him. I hadn't heard him say anything.

"I said, you need to sit in the middle. Brad is riding with us."

"Oh." I had no idea who Brad was.

"You need to pay attention."

I bit my trembling lip and blinked back tears as I nodded.

"Oh, for God's sake. What is wrong with you? Is it that time of the month again?"

"I'm sorry," I said, my voice cracking. I wiped away the tears that had streaked down my face.

He let out an irritated sigh and then grabbed me and hoisted me up onto the seat.

I nearly toppled over before I caught myself with my hands on the grimy fabric. I tried not to cringe as I moved over to the middle and straightened my gown and sweater. Neither were long enough to cover the backs of my legs and protect them from the grime-coated seat.

When the passenger door flung open, I scooted back toward the driver's side. At least as far as I could go, bumping into Henry's arm.

"Company, I see," a guy said with mild interest as he hauled himself into the passenger side next to me. "She'll be a welcome break."

Henry gave him a slight nod.

"For all of us?"

"No, you asshole," Henry replied, sounding irritated. "For me."

"Well, maybe we can watch then."

I stifled a helpless whimper. My eyes felt strained and my brows furrowed. I could feel Henry's gaze on me.

"Yeah, maybe."

I closed my eyes and held my breath, trying to keep myself from crying.

The seat shifted with Henry's weight, but I didn't bother to look up. But then his hand squeezed my arm. Startled, I opened my eyes and stared up at his face. His hardened expression didn't soften. It never did. Even when there were tears in my eyes.

Keeping his voice low, he said, "Pay attention."

Brad burst out laughing. "To what? You think she's going to start driving us around now?"

Henry laughed, too. His hand moved from my arm to my thigh. As he inched his fingers up my inner thigh, he said, "No. I want to hear her moan when I do *this*."

A short sob escaped my lips, causing them both to laugh again.

"That's good enough," Henry said.

My chin quivered and a tear slipped down my cheek. When he removed his hand from my thigh, I spread the gown back over my lap as I stared at the dash.

He grabbed the key from above his visor and then slid it into a slot behind the steering wheel. Glancing my way, he turned the key.

When the engine roared and the truck started to crawl forward, I let my gaze drift. I didn't know why he wanted me to pay attention. Pay attention to what? He'd never let me out of the apartment by myself. If I was able to go outside, he'd be with me. He didn't need me to take over for him. He was perfectly capable of driving himself.

Not that he wasn't also perfectly capable of lathering himself with soap or cooking his own meals. I guessed he figured he could leave the menial jobs to me.

After he drove up an on-ramp and then headed west on the main road, he glanced over at me and set his hand on the top of my thigh again.

I held my breath, expecting him to move his fingers higher up my leg and underneath my gown, but he didn't. As quietly as I could, I let out the breath and tried to relax.

On the outskirts of town, where the trees had started to become thicker, he turned off the highway and headed south. A few minutes later, we passed a dilapidated city sign that read 'Hopewell.'

When I turned my head and looked at him, he glanced my way and hummed, like he was questioning me.

"You work out here?" I asked.

"Every day."

"Doing what?"

"You'll see."

CHAPTER 6

WHEN HENRY PULLED UP alongside a single-story building with a tall, oversized roll-up garage door, he put the truck in park and turned off the engine. Then he opened the driver's door and stepped down onto the pavement. He reached for me, gesturing for me to hurry up.

Quickly, I scooted across the seat, trying to keep the gown covering my legs as I moved. He set his hand on my outer thigh. And then he grasped me by the waist and hauled me out of the truck. I cinched the sweater tighter around my chest as the frigid air rushed over my bare knees and thighs and seeped through my sweater.

When he headed for a small side door, I hurried after him, hoping it was warmer inside the building. I almost let out a soft moan when I stepped inside. Warmth began to ease the chill from my legs.

The door clicked shut behind me and I looked over my shoulder at Henry. He was watching me, his expression blank. I felt my cheeks flush and quickly I looked away, turning my attention to the building's interior. It had a high ceiling with exposed metal beams, and there were five offices, separated by glass and what looked like pull-down shades, lining the far wall. And to the left was a wall of curtains, probably covering more glass and blocking out the view of the warehouse.

Henry grasped my arm, his fingers brushing against mine and making me suck in a breath. When he set his other hand at my back, he guided me across the carpeted floor to the office in the far corner. He pulled out a stool at a long work bench in the center of the room and nudged me onto it with his hands on my hips.

"You brought your girl here? What is this? Take your slave to work day?" a male voice asked with a laugh.

I looked up and saw a guy walking into the room.

He winked at me and gave me a toothy grin. "Damn," he said. "I missed that memo."

I cringed at his implication.

"I like the company," Henry said softly, sliding his hand across my waist. "I don't know why I didn't do it sooner."

I held my breath, worrying about what he would do next.

And then he bowed his head and pressed his warm lips to my neck.

I gasped and my cheeks flushed. As he straightened up and removed his hand, I pulled the edges of my sweater across my chest, covering myself again as much as I could.

"What if she blabs what we're doing here?"

"Who's she going to tell?" Henry asked, catching my eye as he walked around the work bench. "Besides, she knows if she says anything, I'll make her pay for it."

The guy smirked.

I hugged my arms tight to my chest and tried not to cry. I couldn't believe he expected me to sit there all day long doing absolutely nothing. But then again he had said to use my imagination. Did that mean he would be okay with me finding my own thing to do?

While I sat there, I watched them unlock a large storage cabinet on the back wall and wheel out a silver tray stacked with small boxes. The guy kept casting wary glances my way, but Henry seemed to be doing his best to ignore me.

I let out a quiet sigh and then propped my elbow on the bench and rested my chin on my palm. I couldn't just sit there doing nothing, but there wasn't anything else to do. And my imagination had taken an apparent break. My mind was a complete blank, and I felt drained already.

"There's been a change in our schedule," Henry said.

I kept my head down, trying to appear occupied with a spot on the table.

"Everything needs to be loaded in the truck Friday night so I can head out after midnight."

As he spoke, I lifted my gaze and caught him glancing my way. His expression remained blank. And he didn't seem concerned that I was learning about his plans.

Where was he going? And was he taking me with him? I couldn't decide if that would be the better option. But then I supposed it was better to stick with someone I knew than to be stuck with the unknown. He was unpredictable, sure, but it was never really that bad. It could have been a whole lot worse. At least that's what I kept telling myself.

"You really think they can kill every prisoner?"

"Sure, why not?"

The guy shrugged.

"It's their only option to rid society of hardcore felons."

The guy huffed. "A lot of our guys need to end up there."

"Yeah, well, keep doing this after I'm gone and you'll have the ammo to take them out. Save Scott's guys the trouble."

I had no idea what they were talking about. I couldn't remember the last time I had witnessed a conversation involving anything other than cooking, house cleaning, and sex. Well, at least since the gangs took over three years ago.

And I honestly didn't think Henry would want me hearing the information. It made me wonder what kind of threats he would make later. What would he do to me now that I knew things I shouldn't?

I wasn't sure how long I sat there, with my chin in my palm and worrying about what he would do to me. My stomach had worked itself into a tight knot and I felt like I was going to throw up.

"Henry?" I asked, keeping my voice down.

He looked up and asked, "Hmm?"

"Um," I said, casting a quick glance at the other guy. "I have to use the bathroom."

With a slight nod, he turned back to his work. I thought he was going to ignore me, but then he stood up and walked around the table.

I slid off the stool and let him guide me back toward the main entrance and into a short hallway.

When we reached the door which had the sign for the women's bathroom, he pressed it open and then reached in and flipped on the light. There was a toilet and a counter with a sink inside. And an exhaust fan motored loudly overhead.

When I stepped inside and he followed me in, I glanced over my shoulder. "You don't have to come in or even wait. I can…"

"I can't have you taking off by yourself."

"I won't," I said, shaking my head. "I swear."

"I can't have you running into anyone else either. It's not safe for you here," he replied, sitting down on the counter and letting his feet dangle. When he saw me still eyeing him, he smiled. "Bashful all of a sudden?"

My cheeks blushed and I bowed my head as I bit my lip.

"Come here," he said. When I stepped closer, he reached out and snaked his arm around my waist, pulling me to him to stand between his thighs. He lifted his hand and hooked a finger under my chin, tilting my head back.

His gaze drifted lower and then he cocked his head to the side as his brows furrowed. "I was too rough yesterday," he said, grazing my neck with his fingertips. "I'm sorry."

I closed my eyes and swallowed hard. He never apologized for anything he did to me.

"Look at me." When I opened my eyes, he said, "You need to start fighting back."

My eyes widened. I couldn't imagine fighting back. If I did that, things would be worse for me. He'd be worse.

"You're too weak."

Tears welled in my eyes as I looked away. What was I supposed to say? What did he want from me?

"That's why you've changed hands so many times. Guys get bored with the submissive state. They like a challenge."

I bit down harder on my lip. How much more was he going to say in an effort to cut me down?

"I'm not saying I'm bored or that I'll sell you. I'm just saying if you fought back, you'd feel better about yourself."

I wiped away tears from my face, rubbing over the bruise on my cheek in the process and making myself wince. I wasn't sure what to say. Or even think. So, if I fought back, the outcome would be better? Was that what he was trying to say?

"Go pee," he said. "I need to get back to work."

Just like that? Make me cry and then forget it ever happened?

Sniffling, I pulled away and then reached out for the counter on my way to the toilet. I didn't trust my own legs to keep me steady. As I walked the short distance, I kept my head down. I could feel Henry's eyes on me; I didn't need to see him, or myself, in the mirror.

He let out a heavy sigh as his boots clomped on the floor. "I'll wait outside."

I nodded. My lip trembled and more tears threatened to spill out. The door latched, and then I thought I heard his voice from the hallway. It sounded like he was making a joke, but there hadn't been anyone out there when we came through.

Quickly, I wiped my face dry and then pulled off a few squares of toilet paper to blot my nose. With a trembling hand, I lifted the toilet seat and then dropped to my knees on the dirty floor.

When I opened the door several minutes later, Henry was leaning against the wall with his arms crossed over his chest. He turned his head to look at me. His brows furrowed slightly, making him look worried.

I blinked my gaze away and stared down at the carpeted floor. Surely, he had heard me throwing up in the bathroom. And the sobs that I couldn't control.

With a hand at my back, he led me to the corner office. When I went to hoist myself up on the stool at the work bench, he lifted me and set me on the seat, his warm hands lingering at my waist.

"Thank you," I said weakly, lifting my gaze to his.

"Sure," he replied, straightening his back and squaring his shoulders.

I closed my eyes. And then I heard his footsteps walk away.

CHAPTER 7

A COUPLE HOURS LATER, Henry walked over as he said, "Break time."

I eased myself off the stool and then followed him to the back door of the warehouse. Outside, he took my hand and set it on his forearm. I leaned my head against his upper arm. I knew he'd want sex. Wasn't that why he brought me to work with him? To look pretty and be available whenever he wanted me?

He took me to an apartment building several blocks away and then we walked up the flight of stairs positioned just inside the entry. He pulled a set of keys from his pocket and unlocked the second door on the right. When he pushed the door open, I peered inside. There were several packages of food sitting on the island in the kitchen.

"Make lunch," he said, nudging me inside the apartment with his hand at my back.

With a nod, I glanced his way and then headed into the kitchen. There was a saucepan sitting on the stovetop. I grasped the handle and looked inside, inspecting it for cleanliness.

"Everything is clean," he said behind me. "I washed it all yesterday before I went home."

I glanced his way again and then nodded.

He sighed as he leaned his hip against the counter and crossed his arms over his chest. "Don't you have questions? Aren't you wondering what I was doing here yesterday?"

I lifted my gaze to his. He looked annoyed. I swallowed hard. What did he want me to say? "I thought you didn't want me to question you."

"Well, I want to hear them now."

"Okay." My voice came out so quiet. With a trembling hand, I picked up the package of food that was sitting beside the oven. "This one?"

"Yes."

I found the small cut in the packaging and started to tear off the top, but its plastic lining caught. My trembling hands felt so weak. As I struggled with the package, trying to tear it open, I could feel Henry's eyes on me.

"Use the pair of scissors, Kallis," he said.

With a small sigh, I scanned the counter and found the scissors. I tried to keep my hand steady as I cut off the top of the package. After I dumped the contents into the saucepan, narrowly missing the outside edge, I reached for the jug of water. I popped off the cap and then picked up the measuring cup. My hands were trembling so bad I sloshed water on the glass top of the stove.

When Henry set his hand over mine, I gasped.

"Let me," he said, taking the cup from my hand.

"I'm sorry," I said. I tried to move aside, but his arms were blocking me in.

He measured out the four cups of water, then he wrapped his arm around my waist and pulled me backward a few inches as he turned the burner on.

My vision was starting to blur with tears. Sniffling, I covered my face with my hand and bowed my head.

"What's wrong with you?"

I shook my head as I said, "I don't know. I'm sorry."

He turned me around and cupped my chin with his palm and tilted my head back. "Look at me."

A tear slipped down my cheek when I blinked up at him.

His eyes narrowed as he looked at me. "What's wrong?" he whispered.

"It's fine," I replied. He wouldn't want to know that I was tired. Tired of being treated like I was nothing. Tired of being used. And scared that he would hurt me if I said or did the wrong thing.

"All right," he said, reaching past me and readjusting the burner knob.

Quickly, I wiped my face dry. When he turned back to me, I tried to give him a small smile. "I'm sorry," I said again.

He nodded slightly as he eyed me. Then he took two bowls from the cupboard and two spoons from the drawer. He handed me the spoons and then he took the bowls to the dining table.

I followed him and placed a spoon beside each bowl.

Then he went back into the kitchen and leaned against the counter, crossing his arms over his chest again.

"I can do this," I said, brushing past him and picking up the ladle he had resting on the counter.

He grasped my wrist before I could get the ladle inside the saucepan. "Go sit down."

I swallowed hard and nodded as he pried the ladle from my hand. I didn't argue. I didn't want a slap in the face.

Hugging my arms to my chest, I padded across the floor and wandered down the hallway. Once inside the first bedroom on the left, I leaned my back against the wall and sank to the floor. I pulled my legs in toward my chest and rested my cheek on my knee.

I must have been nearing my menstrual cycle, like Henry had said. Days ran together and I couldn't keep track. Or maybe it was because I didn't want to. I didn't want to know how many days of my life were wasted.

And I wasn't this emotional, usually. I had learned how to check out, for the most part, make myself forget about my current life. If I could focus on that, I could get through life, provided nothing changed.

"What are you doing on the floor?"

I jerked my head at the sound of Henry's voice.

He reached down, grasped my arm, and pulled me to my feet. When I tilted my head back and looked at him, he asked, "Hmm?"

"Um," I stammered. I couldn't think of a single good answer. I hugged my arms to my chest and hoped he didn't really care about one.

"Lunch is ready."

"Okay."

"Tomorrow you're cooking though," he added. "So, whatever you have going on, get over it."

"I'm sorry."

"And for fuck's sake, stop saying you're sorry all the time. I don't want to hear it."

I felt my eyes widen. Before I could even come up with a response, he turned away and headed down the hall back to the kitchen. I pressed my hand to my forehead and let out a slow breath.

"Are you coming?" he called over his shoulder.

More tears flooded my eyes as I nodded. On trembling legs, I followed him into the dining room.

He pulled out a chair and outstretched his arm to me, catching me around the waist.

I swallowed the growing lump in my throat and sat down. "Thank you," I said, my voice strained and gravelly. I cleared my throat and said it again, my voice clearer this time.

"Sure," he said, looking down at me.

He looked disappointed or annoyed. I couldn't tell which one.

While he went back into the kitchen, I pressed my cool hand to my cheek for several seconds and then I curled my finger under my eyelid and tried to sop up the tears.

"We can't stay here long," he said, coming back to the table with the saucepan and ladle.

Quickly, I wiped my wet hand on my sweater and then folded my hands in my lap.

"I need to get back to work. I'm sure you caught the part about the deadline."

I nodded. As he scooped the rice and chicken soup into the bowl in front of me, I couldn't stop wondering what he was going to do to me for not doing my job. I knew he would punish me somehow. I just couldn't figure out when or what he would do.

When he was done dishing my food, I looked up and said, "Thank you."

He nodded as he lifted his gaze to mine. He gave me a peculiar look.

"Is something wrong?" I asked, afraid of what he was going to say.

"You're not wondering about the deadline? Where I'll be going?"

Did he want me to wonder? I had been more concerned about his reactions and the punishment he would dish out than about details of a conversation I wasn't supposed to listen to.

But I nodded. "You're leaving?" I tried to make my voice sound disappointed and upset. At least with him I knew for the most part what to expect. With someone else, things could be worse. A lot worse.

He nodded as he ladled the soup into his bowl. "I'm taking you with me."

CHAPTER 8

MY EYES WIDENED and I really hoped I looked surprised and hopeful instead of horrified about Henry's response.

"You've always wanted to leave Detroit, haven't you?" he asked. When I nodded, he gave me the slightest of smiles. "Other cities don't live like this. They don't attempt to sterilize half their population. It's the city's fault the gangs took over."

My jaw flexed. The city had thought it was their right to take away my ability to bear children. For the greater good, they had said.

By slowing down the growth of the population, the city could gradually improve to keep up with the added demand. If the population grew too fast, the city would be unable to handle the significant increases in demand for food and other supplies.

So, it *was* the city's fault that the gangs had taken over, but I was smart enough to know they weren't to blame for what the gangs thought they could get away with.

"You can eat."

As I lifted my gaze back to Henry and picked up my spoon, I asked, "Where are we going?"

Without looking up, he stirred his soup as he said, "Out east. To Wilderness."

I vaguely remembered seeing the city on the map. It was located south of Washington, DC, which had once been the country's capital and now served as the prison for criminals of serious crimes.

"Why there?"

He finished chewing his food. Then he said, "I need to drop off a truckload of ammunition inside the DC prison."

"Oh."

He eyed me. "It's nicer there."

"I've never been there."

"I haven't either." His gaze drifted. "It's warmer there, too. You won't need a sweater in the summer."

I pulled the edges of my sweater tighter together. I was pretty sure he was making a sexual reference.

"I think you'll like it there."

When I glanced his way, he was focused on eating. His head was bowed over his bowl as he lifted the spoon to his mouth.

Pausing, he said, "You need to eat."

I took a deep breath and then nodded. I could feel his eyes on me as I ate. And when he was done eating, he pushed his bowl aside, propped his elbow on the table, and rested his chin in his palm as he watched me.

"Has anyone told you that you are the slowest eater?" When I nodded, he hummed. "My little brother used to take the smallest bites. It would take him forever to eat."

With a small sigh, I set my spoon down in the bowl and clasped my trembling hands in my lap. I thought for sure he'd make a comment about me being able to take bigger bites and spoonfuls—surely word had gotten around from my previous owners. It made my stomach hurt just thinking about it.

"It's fine," he said, standing up. "Finish eating."

"I'm full," I replied, hoping he would believe the lie.

He hummed again. "You only ate half of what I gave you. Eat the rest. I'll clean up."

Shaking my head and starting to stand up, I said, "You don't have—"

He set his hand on my shoulder, forcing me back down. "Do as I say."

"But..." My voice trailed off when I saw the irritated look on his face. I swallowed hard and then nodded.

He sighed heavily. "I'm trying to be nice."

"Oh," I whispered as I turned back to my bowl. "I'm sorry."

"Mm hmm."

With a trembling hand, I picked up my spoon again. I could hear him moving around in the kitchen and setting his bowl in the sink.

When I was done eating, he took the bowl. I eased myself to my feet and walked to the kitchen island. He set a clear lid on the saucepan and then headed my way. With a hand at my back, he led me to the door and out into the hallway. After he locked the door, he took my hand and pulled me toward the stairs.

I found it unnerving that he hadn't used me. Especially after joking about it with Brad. What was his plan? Why was he acting so strange?

And *trying to be nice*?

After living with him for the past year, I honestly didn't think he was capable of it. But then again he wasn't that bad. He wasn't that mean. He could have been a lot worse.

We walked back to the warehouse in silence. He seemed to be lost in his own thoughts, too. What was he thinking? Was he considering his options? Deciding what to do with me later?

I didn't dare ask.

When he set me on the bar stool again, his hands lingered. And then he bowed his head and pressed his lips to my neck.

I sucked in a quiet breath.

"Moan for me," he whispered in my ear. He glided his hand down my hip and over my thigh, over the silk of my gown and then on my bare skin as he cupped my breast with the other and grazed my nipple with his thumb through the silk.

"Henry," I said, out of breath.

"Oh, that's better," he whispered, nibbling at my earlobe.

My skin felt flushed, and I was certain that was his intention considering the guy he had been working with all morning walked through the door and approached the work bench.

"Dang, Henry," he said. "Way to make a guy jealous."

Henry straightened up as he said, "Nothing's stopping you from planning ahead and bringing your own girl here."

Something told me he wouldn't have wanted me to mention that our lunch break hadn't involved sex. I didn't understand why, but I wasn't going to complain even though I liked it, a lot more than I wanted to admit. And why did it matter if other guys thought we were doing it? Did it show he was a stronger leader?

"Maybe tomorrow," the guy said.

"Sounds like a plan," Henry replied. "I enjoy mine."

I tried not to roll my eyes and purse my lips as I propped my chin in my palm again. There was no telling how Henry would react. I knew I was supposed to be accommodating and loyal, look pretty, and gaze up at him with doe eyes. That made me wonder if he really wanted me that way or if he was trying to put on a show in front of the other guys. It was clear that the public display was his goal at the warehouse.

I wasn't sure if the other girls appreciated being used in front of others. I saw them often while we were passing in the hallway—although I tried not to look. At least Henry had never gone that far. He saved the hardcore stuff for himself. Maybe because he had sense enough that that was supposed to be private. Not for public display.

"Kallis."

Startled from my thoughts, I looked up at Henry.

"Come here."

As I nodded, I caught the guy casting him a wary glance. I eased off the stool and walked around the bench. Henry reached for me, setting his hand at the small of my back and nudging me closer.

"Have you been paying attention?"

I started to panic. Had he really expected me to watch him the whole time? I was pretty sure it had only taken me a few short minutes to zone out.

He sighed. "What have you been doing this whole time?"

"Um," I stammered, trying to figure out what to say.

"Thinking of me then?"

I swallowed hard as I blinked up at him. "Yes."

He held my gaze and for a panicked moment I thought he was going to call me out on my true thoughts about him, but then he just hummed and repositioned me to stand at the edge of the counter.

I watched him lean over and pull a box of tiny cylinders across the counter. Then he fished one out and held it between his thumb and forefinger.

"This is a brass casing," he said.

I craned my head back to glance at him.

He stepped out from behind me and picked up what looked like a brass cap. "We fill it with a measured amount of gunpowder and then we cap it."

I caught the other guy watching us as I nodded again. His brows were raised and he looked amused.

"To measure out the gunpowder, we use a scale." He demonstrated the process, fitting a casing into a tiny slot in the metal tool he was using to seal the caps onto the casings. He set a tiny funnel onto the casing and then tapped some gunpowder into it from a small scoop. "See?"

I nodded.

After he set a brass cap on top, he glanced over as he pulled down the lever. The machine clamped the cap in place. He lifted the lever and picked up the bullet and held it out to me. When I held out my hand, he set it on my palm, his fingers brushing gently against my skin and making it tingle.

I turned the bullet around in my fingers. It felt strange to hold something he had made.

"You try it," he said, taking the bullet and setting it in a bin.

I blew out a slow breath as I dug into the box and pulled out a casing. With trembling fingers, I set it into the small slot in the machine. When I went to scoop the gunpowder for the casing, my hand shook.

"Good heavens. Why are your hands shaking?" he asked, grasping my hand in his. "We'll end up with gunpowder all over the damn floor."

I bit my trembling lip. "I'm sorry."

"Why don't you just insert the casings," he said. "Think you can handle that?"

I took a deep breath and then nodded.

"Let me see."

I picked up a handful of brass casings and then set one inside an open slot, barely getting it in there this time. I could feel his gaze on me, studying my every move. When I went to add the next one, it slipped from my fingers and clinked on the floor.

He sighed as he leaned down and picked it up.

When he set it in my hand, I gave him an apologetic look. "Sorry," I said, my voice weak.

He hummed. "What do I need to do to get you to stop shaking?"

"I don't know. I'm sorry." I knew if I didn't find him intimidating, I would feel more relaxed. If I wasn't worried about him punishing me.

"Liquor, maybe." He looked up and caught the other guy's eye.

"I stashed some in the women's bathroom," the guy said, "under the sink."

Henry took my hand and moved it over the box of casings. After I had dropped the casings into the box, he pulled me across the office. Inside the bathroom, he set me on the counter and then crouched down and peered into the cabinets. He reached inside and pulled out a bottle of amber-colored liquid. Then he popped the cork and sniffed the bottle. After he took a swig of the liquor, he handed the bottle to me.

I stared at it. "Do I really need to drink this?"

"It'll help you relax."

"How much do I drink?"

He shrugged. "Depends on how much you can get down that dainty little throat of yours."

I took the bottle and lifted it to my lips. The smell burned my eyes and nostrils.

When I looked at him again, he nodded. "Take a small sip."

I raised it to my lips again. When it trickled over my tongue and the potent fumes hit the back of my throat, I coughed, spraying the liquor over Henry's head.

Quickly, with eyes wide, I covered my mouth with my hand and tried to stifle the coughing.

He sighed as he lifted his arm and wiped his face on his T-shirt. When he looked up at me, his lips were pursed and he looked annoyed.

When I coughed again, trying to clear my throat, he rose to his feet and patted me on the back. "Did you manage to swallow *any* of the whiskey?"

I nodded.

"Try some more."

I took another sip, this time managing to get it down before coughing it out. It burned my throat and nostrils going down. Then it settled into a warm pool in my stomach.

He took the bottle from me, took another swig, and then set it on the counter beside me. He lifted his hand to my chin and rubbed his thumb gently over my throat. "I guess I've sheltered you a little too much."

I swallowed hard. "Sheltered me?" I wasn't sure what he meant by that.

"You can't handle hard liquor." He lifted his hand higher and moved aside wisps of hair from my face. "But maybe that's not a bad thing."

I didn't know what to say.

"Your innocence surprises me sometimes. How can you not know?"

I looked away and then closed my eyes. I hardly would have considered my life to be sheltered. Nor myself to be innocent.

"You're terrified of everything."

I shook my head. "Just you."

He hummed. "And every other man in the city."

I pressed my lips together and hugged my arms to my chest.

He brushed his thumb over my chin.

Blinking up at him, I asked, "Can I go? Please."

He eyed me as his lips jutted out and it looked like he was chewing on the inside of his cheek. Then he lowered his hand, circled his fingers around my wrist, and pulled my arm toward him. Gently, he moved his hand underneath my palm. When he looked back at me, meeting my gaze, he said, "You're still trembling."

"I'm sorry," I whispered.

He picked up the bottle and handed it to me again. "Drink some more."

I honestly didn't think drinking more of the liquor was going to help. If anything it would make me drowsy.

"Maybe I need to bring along the muscle relaxers next time. You weren't trembling last night."

I shook my head. I took the bottle and then gulped down the liquor. It burned my throat. Handing back the bottle, I bowed my head and coughed into my free hand.

He rubbed his hand over my back. After a moment, he crouched down and stashed the bottle back inside the cabinet and then he lifted me off the counter and set my feet on the floor.

My head whirled a little and I reached out to steady myself, my hand landing on his stomach.

"Tipsy already?" he asked, wrapping his arm around my waist. When I tilted my head back and blinked up at him, he cursed under his breath. With a sigh, he leaned down and hooked his other arm under my legs and lifted me off my feet.

Closing my eyes, I rested my head against his shoulder. I couldn't believe that small amount of liquor had made me feel so faint, and so fast. And just the movement of his walking as he carried me through the building to the office made my head whirl.

"She drink too much?"

"Apparently," Henry replied.

"Drunk is a normal state for mine. I've had to hide the booze numerous times."

"I'm sure Kallis would be the same way if I allowed it."

I tried to ignore the fact that they were talking about me like I wasn't even there. When he set me on the stool on his side of the work bench, I leaned over the table and rested my forehead on my arms.

His hands lingered at my waist.

I wanted to help him, to sit up straight and do what he wanted me to do, but I couldn't keep my eyes open. I felt drained. More than I had the night before.

"Well, it was worth a shot," the guy was saying. "Not that I was expecting her to get much work accomplished. That's why women don't do men's work."

"Right," Henry replied, his tone flat.

I clamped my eyes shut tighter. I knew I could do it just fine if my hands weren't shaking. And if I weren't wiped out from the liquor.

I felt so drained I must have fallen asleep because the next thing I knew I was getting nudged on the arm. And then I heard Henry say, "Time to go."

I looked up and saw him stashing the tools inside bins and wheeling them inside the storage unit behind me. Slowly, I eased myself off the stool and then pressed my hand to my forehead.

When he came back, he set his hand at the small of my back and led me across the warehouse to the main doors.

When we reached the truck, I leaned against it while Henry opened the door. After he lifted me onto the seat, I scrambled to smooth out my gown which had bunched up high on my thighs, brushing my hand over Henry's in the process.

"Your modesty around me is amusing."

My cheeks grew warm. "Oh," was all I could manage to say.

"Move over."

"Sorry," I replied, my voice faint. While I scooted over to the middle seat, he hoisted himself in, bumping me out of the way and sitting down on the edge of my gown. I tried to tug the fabric, but it wouldn't budge. "Um, Henry?"

"Yeah." He glanced over at me and then looked down.

When he lifted himself high enough to release my gown, I pulled it out from underneath him and then smoothed it out again just as Brad opened the passenger door.

With a sigh, I leaned closer to Henry.

"How'd her first day go? You put her to work?" Brad asked.

"Nah. She's not good for much," Henry replied, leaning forward and starting the engine.

My jaw flexed. I hugged my arms to my chest and stared at the dashboard.

After he put the truck in drive, he put his arm over the back of the seat behind me. "Made my lunch break more interesting though."

I felt sick to my stomach at the comment. When I turned my head to stare at him, he met my gaze briefly and shrugged.

I knew he had only said that for appearances. He had to make himself appear one way for the sake of his leadership, but that didn't make it okay. Maybe his comment was true, but there was an implication in it. No doubt Brad would take it to mean something it wasn't.

I zoned out for the rest of the trip. At least the best I could.

When the truck came to a stop, Brad hopped out and then Henry turned to me. "I don't want you saying anything about what we did today," he said, squeezing my forearm. "Not to Liana. Or even Hector."

I blinked down at his hand. His knuckles were white and his fingers were pinching my skin.

"Kallis."

Quickly, I shook my head, worried from his firm tone that he would do something to me if I didn't obey him. "Of course I won't." When he didn't reply, I looked up and saw him eyeing me, his brows furrowed slightly. "I won't say anything."

He eyed me a moment longer like he didn't believe me and then he turned away and opened the truck door.

When he stepped down, I scooted across the seat behind the wheel.

He reached out and set his hand on my bare thigh. "Thank you for coming today," he said.

I tried to smile as I gave him a small nod. It's not like I had had a choice. And surely he realized that.

"How about a movie tonight? After dinner and a shower."

With a nod, I said, "Okay."

He smiled. "Your choice."

"Oh. Um." I tried to think of which movie he would actually want to watch. He never let me choose.

"If you were watching it alone, what would you pick?"

"It's okay. I don't mind—"

"Kallis," he said firmly. "Answer the question."

My throat tightened. "I don't know."

He sighed. "Take a look then." He gripped my waist and then lifted me out of the truck and set my feet on the pavement. Then with his hand at the small of my back, he led me into the apartment building and to the stairwell.

I thought he was upset with me for not being able to answer his question. I could never really think straight when he was touching me. I was always expecting something bad to happen. I hugged my arms to my chest as he led me down the hallway past the other guys who were loitering in the halls. I tried to ignore their stares.

When we got back, we found the apartment quiet. Liana should have been in the kitchen preparing dinner, but the counters and stovetop were clear and spotless. I turned to Henry, but he was too busy sinking into the couch and leaning his head back against the cushion.

As I wandered down the hall, I called out her name. Not loud though. I didn't want to upset Henry and risk being punished. I peered into Henry's room. Everything seemed quiet. And I honestly didn't think she'd go in there.

"Liana?" I asked softly when I reached Hector's door. I thought I heard a whimpering sound coming from the bathroom.

Casting a quick glance down the main hallway, I charged through the room and then stopped short when I saw her lying in the bathtub. Her eyes were open, staring up at the ceiling.

"Liana, what are you—" I stopped talking when I stepped closer and saw deep red smeared on the inside wall of the tub.

CHAPTER 9

I STIFLED A SOB with my hand. My stomach twisted and my legs trembled as I walked the few feet to the tub ledge. Her wrists were bloody and streams of blood stretched out toward the drain.

"Liana," I cried, dropping to my hip on the ledge at her side. Tears stung my eyes and blurred my vision as I tried to figure out how to stop the bleeding. She was gasping for breath, starting to panic from the loss of blood, and her eyes were focused on me. Her lips were moving slowly, but no sound was coming out and I couldn't tell what she was saying. If anything.

"Leave her," Henry said firmly, grabbing me around the waist and hoisting me back up.

I clung to his arm. "We have to save her."

"She made her choice."

There wasn't any point to arguing, even though I believed it was possible to save her life. We could have taken her to the hospital. Those were still running. They were run by the gangs now, but people were still able to receive medical care.

"We need dinner," Henry said.

My legs were so weak he practically had to support all my weight as he dragged me back to the kitchen. I felt numb.

"Good grief, Kallis," he said. "Can you not stand up on your own?"

A small sob escaped my lips.

With a sigh, he took me into the living room and let me crumple onto the couch.

I curled onto my side, tucking my knees in, and pressed my face into the back cushion as I cried. He covered me with a blanket and then I heard his footsteps across the floor. I kept waiting for him to decide to punish me for crying or for not preparing dinner, but I could hear him making noise in the kitchen. Maybe the punishment would come later.

And then I heard another set of footsteps walk out of the apartment. I was pretty sure it was Hector carrying Liana.

I didn't stay on the couch long. Maybe fifteen minutes. I knew for sure Henry would see to it that I was punished for failing in my basic duties. I folded the blanket and set it on the stuffed arm of the couch and then I walked into the kitchen. Henry looked over his shoulder at me from his position at the stove.

"I can do this," I said, reaching out for the ladle he was using to stir the soup.

He pulled out the ladle and set it down by the stove and then he grasped me around the waist and lifted me onto the counter.

"Henry." His name came out as a whisper.

"What have I told you about arguing?" he warned, his voice low.

"I want to help," I replied, staring down at my hands. If I were being honest, I didn't really want to help, but I also knew he believed it was my duty to take care of dinner and other household tasks. He would make sure I would return the favor. "Henry, please."

"Nah. I doubt Hector wants you blowing snot into his food."

His tone was serious, but a laugh bubbled up inside me and burst out before I could stop it with a hand over my mouth.

He hummed as a small smile lifted the corners of his lips and brightened his expression. He went back to stirring the soup which he had on a low simmer. Then he pulled out the ladle again and with his hand under it, held it out to me. "What is this soup missing? It's not very good."

I leaned closer and blew on it for a few seconds and then tasted it. "Sodium," I said. "How much broth or salt did you add?"

He shrugged.

I peered into the saucepan at the thick soup. "I would add a cup of broth. It's a little too thick." I went to hop down from the counter, but he held up his hand like he was ordering me to stay.

He retrieved the jar of broth from the refrigerator and then began pouring it into the saucepan. "This enough?" he asked, glancing my way.

"Maybe."

"What do you mean 'maybe'?"

"Well, you didn't measure it," I said hesitantly, worried about how he would react. Before he had a chance to respond, I added, "I'm sure it's fine. If you stir it and simmer it longer."

He hummed. Then he lifted me off the counter and set my feet back on the floor.

Quickly, I smoothed down the gown that had hitched up when he grabbed me.

He reached into the cupboard and grabbed three bowls and then handed them to me. "Go set the table."

With the bowls cradled in my arm, I retrieved spoons from the drawer and then did as he said. Then I unwrapped the rest of the dinner rolls from the day before and took them to the dining room. As I was heading back to the kitchen, Hector walked through the doorway. He looked furious.

"I need a shower. That bitch got blood all over me," he said.

I grimaced at his wording.

"Take your time," Henry called out. "It'll still be hot when you get back."

Hector huffed and then disappeared down the hallway.

"Kallis."

I jerked my head and saw Henry eyeing me. I bowed my head and then walked the rest of the way to his side.

"Watch this," he said. "I need to talk with Hector."

I nodded and took the ladle he was holding up for me.

"It won't be long," he said, turning and heading down the hallway.

As I was stirring the soup, keeping it stirred so it wouldn't stick to the bottom of the pan, a soft knock came from behind me. I looked over my shoulder and saw a young girl standing in the doorway. She was wearing a pair of skinny jeans and a loose-fitting T-shirt and her bleach-blonde hair was bound in a loose ponytail. She couldn't have been much older than sixteen.

"Um," she stammered as she looked around the nearly bare apartment. "I was told to come here and ask for Hector."

I sighed. Seriously, I thought. Liana was getting replaced so soon?

"Is this the right room?"

"Yes," I replied as I stirred the soup. "Have you eaten?"

She nodded as she hugged her arms to her chest and rubbed her upper arm with a hand.

"You should sit at the table."

While she sat down in one of the chairs—incidentally, Liana's chair—I turned off the burner and then wandered down the hall. I could hear muffled voices coming from Hector's room, but when I reached the door, the words were clear.

"There was a delay. I don't know," Hector was saying. "It might be in a few days."

Henry sighed. "I can't believe they've waited this long."

"I was expecting it to happen months ago. Something's been keeping them from making their move."

"Okay."

When I heard footsteps, I panicked. I hurried down the hall, but before I could make it to Henry's bedroom, he called my name. I stopped and slowly turned to face him.

"What were you doing?" he asked, still walking. When he reached me, he grabbed my upper arm, pinching the skin. "Were you eavesdropping?"

"I, um," I stammered. My eyes widened as the furrow of his brows deepened.

He dragged me into the bedroom and then pressed my back against the wall. His eyes bored into me. "Tell me what you were doing." He spoke the words slowly.

"I'm sorry," I said, my voice trembling. "I don't have a clue what you were talking about. I—"

"That doesn't answer my question," he replied, his own voice hushed.

"There's—"

His fingers squeezed my arm tighter, making me cry out.

Tears started to well in my eyes. I bit my lip and looked away as I blinked back the tears.

With a sigh, he released my arm.

I wiped the tears away and then cleared my throat. "There's a girl," I said, my voice trembling just as much as my hand. "She asked for Hector."

"All right," he said with another sigh. He smoothed the sleeve of my sweater like he was trying to soothe my arm. "I'll let him know."

I wanted to stay in the room, against the wall, and wait until he returned, but he nudged me out with a hand at my back. I hugged my arms to my chest and wiped at my face again as I walked with him to Hector's room.

The shower was running, and when we reached the bathroom, we found Hector in the shower stall.

Quickly, I averted my eyes, managing to catch a mere blur of his naked form.

"There's a girl here for you," Henry said above the noise of the shower.

"Send her in."

"Dinner is ready."

"It won't take long."

"All right." Henry guided me back out and then we headed for the kitchen.

When we walked in, the girl, who was still sitting at the table, looked up at us.

"Head down this hallway and go into the room on the left."

She nodded and rose to her feet. "Hector?"

"He'll be out of the shower soon."

She nodded again as she rubbed her hands over her arms and walked across the room.

I tried to give her a weak smile as she walked by, but it didn't look like she had noticed.

"Why is the burner off?"

"What?" I turned my head to see Henry standing at the stove and resetting the burner.

Glancing at me, he said, "The burner. Why is it off?"

"Um."

He sighed. "Why do you look spaced out all the time? Has the liquor seriously not worn off?"

I wanted to tell him it was how I had learned to cope, but I didn't figure he would accept that for an answer. Probably tell me I should get over it.

"Come here." He outstretched his hand. When I walked to him, he wrapped his arm around my waist and pulled me against him.

Hesitantly, I relaxed, wrapping my arms around him and resting my head against his chest. As I closed my eyes, he rested his chin on the top of my head. Finally, I said, "I didn't want the soup to burn in the pan."

"Okay."

I did not understand his behavior. Did it have something to do with what he and Hector were discussing? And whatever it was, he didn't want me listening in. Although he hadn't chewed me out that much and he hadn't even threatened me to not say anything. Not that I had anyone to talk to. Who was I going to share the details with? I wasn't going to go venturing into the hallway by myself.

When I heard footsteps, Henry shoved me away and went back to stirring the soup.

Puzzled, I blinked at him, trying to figure out why he had shoved me, but then when Hector appeared around the corner with his new companion in tow, I realized Henry hadn't wanted Hector to see us so close. It had been the gentlest he had ever been. Something had changed since the afternoon before. But he wasn't willing to let anyone else see it. That was the only logical explanation for his strange behavior.

Hector led the new girl to the table and told her to sit. Oddly enough she seemed intact. The same appearance as when she had arrived. I had expected her to look more ruffled. She looked scared, yes, but not completely terrified that she wanted to slit her own wrists or jump out the window.

I was too afraid of the punishment I would face if I attempted those things and I actually survived. I doubted Henry would nurse me back to health and make no attempts to make me regret my terrible decision.

When I felt a gentle touch on my arm, I gasped and looked up. Henry was beside me, eyeing me.

"Dinner is ready."

I carried the pot holder while he carried the saucepan. With trembling hands, I set it on the table and then backed away as he sidestepped me to set the pan on top. He dished out the soup and then grabbed me by the arm and pulled me to my usual chair. Keeping my eyes downcast, I sat down and then waited for him to tell me I could eat.

After dinner, I helped him clear the table and load the dishwasher. Then I let him lead me to the bedroom. I waited by the door as he closed it. When he set his hand on my shoulder, I tilted my head back and looked up at him.

He stared down at me.

Swallowing hard, I looked away. When I started to head to the bathroom, he followed. He removed his shirt and tossed it to the tile floor. I reached out for the button on his pants. My hands trembled so badly. When he grasped my hands, holding them firmly in one of his, I gasped.

He took over and loosened the button and zipper.

I stared down at the floor while he removed his jeans, boxers, and socks, and then stepped past me to the shower stall.

He reached inside and turned the faucets. Then he reached out and grabbed my arm.

With a ragged breath, I stepped closer.

He slid my sweater over my shoulders and down my arms. Then he tossed it over the tub ledge. Turning back to me, he reached his hand behind my head and fumbled with my hair tie. When he pulled it and made me wince, he stopped and sucked in a breath. "Sorry," he whispered, lowering his hand.

Backing away from him, I lifted my hands to the back of my head and carefully pulled the tie from my hair.

He took the tie from my fingers and set it on the tub ledge beside my sweater, and then he coaxed me closer with his arm around my waist and nudged me inside the shower stall.

The hot water pelted my head and shoulders, making me squeeze my eyes shut as water drizzled down my face. I stepped out from under the stream and wiped at my eyes, trying to dry them.

Henry stepped in behind me. "You're coming with me again tomorrow," he said, gliding his fingertips over my shoulder and sweeping my soaked hair aside.

I turned my head to the side and nodded. I didn't think he'd care to hear that I had enjoyed the fresh air, even though it was frigid. And now with Liana gone, I didn't want to stay in the apartment by myself.

He wrapped his arm around my waist again, gently drawing me back against his chest.

I wasn't sure what was happening. He hardly ever treated me gently. It set me on edge. My punishment was coming. I could sense it.

He pressed his head against mine as he wrapped his other arm across my chest. He wasn't trying to make my body betray me, to respond against my wishes. He was just holding me. I didn't want to ruin the moment by asking him a question or making a comment about it. And I hoped he wouldn't say anything either. I hoped he wouldn't come to his senses and do or say something that would ruin everything.

Gently, he turned me around to face him and then he hooked a finger under my chin and tilted my head back to look at him.

I held my breath as I searched his eyes.

And then he bowed his head and pressed his lips to mine. For the first time.

I didn't understand why. Why now after all this time? After more than a year? He had never kissed me before. And he had never been this gentle. He had only ever taken what he wanted or tried to make my body betray me. It always did. No matter how rough he was. It was like his little game.

His hands moved down my sides and then he was prying the soaked nightgown up and over my head. "Turn around," he said softly.

I turned around to face the shower wall and then hesitantly I pressed my palms to the tile, expecting him to use me.

He moved behind me, blocking the stream of water so it wasn't pelting me. And then he grasped my upper arm and pulled me back.

Startled, I gasped and turned my head. When he pressed the sponge to my back, I flinched and glanced over my shoulder, catching his eye as he lifted his gaze to mine.

He returned to his work of lathering my skin with the soap and making my heart race.

What was he doing? I wanted to ask him what was going on, what was happening. And what would he expect in return? But I was afraid he would snap out of it.

A soft moan escaped my lips when he grazed the sponge over my breasts. My body trembled. When he was done with the sponge, he squeezed shampoo into his palm and then worked it into my hair. I closed my eyes and tilted my head back. He had never done that before. It was always me bathing him and then he would leave me to shower alone. I couldn't stop wondering what had made him change. And would he be like this from now on or was this temporary?

He nudged me underneath the water and then ran his hand over my head, rinsing away the shampoo.

I studied his face, trying to figure out what he was thinking, but he stayed focused on his task.

When he was done and I reached for the sponge, he took it from my hand and began scrubbing it over himself. I watched him and he held my gaze, but he didn't explain.

He turned the faucet knobs, shutting off the water, and then he reached outside the stall, retrieved a towel, and handed it to me.

"Thank you," I said, hugging the towel to my chest. "And for bathing me."

He smiled.

After I dried off and wrapped myself in the towel, he grasped my arm and guided me out onto the bath rug.

He tossed his towel on the ledge of the bathtub and then tugged my towel free. After tossing it aside, he wrapped his arm around my waist and pulled me against him.

My heart was racing so fast I thought for sure he'd notice.

He bent down and hooked his arm under my knees and then he lifted me in his arms and carried me into the bedroom. Setting me down on the bed, he asked, "What movie would you like to watch?"

"I don't…"

"I'll pick it for you then." He pulled the covers up over my legs and tucked them around my waist.

Closing my eyes and bowing my head, I hugged my arms to my chest and rubbed my hands over my arms, warming them from the chill in the room. I could hear him opening a movie case and the player powering on. Then a blanket wrapped around me as the mattress shifted.

I looked up as Henry positioned himself behind me with his legs on either side. Once he was situated with his back against the headboard, he wrapped his arm around my waist underneath the blanket and pulled me closer. As I leaned against his chest, he pulled the blanket back up and tucked it around my shoulders.

"Comfy?" he asked, his stubble grabbing at my hair as he reached for the remote.

"Yes," I murmured back. When the movie appeared on the screen, I frowned. It looked like a Turkish romantic drama with subtitles. I craned my head back to look at him. "Where did you find this?"

He smiled. "Out scouting a few weeks ago. It better be good."

"You brought it back for me?"

He nodded. "I'm pitching it though if it sucks."

I huffed. That's what he had said about the last one, but he let me keep it.

When his hand brushed over my arm, he sighed. "Why is your arm so cold?"

"It's cold in here," I said, my voice quiet. "It's always cold in here."

He hummed. As his hand moved over my thigh, he sucked in a breath. "And your leg."

I moaned. The warmth of his hand felt so good I couldn't help myself.

When he leaned forward, forcing me over with him, the blanket slipped off my shoulders. I hugged it to my chest as he tucked his hands under my thighs and lifted my knees.

For a moment, he rubbed his hands over my shins, warming them. Then he wrapped his arms around me like he was trying to bundle me in heat.

As I started to warm up, I leaned back and rested my head against his chest.

"Better?" he asked.

I nodded and craned my head back to look at him. "Thank you."

He smiled.

When he bowed his head and kissed my forehead, a tingling sensation flooded my chest. Was this what it was supposed to be like with a guy? A warm, fuzzy feeling in your chest and stomach? Was that what love felt like?

"I'm not as mean as you think," he said softly as if reading my mind.

That could have fooled me. But he had been acting strangely. Ever since the previous night. Why was he being so nice to me? He was still a bit abrasive, but this was nothing compared to before.

Halfway into the movie, he repositioned, lifting me and setting me at his side. He fluffed the pillow and then stretched out. He guided me back down so I could rest my head on his chest. Then he pulled up the covers and draped his arm over me as he raised his other arm over his head.

When the movie was over and the credits played, we lay in silence. I tilted my head back to look at him. "What's wrong?" I whispered, tracing my fingertip over his chest.

"What do you mean?"

"You don't want to…" I let my voice trail off.

"Can't we just lie here?"

"We never do."

"Why are you arguing?"

"I'm not arguing. I just don't understand what's happening."

"Let's not talk about it," he said with a sigh as he leaned over and turned off the light. Then he slid down and wrapped his arms around me again. He pressed his lips to my forehead. "Good night, Kallis."

I spent a good portion of the night trying to figure out what was going on. After a couple hours of lying awake and studying the bedside clock, I finally drifted off to sleep.

CHAPTER 10

THE NEXT MORNING, I awoke to Henry's side of the bed cold and empty. I lifted my head and tried to listen for sounds, but the apartment seemed quiet.

As I crawled out from underneath the warm covers, I spotted a nightgown laid out on the bed. It was one of the longest ones I had, with a hem that reached my knees. But the fabric was nearly sheer and the bodice offered little coverage, barely enough to cover my nipples and nothing in between.

I sighed. I should have been used to wearing nightgowns made with thin, silky fabric, but I longed for the days I would be able to choose for myself what to wear.

After a quick trip to the bathroom, I wandered out down the hall and found Henry in the kitchen. He was gathering up some packaged foods and stuffing them inside a small black bag.

He looked my way. He must have noticed the way I was hugging my bare arms to my chest because he slung the bag's strap up onto his shoulder and walked over and rubbed his warm hands over the goosebumps on my arms.

"How long have you been up?" I asked. "I missed waking up beside you."

He smirked. "A few hours. Ready?"

I nodded.

He pulled out my sweater—the one I had worn the day before—and then walked around me. "Put your arms back," he said. When I did, he slid my sweater up and then over my shoulders.

I wrapped the edges around my chest, seeking any warmth I could get.

He led me out of the apartment and into the main hallway. This time, he stayed beside me with his hand at the small of my back.

I ignored the stares and kept my gaze straight at the stairwell ahead. His mood seemed so strange. Like he was expecting something bad to happen.

Outside, he lifted me onto the seat of the truck and then shoved the bag underneath the driver's seat. He hopped in beside me and rested his arm on the backrest behind my head. When I scooted closer, his fingers brushed through my hair.

Startled, I looked up.

He smiled. And then he leaned over and nuzzled my neck with his lips.

As I giggled there was a loud rap on the window. My body tensed.

"Damn," a male voice said.

Henry lifted his head and sat back in the driver's seat as Brad hauled himself up onto the seat beside me.

"Didn't you take care of that this morning?" Brad asked.

"Actually, I've bent her over the bathtub ledge twice already."

Brad laughed.

My jaw dropped as I lifted my gaze to meet Henry's. He winked at me.

"Good," Brad said. "I should try that with mine."

"It's fun," Henry added as he turned the key.

"Real fun," I muttered. My body was trembling with a quiet rage. How could they joke about that? Even if it wasn't true, those details were supposed to be private.

As the engine roared, Henry glanced at me. Through the blur of tears, I couldn't see his expression. Not to mention, I was too busy staring out the windshield.

When he got on the highway, he draped his arm over my shoulders and rested his hand on my upper arm.

I felt my body tense as I sucked in a quiet breath. I knew he was just putting on a show for Brad, talking it up to make himself look like a leader who was in control of his life and everyone else in it.

But that didn't make me feel better.

When were we ever going to stop pretending? When was he ever going to be honest about our relationship and the things we did? When was he going to stop acting cruel just to keep me in line? He knew that if I spoke up about the truth, I'd be expecting to be punished for it.

It did make me wonder what he would do. And honestly, how much worse could it get?

But I stayed quiet. If I did speak up, who's to say he wouldn't try to make me look unstable and unable to recall events correctly. And no doubt Brad would believe him.

When a tear slipped down my face, I bowed my head and brushed my fingers gently over my bruised cheek.

Henry gave my arm a light squeeze.

I couldn't be sure if it was meant to be for comfort or a warning.

I pressed my knees together and cupped my elbows with my palms as I tried to keep my breathing calm and my body from trembling. Anything to avoid drawing attention to myself. I didn't want Brad making a comment.

They spent the drive talking about the policies of the gang in the next district over. It was the first time I had heard about the other gangs. Nothing of interest was ever discussed with me around. If the guys needed to discuss something, they did it in private.

When we approached Hopewell, Henry moved his arm over my head and gripped the steering wheel as he leaned forward and peered out the windshield. I followed his gaze toward a truck that was parked on the side of the road.

I glanced at him, but he didn't seem interested in sharing his thoughts. I caught him glancing at Brad over my head.

Had the truck been there the day before? Was that what he was worried about?

He kept driving and then he stopped in the road in front of the warehouse. Looking over at Brad, he said, "I'll pick you up here at five o'clock."

After Brad got out and secured the passenger door, Henry kept driving. When I looked over at him, he glanced my way and raised his eyebrows but didn't say anything.

"Where are we going?" I asked, my voice quiet.

"Somewhere no one will expect us to be."

I sighed. How many questions did he expect me to ask to get the answers I was looking for?

"The truck back there," he said as if reading my mind, "was a warning."

"I don't know what that means."

He studied the road ahead, peering at the two- and three-story buildings that made up the town of Hopewell.

"Henry," I whispered, casting him a sidelong look.

"Just a second."

I sighed again as I stared out at the quiet street.

Finally, he parked the truck and stepped out onto the pavement. When he reached for me, I scooted across the seat and let him lift me out. After he set me down, he quietly latched the driver's door and then grasped my hand. He pulled me across the cracked pavement toward what looked like an apartment building. I hadn't really been paying attention, but I was sure it wasn't the same building as the day before.

I thought we were heading for the main door, but then he pulled me alongside the brick exterior to an alleyway. I cinched the edges of my sweater tighter together to stop the cold air from coming in, but it just seeped through the soft fabric anyway, chilling me.

When we reached a small staircase, he pulled me up and then he unlocked a metal door and nudged me inside.

I sucked in a breath. It was just as cold inside as it was outside. I rubbed my hand over my arm and waited for him to lock the door behind us.

When he turned back to me, he guided me to the second floor and through a door on the left. It turned out to be a furnished apartment. When he closed the door behind us, he released me and then raised his arms and clasped his hands at the back of his head as he let out a heavy sigh.

I was too afraid to ask him what was wrong, so I hugged my arms tighter to my chest and waited for him to tell me what to do.

Reaching out his hand to me, he said, "Come on."

I stepped closer. This was new territory. He was acting strange, and I had no idea how to respond or what he wanted.

He rested his hand at my back and led me into the living room. "Sit down."

I did as he said and nearly toppled over his lap when he sat on the cushion beside me. He chuckled and draped his arm over my shoulders. When I tried to scoot closer so I could rest my head on his chest, he slid his hand under my legs and lifted me onto his lap.

My nightgown hitched up. I tried to straighten it, get it back under my bare backside.

"There's no one else here," he said, grasping my wrist and holding it still. "And I locked the door."

"Oh."

"Put your head down." His voice was soft.

I let my body relax and rested my head on his shoulder.

He rubbed his hand over my arm. "I'm so sick of pretending."

"What?" I asked, confused.

"Being an asshole all the time," he said. "I wouldn't have been able to be so rough with you if you hadn't liked it."

"I don't like it."

"Your body says otherwise."

"It scares me," I whispered. "When you grab my neck."

"I've seen the fear in your eyes."

"Why?" I croaked. "Why do you do it?"

"It scares you, but it gives you pleasure. I know that, too."

My face grew hot. I hugged my arms tighter.

"It's not a sin, Kallis," he said softly. "I don't want to like it either, but it's not shameful to like it."

I wanted to believe him. But I knew it was sinful for us to be having sex outside of marriage, and we weren't married. That's not how the arrangements worked. Not that I had a say in how my life played out. As far as I knew, he wasn't sleeping with anyone else—I thought for sure he'd have made a point to tell me, to punish me, if that were the case—but whenever he tired of me, I would be sold to someone else. I also knew that for whatever reason, God was letting it happen. It was either this or death. Or more humiliation.

"I won't ever sell you. I hope you know that."

"Why won't you?"

"I don't trust anyone else."

"What do you care?"

"I know I've been rough with you. I've made you cry. I've made you hate your life. But I also know others would be worse."

I wasn't totally sure that was true. Did I really deserve to spend my whole life with someone who made it his personal mission to control me and make me cower? I was so afraid of what would happen. And I was afraid of doing the wrong thing. I tried to please him, to do what he wanted.

Sometimes that was enough.

Several times a month he wouldn't return until late and it always made me wonder if he was seeing someone else. I would sit at the end of the bed waiting for him to tell me what he wanted from me and he'd walk across the room and crawl into bed without even glancing my way. If he was seeing someone else, why did he need me?

"Am I the only one?"

"Only one what?"

"The only girl you're sleeping with."

"There hasn't been anyone else since you came to live with me."

"Why?"

"What's with all the questions?"

"I just don't understand."

He sighed. "I'm not as bad as you think, Kallis. And despite what I've done and said to you, I *do* care about you. A great deal. I know that doesn't make up for anything though. You probably hate me. And I only have myself to blame."

"I don't hate you." I couldn't believe I was saying those words. I *had* hated him. I had wanted to figure out a way to escape. And I should have still hated him for everything he had done, but deep down, I just wanted him to care about me. To like me. To protect me. And if he did those things, maybe I would be happy. Content.

"I don't believe you," he said, his voice soft as he rubbed his hand gently over my arm. "But that's okay. I'm sorry."

"I mean, I did. But if you would just be nice to me..."

"Things would be different?" he asked, finishing my statement.

"Maybe." I craned my head back to look up at him. "If you would just love me."

Slowly, with his hand supporting my back, he sat up. He hooked his finger under my chin and then he bowed his head and pressed his lips to mine.

My eyes flooded with tears and a soft sob escaped my lips. I lifted my hand to his cheek and brushed my thumb over his stubble as I returned every kiss.

Why couldn't he have done all of this before? Why couldn't he have loved me, protected me? Why did he have to wait until now?

His fingers slid through my hair and cradled my head as his lips brushed slow, gentle kisses over mine. After a moment, he pressed his forehead to mine. "I don't deserve you," he said softly. "You need someone who is worthy of being yours. Someone who doesn't make you cry."

"No." The simple word came out strained and desperate.

"You can't love me. It isn't right. Not after everything I've done."

I bit my trembling lip and fought hard to steady my breathing. I had no idea how he expected me to find that guy. Surely, I wouldn't find him in Detroit. Was Henry going to drive me around Wilderness so I could find him there?

When he lifted his head, I opened my eyes. He gave me a sad smile. He looked so regretful. If he would always be this gentle and loving, I could easily forgive him. Maybe I already had. Or maybe I was deceiving myself.

"We need to go," he said. "I think we've waited long enough."

With a nod, I looked away. When we got back outside, in front of everyone, would he go back to the old way? Would he humiliate me to show everyone that he was in control?

Gently, he grasped my arm and pulled me up straight. I took that as my cue to get up and stretched my leg out toward the floor. When I braced my hand on his shoulder, he gripped my hips and helped me up.

At the door, as he turned the deadbolt and grasped the handle, I looked up at him and asked, "What happens out there? In front of everyone again."

"We pretend like I'm still an asshole."

I sighed. "Why do you have to pretend?"

"That's not the way our world works now. If I show mercy, I'm showing I'm weak and that I can't lead."

I looked away and hugged my arms to my chest.

He turned back to the door, but before he had a chance to open it, the distant sound of gunshots broke through the silence.

CHAPTER 11

I JUMPED. Eyes wide, I stared at Henry as he cursed under his breath and pressed his forehead to the door. "What's happening?" My voice trembled.

He cursed again and then let out a heavy breath. "We have to get to the truck," he whispered.

"But…"

Ignoring me, he removed his handgun from its holster and screwed a suppressor cylinder onto the barrel. Then he opened the door and peered out. Turning to me, he gripped my arm with his free hand and said, "Everything is going to be fine."

I blinked up at him, too stunned to speak.

Releasing my arm, he stepped out into the hallway and motioned with a head nod for me to follow.

My heart raced as we hurried to the stairwell at the back of the building. There was more gunfire and men screaming and yelling. It sounded like the noise was coming from outside, several blocks away.

Henry wouldn't explain what was going on. And I didn't understand why we couldn't stay inside the room and wait it out.

Slowly, he opened the stairwell door and peered inside. Then he held the door open and nodded his head toward the stairwell, motioning for me to walk through.

I hurried inside and reached for the railing. My legs were trembling so bad I didn't think I'd be able to make it down the stairs. He grabbed my arm, supporting me as I made my way down the single flight of stairs to the main floor.

As he pressed the bar, he whispered, "Stay right behind me, okay?"

I nodded quickly.

He opened the door and after a brief moment, he stepped out and held the door for me. When I stepped through into the lobby, he grabbed my arm again and ushered me toward the front desk.

When I heard faint voices coming from somewhere out front, Henry cursed again and pulled me down behind the desk.

I dropped down hard on one knee on the tile floor, the jolt reverberating up my thigh. When I cried out, Henry shushed me. I covered my mouth with a hand as I rolled down onto my hip. I stifled another groan when the chill of the tile seeped right through the thin fabric of my gown.

The voices got louder.

He peered around the desk and then quickly came back, cursing under his breath again. He closed his eyes and pressed his forehead to the counter's edge. Then he whispered, "We have to go out the back."

I nodded but I knew he couldn't see me.

And then I heard the sweep of the door.

I held my breath as footsteps crossed the threshold.

"How are we supposed to find Henry inside an apartment building? He could be in any one of the rooms."

As the man spoke, Henry turned to me. His throat bobbed as his eyes bored into mine.

I couldn't tear my gaze away. He seemed so calm.

"Hector said he'll probably be on the second floor."

"Really narrows it down," the first guy replied.

Henry's lips parted and I could hear him release the faintest breath. As the footsteps grew closer, he turned away and then when the two men appeared, he fired off two shots.

Startled at the loud bang of the gunshots, I yelped into my hand and stared at the men as they dropped to the floor of the lobby. Blood spatter marred the walls and floor, and the dark liquid began to pool across the tile and creep along the grout lines.

My stomach twisted and then I felt my body heave. I rolled over just in time to throw up on the tile, narrowly avoiding the edge of my long sweater. I coughed on the bile, my throat raw, as I wiped my mouth with the back of my hand.

Henry grabbed my arm and hauled me to my feet. And then he dragged me down the hallway to the back of the building. I tried to lighten my steps, but the quick pace was too much. My boots sounded like they were clomping across the hard tile. Even Henry's steps were quieter than mine.

When we reached the back door, he opened it quietly and peered out. Then we were running again, down a dirty alleyway toward the street.

I honestly had no idea where we had parked the truck in relation to the building. But thankfully he wasn't relying on my memory to get us there.

At the street corner, we turned left. And then I saw the truck, parked along the curb up ahead. I let out a relieved sigh, but then I heard running footsteps behind us.

Henry whirled around as gunfire rang out, its ear-splitting noise bouncing off the buildings around us. He cried out, hunching over and pressing a hand to his stomach.

My eyes widened. I cast a quick glance down the street. A man was lying on the sidewalk, his legs sprawled out.

With a groan, Henry dropped to his knee. He was cursing under his breath between gasps. Gritting his teeth, he hauled himself back to his feet. And then he caught my arm and dragged me the rest of the way to the truck.

At the passenger door, I fumbled with the handle and then pulled the door open.

"Get in!" he said, his voice strained.

Frantically, I scrambled up into the passenger seat. I was about to sit down when he came up behind me, shoving me out of the way.

"Drive!"

The door slammed shut as I scrambled on my knees to the driver's seat and fumbled for the ring of keys he had stored on top of the visor. It slipped from my hand and landed on my lap. As quickly as I could and with a trembling hand, I shoved the key in the slot and turned it. The engine roared to life.

When I grasped the lever, ready to put it in drive, Henry said, "Put your foot on the brake."

I lifted my foot and set it on a pedal. The engine roared even more.

"No, not that one. The other one!"

"Um," I stammered, peering under the wheel. I moved my foot to the left pedal.

"Press it. Hard."

My leg was trembling so bad I didn't think I'd have the strength to do that. With my foot pressing the pedal as hard as I could, I fumbled with the lever.

He groaned. Gasping, he said, "Pull it toward you and then down."

Nodding quickly, I did as he said. But then I didn't know what to do with it. "What do I do?"

"On the instrument panel where it shows a line of letters…"

I scanned the panel in front of the wheel. "Which one is it?"

"D. D1."

As I set it on D1, he groaned again and mumbled. I thought he said, 'I'm gonna die,' but I wasn't sure. "What?" I asked.

He let out a sob or a cry as he clutched his stomach. "Drive!"

When I stepped on the pedal on the right again, the truck lurched forward.

He groaned. When I glanced over at him, his eyes widened. "Oh, God. Drive straight." He reached for the dash with one arm. "And put your seat belt on."

I tried to keep the truck inside the faded lines on the road, but the bumps in the pavement jostled me in the seat, making me jerk the wheel. And I couldn't figure out how to put my seat belt on without taking my hands off the wheel.

"Slow way down," he said. "And turn left at the stop sign up ahead."

I nodded as I let off on the gas pedal. "Do I have to stop?"

"No," he said through gritted teeth. When we got closer to the turn, he yelled, "Slower!"

When I pressed the brake pedal, the truck jolted us forward in the seat. Henry gripped the handle on the passenger door. He was grimacing and sucking in a short breath.

I heard a loud ting behind us, like something was hitting the back of the truck.

When I made the turn, the tires squealed as the truck slid through the intersection. I thought I heard Henry cursing from the passenger seat. My heart was racing so fast, and my leg was shaking so bad I couldn't keep it on the pedal.

"No, no, no," Henry said, sounding panicked. "Baby, don't slow down."

"I can't..." My eyes were starting to blur.

"Yes, you can. You're doing great."

I shook my head.

"Kallis, you have to drive."

I wiped the tears from my face.

"Come on. Put your foot on the gas. They're right behind us."

When I stepped on the gas pedal again, the truck lurched forward. I tried to keep my foot steady, but my leg was shaking uncontrollably.

Another ting bounced off the back of the truck, making me flinch.

"Faster!"

I pressed my foot harder against the pedal. I fought to keep the wheel steady and loosen my grip so I wasn't jerking it with every bump.

When the truck swerved and the right front tire went up over the curb, he yelled, "Stay off the sidewalk! You have the whole fucking road!"

"I'm sorry."

"That's TWO lanes!"

Quickly, I nodded. He was gasping for air now. And his eyes seemed even wider than before. I dared a glance in the side mirror. A dark blue truck was behind us and seeming to gain on us.

When I pressed harder on the gas pedal, the engine roared louder. My heart was racing so fast. If we didn't get away, Henry would die and I would be given to someone else. Maybe that was the better option. Maybe it wouldn't be so bad.

"We need to lose these guys," Henry was saying. When I glanced over at him, he was peering over the back of the seat.

I didn't know how we were going to do that. If I slowed down to make a turn, they'd catch us.

"Turn up here," he said. "Take a right."

"I can't slow down." My voice shook as badly as my hands.

"You have to."

I blew out a slow breath as I set my foot on the brake. I had no idea how slow I was supposed to go.

"Step harder on the brake!"

I did as he said, getting the truck to slow way down. But before I could reach the turn, the other truck rammed our tailgate, making me yelp.

Forcing myself to keep my eyes on the road, I jerked the wheel to the right for the turn. The tires slid on the pavement and rammed into the concrete curb.

Henry was cursing under his breath again.

I stepped on the gas pedal, propelling us forward as I turned the wheel back toward the left. I got us going straight again and plowed through a faded orange barrel, sending it flying across the sidewalk.

As I chanced a quick glance in the side mirror, the truck reappeared around the corner behind us.

I knew we had to lose them somehow. If I could find a place to pull in, maybe we could sit and wait for them to pass and give up. I kept a lookout for a place to go. Somewhere to turn off. Up ahead there was a subdivision of houses. A compact cluster of apartment buildings and single-family homes. But if I stopped, couldn't they search every house? They could find us easily, especially with Henry injured. Our only option was to outrun them.

"Don't stop," Henry said as if reading my mind. "There's an on-ramp for the interstate up ahead. Take that and head south."

Quickly, I nodded and stepped harder on the gas pedal.

"I'm hoping they give up," he added.

Seconds later, the truck rammed us again.

He cursed out loud. And then he pulled out his gun and aimed it through the open center window. When he fired off a shot, the casing flew over my head and tinged against the dashboard. He collapsed back onto the seat, breathing heavily.

I looked in the mirror again and saw the truck veer off the road and crash into the corner of a building. My eyes widened at the sight. I cast a quick glance at Henry. Apparently, he had managed to shoot the driver.

When I saw the sign for the interstate, I slowed down, making sure I didn't miss the turn. Once I got onto the interstate, I pried the fingers of one hand off the steering wheel. I had gripped it so tight. I flexed them, trying to get the blood flowing.

I had no idea where to go. Did he want me continuing south? I couldn't remember the geography of the area and I honestly didn't know how far south we had to go to get past the lake.

"Henry?"

He groaned.

"Where do I go?"

He let out a heavy breath. "South."

"I know, but..."

"Toledo."

"Oh." I glanced over at him. His eyes were closed and he was grimacing. Somehow we needed to find a doctor, but out of the city that would be nearly impossible. If I wanted him to get medical treatment, I had to take him back to Detroit, to the hospital. "We need to go back."

"What? No!"

"You need a doctor."

"I can't protect you there."

"Yeah, well, you can't protect me out here either," I mumbled.

"I took care of those guys back there."

"You're no good to me if you're dead."

"Kallis, we cannot go back to Detroit. I'm a traitor. They'll kill me and sell you."

"I have to take you back. You need help."

"Do not turn this truck around," he said slowly, a warning in his tone.

"What are we supposed to do?" I asked, my voice loud and trembling.

"We'll find some other place. Just not Detroit. Keep driving."

CHAPTER 12

WITH A HEAVY SIGH, I relented. Henry was in no condition to tell me what to do or even punish me for going against his wishes, but I kept driving anyway.

Maybe he was right.

Maybe when we got back to Detroit, they would just kill him instead of treating him. And who knew what would happen to me. I wanted to believe that someone would help us, but the gangs had control of the city. And they'd know everything that went on.

I drove for over an hour, following the signs for Toledo. Someone must have cleared a straight path through all the parked vehicles on the road. I tried not to look inside any of the vehicles, but sometimes that was hard to avoid. All of those people, caught out on the road when the poisonous gas filled the air and left to rot inside their cars.

It made my stomach twist. I had never seen so much death before. Being inside the city had kept me from seeing the side effects of the meteor disaster that had happened years ago. My father, being a guard for Detroit, had received ample warning. I remembered he had taken us to an underground bunker reserved for the city government.

When a red light popped on behind the clear screen, I glanced over at Henry. He had his eyes closed and his head resting against the back of the seat. I cleared my throat, trying to get his attention, but he didn't react. "Um," I stammered. "Henry?"

"Hmm?"

"A red light popped up on the dashboard."

"What does it say?"

I glanced his way. His eyes were still closed. "I don't know."

With a sigh, he leaned over to look. Then he groaned. "We're almost out of fuel."

"How do we get more?"

"We can't."

"What do you—"

"Look around, Kallis," he said, sounding annoyed. "You see any fueling stations around here?"

I bit my lip as I shook my head. My face flushed with heat, and tears were starting to well up again. I drew in a ragged breath.

"Any vehicles out in the middle of fuckin' nowhere?"

I wanted to argue, to tell him that if he just sat up and looked out the damn window, he'd see all of the vehicles I kept driving past. But when I looked over at him, he had his eyes closed and his face scrunched up like he was in excruciating pain.

When a tear slipped down my face, I quickly brushed it away. I curled my fingers around the wheel again, but my hand slipped. Quickly, I rubbed my hand over the wheel, trying to dry it out with the friction.

We rode in silence for a little while. A few miles maybe. I wasn't paying attention other than keeping my eyes on the road and the wheel straight.

"I'm sorry," Henry said, breaking me from my thoughts.

I bit my trembling lip as I nodded. I didn't bother to reply. And I didn't dare tell him we had missed our opportunity to siphon fuel because I was too afraid of what he would do to me if I argued with him again. We had passed the last vehicle on the road a mile back.

When the truck started to sputter, I let out a helpless breath. And when it died and came to a stop in the road, I pressed my forehead to the steering wheel. I heard Henry move in the seat and then the creak of the passenger door opening.

"Get the bag from under the driver's seat."

Looking up, I saw Henry easing himself out of the truck. I leaned forward and ran my hand under the seat and felt thick fabric. With trembling arms, I pushed the heavy door open and nearly fell out of the truck getting out. I reached back inside and tried to pull the bag from underneath the seat, but it was wedged in tight.

"Lift the seat."

I looked over my shoulder and found Henry leaning against the truck behind me. He had his hand pressed to his stomach. And the back of his hand was covered with dried blood.

Before I could get the seat up, my stomach churned and I was falling to my knees and throwing up again. Sitting back, I pressed a trembling hand over my wet eyes.

"You all right?"

I shook my head.

"Come on. You have to get up."

I blew out a slow breath and then pushed myself up. I thought Henry would be angry with me for being so weak, but he looked concerned.

After a brief struggle to push up on the seat, it folded and I was able to pull out the bag.

"Open it."

With a nod, I fumbled with the zipper and then peered inside, finding the bag stuffed with jeans and shirts. When I glanced over at Henry, he was watching me. "You did this for me?"

"You think I *want* you wearing that sheer nightgown in public?"

I frowned as I looked around. "Public?"

He sighed as he leaned his head back against the truck and stared across the highway. "Just hurry up and get dressed. We need to keep moving."

I pulled out the clothes, finding undergarments, too. Glancing his way to make sure he wasn't looking, I shrugged out of the sweater and slipped off my knee-high boots and set them all on the seat.

When I pulled the nightgown over my head, Henry grabbed it from my hand.

I gasped and shrank back, trying to cover myself with my arms. "I thought you weren't looking."

"Relax," he said, eyeing me. "It's not like I haven't seen every inch of you already."

I let out a ragged breath. When he busied himself with slicing the fabric of my gown with the blade he always carried in his boot, I fumbled with the clothes. As quickly as I could, I got dressed in the skinny jeans and shirt and slipped back into the boots.

"Help me with this," he said, out of breath as he held up a strip of fabric.

While he pressed the excess fabric to his stomach and back, I wrapped the strip around his waist and then tied it tight.

He winced.

When I looked up at him, his eyes were glistening and his jaw was clenched. Seeing him in pain brought fresh tears to my eyes. "I'm sorry," I whispered.

His throat bobbed. "It's not your fault."

I wanted to say, "that's not what I mean," but the more I thought about it, the more his comment made sense. It really wasn't my fault. I hadn't been the one to shoot him. I hadn't even been the one in charge of the whole mission. I was just an innocent bystander caught up in the mess. And that reminded me of the ammunition.

"What about the ammunition?" I asked. "Don't you have to take it out east?"

He looked at me like I had lost my mind. "There's no way we can go back to Hopewell to get it. Even if we could, I doubt I'd make it all the way to DC."

I sighed.

"They'll have to come and get it themselves." He closed his eyes. "Besides, the gangs have probably found it."

Not that I wanted to go back north, but didn't he have an obligation to deliver the ammo? Or at least attempt to do it? He had made the arrangement. Didn't he have to fulfill it?

"But..."

"We can't do it, Kallis," he said. "It's too late. I'm not going to make it."

I shook my head. "That's not true."

"Look at me."

I clamped my eyes shut. I couldn't look at him without seeing the paling of his face, the blood soaking his clothes and seeping between his fingers. Didn't gunshot wounds always look worse than they really were? There always seemed to be more blood than what it really was. I had seen it happen three years ago. I had thought for sure Carl would have died from his stab wound. It seemed he had lost so much blood, but he had still lived. Which was unfortunate for me.

But Henry... I felt like I was tied to him. He had kept me for over a year. And he had planned to take me with him out east. That had to mean something, right? He wasn't a great guy, I knew that. He had a way of tearing me down with his words. They were all honest words, but did he really have to say them? And did he say them to hurt me or was he just being honest?

He sighed. "You need to understand what I'm saying. We cannot go back. Even if I make it, they will kill me and sell you to someone else. Do you want that? To be some other man's slave? And who knows who it would be this time. Another guy who beats you. Treats you like shit because he can?"

I cringed at his words. At the bite in his tone. I knew what he was saying was true. And I would rather be his than be sold to anyone else. If avoiding Detroit was going to keep that from happening, then I was all for it.

"Is that what you want?"

Sniffling, I shook my head.

"I didn't think so. Besides, there are no hospitals anymore. We shut them down months ago."

"But..."

"The city is faltering, Kallis. We were running out of food. Eventually, another few weeks, maybe a month, two at the most, people will be dying of starvation. That's why we left."

I felt my eyes strain as I stared at him. I was so confused by what he was saying. Had things changed that much?

"The gangs made a mistake killing off the people who had been running the city."

I pressed my hand to my forehead. "What happens to me if you die?"

"You fight like hell to survive."

"Why?" I asked. "Why would I do that?"

He narrowed his eyes as he stared at me.

"I don't know where to go. I don't know how to get to this place you keep talking about."

"You figure it out."

"Why would I even bother? Why is it so important that I live? Why me?"

He leaned over and grasped my hand, squeezing it tight. "Listen to me. You deserve a good life. I'm sorry I hurt you. I'm sorry I never made you feel worthy. You lack the confidence to be yourself and I'm partly to blame."

As he spoke, my eyes flooded with tears. I wanted so much to believe him, but deep down I didn't feel it.

"Come here," he said. When I stepped closer, he wrapped his arm around me as his other hand cupped my cheek.

Sniffling, I rested my temple against his chest.

"Look, I'm sorry," he said. "For everything I did to you."

"But…"

"And for being an asshole."

"I—"

"You think I wanted to hurt you?"

"Didn't you?"

He sighed. "No."

"But you did," I said, pulling away.

"I know." He brushed his thumb over my cheek and then he lowered his hand to his side.

I wiped at my face and then rubbed my hands over my jeans, drying them. Taking a deep breath, I grabbed my sweater off the seat and then stepped around the truck door. I paused to make sure Henry was going to follow and then I started to walk south.

After a few minutes of walking in silence, he groaned.

I turned around and saw him bracing himself against the guard rail. His forehead glistened with sweat.

"Kallis, you need to leave me here."

CHAPTER 13

IGNORING HENRY, I kept walking.

"After everything I did to you, I don't deserve your help." His voice was strained, his breathing labored.

I stopped. I hugged my arms tighter to my chest. Without him, what would happen to me? How would I survive on my own? I had wanted so much to be free, but now that I was, I didn't know how I would manage.

When he touched my arm, I flinched.

"I'm not going to make it. You can travel to Wilderness quicker without me."

Tears slipped down my cheeks. I wiped them away with my hand as I turned around to face him. "We have to find the hospital."

"There's nothing out here for hundreds of miles, Kallis. There's no one who can help."

"Medications," I said.

He sighed heavily as he looked away.

"What am I supposed to do without you?" I asked, my voice strained. "I've never been on my own. And for the last three years, I've been told I'm only good for two things."

He raised a trembling hand to his face, covering his eyes.

"At least maybe I won't starve. If I can actually find food."

When he lowered his hand back to his side, his eyes were watery. I wasn't sure if he felt bad for me or his situation or if the tears were from the pain.

"And if I do run into anyone, maybe I can offer sex as a form of payment. We all know how I like that." I was on a roll. I had never spoken so much all at once. At least not since the gangs took over. With him nearly exhausted from the car ride and walking the last fifty feet, it was unlikely he was going to punish me for finally speaking my mind.

"All right," he said quietly. "I'll keep going until I drop dead."

I blinked back more tears at the thought of him dying. "You just need medicine."

"Okay."

"If we can find a city map, wouldn't it show where the hospitals are?"

"Sure."

I sighed. His flat tone didn't instill any confidence. I tried to remember my life before the gangs. It had become a distant memory. For the last three years, I had been too worried about being punished to think of anything else. I had to tiptoe, I had to be weak, I had to apologize for everything, I had to plead. I had never known what was going to happen or what to expect. One minute things were fine and the next I was getting grabbed by the arm or slapped in the face.

"Come on," Henry said.

I walked beside him, keeping an eye on his staggered walk. I thought he was doing well for no painkillers. But I guessed that was what made him a leader. He was tough. Not easily brought down.

But if he didn't get medicine or treatment, I was almost certain he would die. We had to find the hospital right away. I didn't know how much longer we had to walk to find another town. And hopefully it was large enough to have a hospital. Or a clinic. Or what about an animal clinic? They had to stock medications for infections and pain. But once we got to the city, how were we going to find the hospital without walking in circles?

I looked over at Henry as I said, "Um."

"What?" he asked, out of breath.

"How are we going to find a map?"

He cursed under his breath and followed it up with an annoyed sounding "I don't know."

"I saw a sign for a hospital when we were on the road. It said the next exit. Five miles." I tried to do the quick math estimate in my head. If we had walked for twenty minutes, surely we had traveled a mile. If we kept at that pace, we'd be there in less than two hours.

"One mile."

I turned my head to look at him. "What?"

"One mile to the next exit. Hospital is four miles off the highway."

"Oh. But…" My voice trailed off as I looked around. There was city all around us, but there wasn't anything that resembled an off-ramp. "Did we pass it?"

He lifted his hand and pointed straight ahead.

I followed his gaze, but I couldn't see anything.

"There's another sign. I guess you probably can't see it from way down there."

I cast him an annoyed look. "*Way down there?* I'm not *that* short."

He huffed as the corners of his mouth turned upward. "I'm teasing."

"Well, keep it to yourself."

"You've gotten awfully bold."

My jaw clenched. I could never have been so vocal before. At least not without some form of punishment. He would have grabbed me by the arm and pressed me against the wall. Told me to remember where I was and what my life had been like before him.

But he couldn't do that now. He was weak from the pain and loss of blood.

Finally, I asked, "What does the sign say?"

"Another quarter of a mile. It must be around this bend."

I let out a heavy sigh.

We kept walking and followed the sign for the hospital. I wasn't sure how good the signs were. And I didn't want to miss a sign. The farther we walked, the less I could rely on him to pay attention. He was in pain and it looked like he was struggling to keep going.

When we reached what looked like the downtown area, I looked around, trying to figure out if we were heading in the right direction.

"I'm in pain, Kallis. I don't know how much longer I can walk."

My jaw clenched. "Do you remember that first night? After Carl was released from the hospital."

"Of course I do. I've regretted it ever since."

I blinked back tears at the memory. The way Henry had clenched his fist in my hair and tugged it so hard it made me cry out. The way he had tied my wrists to the bed post when I struggled against him. I wiped my face dry and released a slow breath.

"Remember that the next time you want to complain about being in pain."

I couldn't bring myself to look at him. And I sure as hell didn't want to hear him justify his behavior. Or the behavior of the rest of the guys. I had wanted to die that night. The old memory still burned in my mind, and everything after it paled in comparison. That day, Henry had taken my innocence while Carl and nearly the rest of the guys in the building watched. The whole point was to watch the daughter of a city guard, the guard who had stabbed Carl, suffer. I had had no idea how sheltered my life had been up until then.

Fresh tears were swimming in my eyes now as I turned to face him. "How could you pretend?"

His throat bobbed. "I wasn't. Not then."

I turned away again as I shook my head, too disgusted to look at him.

"Kallis, I'm sorry. I hate myself for what I've done to you."

I sniffled. "When we get to Wilderness and I find a place to live, you can leave."

He sighed. "Okay."

"If you survive that long."

He let out a helpless breath. "Sure."

Maybe I should have cut him some slack. I was starting to get the hang of being mean. Maybe it wasn't as hard as I had thought. But then when I looked at him and saw his pained expression, I felt bad. "I'm sorry."

"You shouldn't be," he said. "I know I deserve every mean thing you could say. And even all the things you won't."

When we reached the city street, I looked up and down the road, trying to figure out which way we should go.

"The hotel," Henry said.

As I glanced his way, I spotted the hotel sign.

When I gave him a questioning look, he said, "There might be a city map. In the entryway."

With a brief nod, I hurried along the sidewalk to the main entrance. I wasn't expecting to find the door unlocked, but it opened with ease when I pulled on the handle.

Casting a glance over my shoulder to see Henry leaning against the brick wall, I slipped into the entryway. Sure enough there was a limited display of faded flyers and brochures featuring local attractions and a short stack of phone books sitting on a small bookcase.

I grabbed a phone book and flipped through it, searching for a city map that pointed out where the hospital was located. I breathed a sigh of relief when I saw a color printout of the streets with indicators pointing out important buildings and locations.

Moving my forefinger over the page, I studied the map. When I found the hospital, I ripped the page from the book and then hurried back out into the street.

I was expecting to see Henry standing where I had left him, but he was gone.

CHAPTER 14

FEELING CONFUSED, I looked around at the empty street. "Henry?"

How long had it taken me to find the map? It couldn't have been *that* long. Which meant he couldn't have gone far, not with his gunshot wound. Right?

Going door to door, I yanked open each one and yelled his name. My heart had started to race at the thought of him disappearing, leaving me to fend for myself. But I kept reminding myself that he was injured. Without medications, his wound would become infected. Without my help, he would die.

With the image of oozing pus, my stomach clenched. I cringed and shook my head, trying to block out the thoughts. But I couldn't shake the idea of him dying.

I wiped away fresh tears with one hand as I opened another door with the other. I squinted my eyes as I peered inside, trying to see into the dark store. "Henry?" My voice came out strangled and weak.

"In here."

I let out a cry of relief at the sound of his voice as I collapsed against the door. "You scared me."

"You've said that already."

"I thought you were gone." I couldn't keep the panicky tone down. "I thought you left me."

He walked back to the door, to me, and wrapped his free arm around me, pulling me into a weak one-armed hug. "I won't leave you. I promise. Okay?"

I let out a heavy sigh. Then I nodded my head against his chest. "What were you doing in here?"

"Looking for food, water."

Pulling away, I wiped at my face. "I found the map. The hospital is only a few blocks away."

He lifted his hand and hooked a finger under my chin and tilted my head back. He searched my eyes as his throat bobbed. His face looked pale and the corners of his eyes glistened.

I swallowed the growing lump in my throat and jerked my head away as fresh tears blurred my vision. "We're almost there. And you need rest."

"Okay." With a slight nod, he lowered his hand and stepped past me through the doorway. As he did, he grazed his fingertips over my hip.

I sucked in a breath. How could he make my skin tingle with a simple touch? He was supposed to recover so he could get me to Wilderness and then leave me alone for good. He owed me that much.

But did I want that? I should have.

"Which way?" he asked, breaking me from my thoughts.

I pointed to the right.

He nodded slightly and then headed that way, setting his hand on the brick siding for support as he went.

I kept an eye on him as we walked. It seemed we were going slower and slower the closer we got to the hospital. And my mind wouldn't stop thinking about what I was going to do if the doors were locked. How was I getting inside the hospital for the medications if the doors were locked and the windows were made of strong glass? I had no idea how to pick a lock. I doubted Henry knew how to do it either. And he could die by the time I figured it out. The returning thought of him dying made me panic even more.

I craned my neck and spotted the hospital sign up ahead. If there were no drugs inside, all of the walking we had just done would be for nothing. That was something I hadn't considered before. I was hoping the poisonous gas had struck suddenly and quickly, knocking out so much of the population that none of the city guards had bothered to touch this hospital to acquire the drugs or medical supplies.

"Kallis." Henry's voice came out strained.

As I turned to look at him, I saw him collapsing to his knees. I hurried to his side as he dropped down to his hip. He had his hand pressed to his stomach and he was breathing heavily.

I looked around, not knowing what to do. If I could get inside the hospital, I could bring out a wheelchair.

"I'll be right back," I said, starting to get up.

He grasped my arm, holding me down. "Look," he said, breathless.

"What…" The question faded as I followed his gaze and saw the hospital's main door opening.

CHAPTER 15

MY HEART RACED as I stared at the opening door and prayed for someone who could help us. And then I held my breath as I watched a man wearing jeans and a loose-fitting gray T-shirt walk outside.

I heard a jangle of keys as he turned around and slid a key inside the slot.

When it looked like he was about to step off the sidewalk, he turned his head and stared at us, squinting his eyes and looking confused like maybe he hadn't seen another person in ages and didn't know what to do. Finally he asked, his voice loud, "Do you need help?"

I tried to nod.

"Is he hurt?" the man yelled. He lifted the strap of his bag off his shoulder and then set the bag on the sidewalk by the door.

"Help," is all I could manage to say.

The man jogged toward us.

"Get my gun," Henry wheezed.

I fumbled with the holster at his hip, but I couldn't release the snap that held his firearm in place.

"I'm a doctor," the man said. "Let me help."

Giving up on the snap, I stared at the man as he crouched down beside us. His short-cropped dark hair was peppered with silver and the corners of his eyes were creased with age. He must have been in his fifties, if I had to guess.

"I'm Reese," he said, pressing his fingers to Henry's wrist. Then he looked up at me. "Wait here. I'll come back with a wheelchair."

I nodded. I watched him run back to the building and disappear inside. Then I turned to Henry and cradled his face in my hands. It looked like he was struggling to keep his eyes open and he was breathing heavily through his mouth. "He's going to help us," I said. "You'll be fine."

"Go. Before he comes back. You're better off without me."

"No," I cried, shaking my head. "I don't know how to be on my own."

"It's not hard," he said, his voice so faint I could barely hear it.

"Stop it," I whispered. "I need you."

He lifted his gaze, barely, and blinked at me. It looked like he was trying to smile. He whispered something that sounded like, "Okay."

Before I knew it, Reese was hurrying back with a wheelchair. "Help me get him up."

By the time we had him sitting in the chair, we were gasping for air. Then with Reese pushing the chair, we headed for the door which he had already propped open. "Close the door after us, please."

I nodded and toed up the door stop. After it had closed on its own, I hurried after them down the dim hallway, lit only by room windows on the right.

Reese wheeled Henry into a room with a hospital bed and helped him up onto the mattress. Then he turned to me. "Stay here with him. I need to go turn the power on."

I nodded. When he left the room, I turned to Henry. His forehead was glistening with sweat, and his eyelids were drooping.

Reaching for my hand and closing his fingers around mine, he said, "I don't want you leaving my side."

"Why?"

"Just don't wander off. Okay?"

"Fine," I replied with a sigh as I sank down into the chair beside the bed.

Finally after about ten minutes, Reese came back and flipped the light switches by the door. The room illuminated as he hurried across the room and put on a pair of latex gloves. Then he lifted Henry's shirt and cut away the strips of fabric from my gown.

"Gunshot wound?"

Henry nodded.

"Are you injured anywhere else?"

"No," Henry replied.

The man nodded slightly as he inspected the wounded area with gloved hands. "I'm going to roll you onto your side a little to check for an exit wound."

I watched Henry grimace as the man rolled him over onto his side.

"Are you on any painkillers now?"

"No."

"Well, the good news is there is an exit wound, so the bullet made its way out. The bad news is I have no way of scanning to assess internal damage. I'd prefer to run you through an MRI to make sure the bullet didn't hit anything major. But you are doing remarkably well for having been shot, and aside from the wound itself and an acceptable amount of surrounding tissue, I see no signs of internal bleeding. The bullet must have been far enough over to cause minimal damage."

I stared at the man as he spoke, waiting for him to share details of what we were supposed to do next.

"So, anyway, I'll put you on an antibiotic and painkiller through a drip. And then I'll get to cleaning the wounds."

When Reese left the room, I reached out my hand and touched Henry's arm. He rolled his head on the pillow to look at me. His eyes were red and glistening, making my face flush with heat. I stood up and stepped closer as I gazed down at him. It looked like he was trying to smile despite all the pain.

I cupped his cheek with my palm. I didn't know what to say. Or if he wanted me to say anything at all.

"I hate feeling so vulnerable."

The word *karma* slipped out before I could stop myself.

He hummed. "I guess so."

"I'm sorry," I said. "I didn't mean to say that out loud."

"What did I tell you about saying you're sorry all the time?" When I didn't say anything, he added, "You need to speak up for yourself. Don't apologize."

I pulled my hand away. "How can you say all of this now? You would have beaten me before for doing that."

He frowned. "*Beaten* you?"

I pursed my lips and looked away. My chin quivered.

"I hit you once. I wouldn't consider that a trend."

My eyes almost bugged out at his statement. Did he seriously not get it? Did he not understand what it was like living with him?

"Kallis."

I clasped my hands together, needing to hold onto something, as I shook my head, more from anger than anything else. "I feared what you would do to me for doing the wrong thing. I can't go a single day without worrying about it."

He sighed. "I'm done pretending. I told you that already."

"That doesn't erase the last year," I said, my voice cracking. "It doesn't make up for the last three years of my life."

"I know," he said quietly.

I swallowed the growing lump in my throat and wiped away a tear that had slipped down my cheek. I sat back down on the chair and crossed my arms over my chest to wait for the doctor to get back.

Either Henry realized I didn't want to talk to him or he was too tired to argue or attempt to make me feel better.

Finally Reese returned, wheeling a cart into the room. I watched him prepare the medical supplies and then rub a swab over Henry's arm. The smell of rubbing alcohol permeated the room, burning my nose. He hooked a bag of fluids to a tall pole and then he grabbed the needle from the tray.

My head whirled and I felt sick to my stomach. Quickly, I looked away and closed my eyes as I held a hand to my mouth.

"Kallis." It was Henry. His voice barely a whisper.

Without looking up, I nodded. "I'm fine," I croaked.

"This will sting for just a second," Reese was saying.

I heard Henry suck in a breath. And then there was the sound of ripping tape. I peeked an eye open and saw the doctor attaching the IV tube to a port at the crook of Henry's arm.

"All right. While the meds do their magic, I'll start cleaning the wounds."

"Thanks," Henry replied, his voice hoarse.

"It's lucky you caught me before I left. I don't make it out this way often. Just stopped in for some supplies."

I eyed him as he spoke. Not that I was the best at reading people, but it didn't seem like he was being truthful. It was almost like he had something to hide. And he cast me a seemingly cautious glance, too. Maybe it was my own cautious stare that had him on edge.

While the doctor cleaned Henry's wounds, he tried to make small talk. And when Henry closed his eyes, Reese turned to me. I wasn't in the mood for chatting, either. Not to mention, I didn't feel comfortable talking with people I didn't know. For the last year, the only people I had really talked to were Liana and Henry. And even then, I held back, afraid of saying the wrong thing.

When it was clear I wasn't interested in talking, Reese fell silent as he started bandaging the wounds. Finally, he pulled off his gloves, set them on the tray, and then said, "I'll leave you two alone."

I nodded and watched him leave the room and close the door behind him. When I turned back, Henry was reaching out to me. I took his hand and then carefully crawled up onto the bed with him. He wrapped his arm around me and set his hand on my hip as I rested my head on his chest. I couldn't bring myself to close my eyes, not with Reese inside the building with us, so I stared out the window instead.

"I don't want you to wander off without me. I can't protect you if you're not with me."

I nodded slightly. There was no point in arguing with him. Instead, I asked, "Don't you trust him?"

He sighed. "It's too late now. And I don't really have a choice. But no. Not when it comes to you."

"I don't. Trust him, I mean."

"I think you're overly skeptical of people."

"I haven't exactly been impressed."

He sighed and turned his head, pressing his lips to my head. "I know I'm to blame for that."

"You're not the only one."

"I know that, too." He rubbed his hand over my arm. "I'm sorry I didn't get you out of there sooner."

"It's over now." I really didn't want to argue or speculate on what my life could have been.

"Three years ago. Before it all started."

I clamped my eyes shut. "Stop. Please." I didn't want him to keep talking. To tell me he could have saved me from a life with the gangs if he had just acted sooner. It wasn't fair. We couldn't go back in time and change anything. What was done was done. I didn't want to dream about something I could never change.

We lay there in silence and after a while, I realized from his steady breathing that he had fallen asleep. When I snuggled against him again, he turned his head, catching strands of my hair with his stubbled chin.

CHAPTER 16

WHEN I HEARD SOMEONE whispering my name, I clamped my eyes tighter and snuggled my face deeper.

"Kallis." The voice sounded panicked.

I jerked awake, realizing it was Henry. I lifted myself onto my elbow and looked up at him.

"I have to get up," he said.

With a quick nod, I eased off the bed and helped him sit up by trying to lift his shoulders.

He grimaced and then blew out a heavy breath when he hunched over. "I don't think you were even helping."

"Well, maybe if you had stopped growing at the age of ten, I'd actually be able to help."

He huffed.

I couldn't tell if he thought my comment was funny or if he was annoyed by my inability to help him. It wasn't *my* fault he weighed so much. And of course he never thought anything was funny unless he was joking with the guys. Even then, maybe it was forced. Just for show.

"Go find Reese."

I nodded and left the room. With slow, quiet steps, I walked down the hall, listening for sounds and keeping an eye over my shoulder. Surely, Reese hadn't left us inside the hospital by ourselves. He would stay to continue any necessary treatment. See to Henry's wounds.

When I neared an open door, I heard an odd chopping sound. And then I peered inside, finding a lounge with chairs and couches. And a long table near a kitchenette.

And Reese was sitting in a dining chair.

Not seeming to notice me, he leaned forward and breathed in a powdery-looking white line on the table.

My jaw dropped. I wasn't sure how long I stood there, maybe only mere seconds, but then I quickly retreated and pressed my back against the wall.

I held my breath. Surely, he had heard me. Maybe he could still hear me and the sound of my blood racing through my veins.

I crept back down the hallway about ten feet and then called out the doctor's name. Maybe that would give him enough time to straighten up and wipe the cocaine or whatever he was snorting onto the floor. If he could handle his drugs well, I figured he'd be able to help Henry with more painkillers.

I peered into the lounge again like it was the first time and then let out a surprised *oh* when I saw Reese washing his hands at the sink.

He looked over his shoulder. "Everything okay?"

"Um," I stammered, bracing myself with a hand on the doorjamb. I cleared my throat. "Henry needs help."

He eyed me briefly, his gaze seeming to drift.

I shifted my weight to my other leg and hugged my arms to my chest.

As he turned back to the sink, he said, "I'll be right there."

"Thanks," I said, my voice weak. I backed away and then hurried to the room. I stepped inside, finding Henry where I had left him. My cheeks blushed as he watched me walk across the room. Bowing my head, I tucked my hair behind my ear.

"What's wrong?" he asked, keeping his voice low.

I looked up, feeling panicked. "Hmm?"

"When you walked in, you seemed upset."

"Oh, um," I said, quickly glancing over my shoulder. I could hear Reese's footsteps approaching. I leaned in and whispered, "Not here." I cupped his cheek with my palm and then gave his temple a gentle kiss.

There was a soft knock at the door as I pulled away.

"You're up," Reese said as he walked in. "How are you feeling?"

Henry blew out a heavy breath and grasped my hand, squeezing it tight. "I just need to get up."

I thought his response was odd. He seemed to need a lot more than that. But then again he wasn't one to highlight his weaknesses.

"Sure," Reese replied, walking around the hospital bed. He wheeled the IV pole aside and then helped him off the bed.

Henry gritted his teeth.

"Where to?"

"Bathroom," he croaked.

As they hobbled across the room, I stepped around the bed and wheeled the pole behind them.

When we reached the doorway, Henry thanked him. "Kallis can help me now."

"Are you sure?"

Henry nodded. He grasped the support bar attached to the wall next to the toilet and took another slow step. He seemed to be walking more steadily now.

"All right. Just holler if you need anything. I'll hang out in the hallway."

When he left, I closed the door and locked it.

Henry stared at the door for a moment and then his gaze shifted to me. He looked tired and his face was scrunched up a little, no doubt from the pain.

After I positioned the pole out of the way, I leaned down and lifted the toilet seat. Then I tried to figure out what else to do. I couldn't really support his weight.

He fumbled with the button of his jeans with his free hand while he held onto the support bar with the other.

"Let me," I said quietly, reaching out and touching his hand.

He sighed. "I hate feeling helpless."

"I know." With both hands, I unbuttoned and unzipped his pants. Before I could do anything else, he grasped my hand. Startled, I looked up.

"That's enough." His voice was hoarse.

Blinking away, I nodded and took a step back. "Do you want me to leave?"

"No."

I hugged my arms to my chest as I looked around the small space, trying to find something—anything—to direct my attention. Finally, I spotted some black mold along the bathtub ledge. It didn't occupy me enough to block out the sounds though. I wasn't sure why he had wanted me inside the bathroom with him. But then again it wasn't anything new. He had never been shy. Except now he didn't want me removing his pants for him. And that didn't make any sense to me.

When the toilet flushed, I jumped, jerking my head over my shoulder. Henry didn't seem to notice. He was too busy making his way to the sink. He turned the faucet on and let it run. When he set his hands on the edges of the sink, bracing himself, and lifted his head to look in the mirror, he blew out a slow breath. His face had regained some of its color, but it still looked pale, almost grayish.

I took a hesitant step closer. "You're looking better," I said, trying to sound optimistic.

He shifted his gaze and looked at me through the mirror's reflection.

I swallowed hard and bit my lip, unsure of what he would do next. I thought his eyes looked glassy.

He let out a ragged breath as he bowed his head.

When I touched his arm, he flinched and jerked his arm away.

"Don't," he warned. His tone was only about half its usual force.

"I'm sorry," I whispered, hugging my arms to my chest again. My chin quivered and I bowed my head as I pressed my palm to my warm cheek. He had been fine with me helping him before, but now that he was actually injured and feeling helpless, he apparently couldn't stand it. I didn't understand him.

I heard the sounds of splashing and swishing water and then the squeak of the faucet knob. When I glanced his way, my breath caught in my throat. He was pulling his blood-stained shirt over his head, revealing the rippled muscles of his abdomen and chest. The area surrounding his bandaged wound was still stained yellow from the iodine, and blood had soaked through the bandage.

When his shirt caught on the IV line, he groaned.

I stepped forward then and touched his arm. Then I unscrewed the line from the port and pulled it loose from the shirt sleeve.

"Thank you," he said.

I tried to smile as I gave him a slight nod. Then I reattached his IV line.

"You should shower," he said. "If you want."

I looked over my shoulder, at the stack of white towels covered in a layer of dust.

"There's a change of clothes in the bag," he added. "Lock this door behind me."

CHAPTER 17

I WANTED HENRY TO STAY. Especially after discovering Reese's apparent drug habit. What if Reese killed Henry while I was in the bathroom? Then again, if he was going to kill him, wouldn't he have already done that with the first dose of medications?

Before I was able to protest, Henry was closing the bathroom door. And then I heard Reese entering the room.

With a sigh, I turned the lock and then undressed, setting the folded clothes on the sink ledge. I grabbed a towel from the stack and shook out the dust—or at least as much of it as I could.

After I let the water run for a few minutes, I got in and scrubbed myself clean, using the shampoo, conditioner, and body wash already sitting on the shelf inside the shower.

When I peered out of the bathroom, Reese was gone and Henry was lying on the couch by the window with his arm raised and the back of his wrist resting on his forehead.

I crept to the main door and closed it, securing the lock. There were glass windows looking out into the hallway—albeit covered with curtains—so we didn't have total privacy, but at least Reese couldn't walk in.

As I looked around the room for the bag, Henry said, "It's by the bathroom door."

I turned around and saw it then. But as I was hauling it into the bathroom, he said, "Come here."

I left the bag by the sink and then padded across the floor to the couch. His outstretched hand hooked around the back of my thigh, gliding over my bare skin. I cinched the towel tighter around my chest and sat down on the couch, facing him. He rested his arm over my legs.

"What was wrong earlier?" he asked, looking concerned.

I turned my head toward the door and covered windows. I couldn't see Reese out in the hallway. Maybe he had gone back to the lounge. Finally, I said, keeping my voice down, "He's a drug user."

His lips pursed as his brows furrowed.

I looked away. "You don't believe me."

"I do," he said, his voice soft. "I'm just trying to figure out how to get you out of here."

"We can't leave. Not with your condition."

"I can heal somewhere else."

I sighed. "We need to find another vehicle. So you don't have to walk."

"What do we say to Reese though?"

I shrugged. "I don't know. You're the gang leader. You should be good at making speeches."

He huffed. "What was he using?" When I gave him a questioning look, he added, "What drug?"

I shrugged again. "Snorting it."

He set my hand back against his cheek and then hooked his finger under my chin and bowed his head. He pressed his lips to mine.

I kissed him back, moving my lips against his. My eyes felt strained behind my lids and tears were welling up again.

"I'm sorry," he whispered, caressing my cheek with his thumb. "For never telling you the things you deserved to hear."

"Why are you telling me this now?"

"It's gone on too long. I can't keep denying you all the things you want and need." He kissed me again, soft and gentle. Then he pressed his forehead to mine. "Go get dressed, Kallis."

I wanted to ask him if he still wanted me, but all I could do was nod as I covered myself with the towel and tried to stand up. He gripped my waist and lifted me off his lap. I padded across the floor, trying to make it look like my legs weren't trembling as badly as they were. I looked over my shoulder, expecting him to be watching me, but he had his bare feet on the floor now and his head bowed in his hands with his elbows on his thighs.

So much had changed. How could someone change so dramatically almost overnight? He had said he was done pretending, and he wasn't perfect now—he still made harsh comments, and the drive out of the city had been stressful for both of us—but it was like he had flipped a switch. Now all of a sudden he actually seemed to care about me. But maybe he had before, just not in an obvious way.

After I got dressed in the clean clothes I found in the bag, clothes he had clearly picked out earlier, and then fingered through my hair, I went back to the couch and sat down beside him.

I kept wondering when he would grab me again. Was it his change of heart or the pain that he was in that was keeping us from doing what we did every day? A mixture of both, maybe.

"We need to keep moving. If someone finds the truck, he'll know we stopped in the nearest city. And they probably already know I was shot. They might expect to find us here."

"In your condition?"

He looked over at me and said, "I'll be fine."

I bit my lip to keep from smiling.

"What?" he asked, his tone sharp.

I cleared my throat. "You act so tough."

"I don't care to be anything else."

"And yet you demanded I leave you behind because you thought you were going to die."

"Momentary weakness," he replied. "I won't let it happen again."

I smiled then.

"I'll get you to a safe place. I said I would."

I nodded. "What do we do about Reese? We can't ignore him, can we?"

"Maybe we can get something to eat first and then decide. I'm starving."

I stood up and headed for the wheelchair that was parked near the side of the hospital bed.

"I don't need that," Henry called out.

I looked over my shoulder and saw him easing himself to his feet. I bit my tongue and looked away as I kept him in my periphery. If I could have ignored his pained expression, I might have been able to believe him.

"Get the door."

I hurried to the door and unlocked it. Then I held it open.

He gripped the doorjamb and paused to catch his breath before he walked through.

I eyed him as we walked down the hallway back toward the entrance. Sweat had sprouted over his forehead, and it looked like he was struggling with each step.

"We should go back," I said quietly, reaching out to him and touching his arm.

He fumbled for my hand and squeezed it firmly, but not tight enough to crack my knuckles.

"Henry," I whispered.

"I'm fine."

His hushed and breathless tone had me thinking otherwise, but I didn't argue. What was the point? He was in control. He always was. And stubborn as hell. I'd never be able to convince him of anything he didn't already believe.

I let out a soft sigh and got a quick, annoyed glance cast my way in return, which I ignored.

When we reached the lounge, we found Reese sitting on the sofa flipping through a magazine.

He looked up and smiled, his gaze raking over me before settling on Henry. "How are you feeling?" he asked, setting the magazine aside on the cushion.

"I've been better," Henry replied. His hand gripped mine tighter, making me wince. He reached out for the dining table and then eased himself down onto one of the chairs. Still holding onto my hand, he pulled me onto his lap and wrapped his arm around my waist.

I wasn't sure if he was using me as an anchor—he was leaning some of his weight on me—or if he intended to make it clear to the doctor that I was his.

Reese eyed me thoughtfully. Then he directed his attention to Henry and said, "You'll likely experience discomfort for a couple weeks. And you'll need to take it easy for a while. Stay off your feet. And absolutely no heavy lifting."

"How heavy?" I asked, my voice quieter than I had expected. But I had to ask. I knew Henry wasn't going to do it.

His gaze shifting to me, the doctor pursed his lips and shrugged. "Nothing more than ten pounds."

When I looked over my shoulder at Henry, I met his gaze. I was going to comment that he needed to listen to the doctor, but his unimpressed expression suggested he didn't want my input. I released a small sigh as I turned again and leaned against him. I almost moaned when he released my hand and then wrapped his arm around me, grazing the swell of my breast with his forearm and trapping my arms to my sides.

I caught Reese's gaze lingering toward my chest and I thought it was too long before he stared back down at his magazine. After a moment, he asked, "So, where did you two come from?"

I turned my head again toward Henry and waited for him to reply. I wasn't sure how much information he wanted to share.

Finally, Henry cleared his throat. "Detroit."

Reese cocked his head slightly. "What are you doing out here?"

"Getting away from the city."

"No one is allowed to leave their designated cities."

"And yet here you are. Right where we are."

Reese's eyebrows lifted a hair at Henry's comment. "Well, I have no intention of turning you in, so you needn't worry about that. So long as we both agree."

"Sure."

"Are you hungry?" he asked, standing up. "I can scrounge up something to eat."

"All right."

After Reese left to find food in one of the supply rooms, I craned my head back and caught Henry's eye.

He lifted his hand and brushed my hair aside with his fingertips. His palm settled on my cheek, warming my skin. "You look tired."

I nodded. "I am."

He pressed his lips to my forehead.

I let out a slow breath. With the tender way he was touching me, I wanted him to do more. He wasn't trying to make my body respond against my wishes; he was being gentle now like he actually cared about me. I knew he was in pain, and probably doped up from the painkillers. If he had attempted to take it farther, I was sure I'd let him, even with Reese no doubt on his way back with the food. I just wanted to feel him, feel his skin on mine. This was different from all the times before. Or maybe it was just that I wanted to believe it was.

"Why don't you look for plates?" Henry said, breaking the silence and killing my fantasy.

I opened my eyes and gazed up at him. He seemed to be avoiding eye contact now and he was lowering his hands to grip my hips. "Okay," I said with a small sigh as I lifted my head off his chest and leaned forward.

With my hands bracing the tabletop, I pulled myself up and then went across the room to check out the cupboards. When I glanced over my shoulder, I saw him raising a trembling hand to his face. He wasn't used to being a victim, being vulnerable, weak. He was a leader. He got his way and men respected him. It was upsetting seeing him in his new condition.

Before he could catch me watching him, I turned away and focused on searching the cupboards for anything useful. It didn't take long to find things we'd need. By the time Reese returned, I had ceramic plates and bowls, silverware—the real stuff, not plastic—and a small collection of salt and pepper packets piled up on the counter that I had sterilized with a cleaning spray I had found under the sink.

"We're in luck," Reese said as he walked into the lounge carrying a box of packaged items. "I found a whole pantry full of food and cooking supplies."

I peered inside the box as he set it on the counter. There was a saucepan and ladle surrounded by numerous packaged meals.

"I'll be back with the water."

I nodded and watched him leave the room again. Then I picked out the meals one-by-one and set them on the counter beside the plates as I assessed our meal options. I knew Henry wouldn't care which one I chose—he wasn't picky about food—so I selected the cheesy potato and beef soup. I dumped the contents into the saucepan and retrieved the measuring cups I had found in one of the drawers.

Reese came back with four one-gallon jugs of water. While he slid them across the counter by the stove, he said, "There's plenty more water in case we run out."

"Thank you," I said.

After he removed the cap from one of the jugs, I measured out the water and poured it into the saucepan and set the burner on low.

He picked up the teapot from a back burner on the stove and then removed the lid and peered inside. With a shrug, he looked at me. "It seems all right."

Keeping my eyes downcast, I took the teapot from him and turned to the sink to wash it with soap.

While I turned the faucet knobs and waited for the water to warm, he searched the overhead cupboards and retrieved a box of tea packets and set it on the counter. Then he said, "I'll leave you to it."

The implication was annoying, but I let it slide. I didn't want him hovering over me anyway. He may have been a doctor, and someone who could help us, but I didn't trust him. There was a strange vibe about him.

I had learned not to trust anyone, but this was different. The other guys seemed immature and curious with what they could get away with, what they could get a woman to do. They weren't evil; they were just stupid and mean.

But Reese...

He was too smart for that. There was intelligence in his eyes, in what he did, but there was also something else.

Something calculating. Thoughtful.

It made me wonder why he was living outside of the city by himself. Was he running from something? Hiding from someone? What was it?

After I had the teapot washed and rinsed, I filled it with the bottled water and then set it on the stovetop to heat. While the food and water heated, I busied myself with examining the cupboards and drawers again. And tried to ignore the guys as they talked about surviving on the outside.

When the teapot whistled, I took it off the heat and poured the steaming water into three mugs. I dropped a mesh tea packet into each mug and then carried two to the table.

Henry looked up and gave me a small smile. "Thank you," he said, taking one of the mugs from me.

With a nod, I set the other mug in front of Reese and then went back to the stove.

"You have quite the little homemaker, don't you?" Reese said, eyeing me over his steaming cup of tea.

I felt my throat tighten and my face flush. I shifted my gaze to Henry. It seemed his expression had hardened with the comment as he held his own mug midway to his lips. He turned his head to look at Reese and I thought I saw his eyes narrow. I held my breath, waiting for him to reply.

But he said nothing.

I supposed that was better than him agreeing to the comment. Not that it was untrue. I cooked and cleaned. I made the bed. I did all the things that a woman in Detroit society was supposed to do. I just wanted to be recognized for my brain, not my body or my cooking skills.

Biting my lip, I turned back to stirring the soup. Henry's words filled my head. *Know your place, Kallis. Don't expect anyone to tell you.*

I knew I was smart. At least I *had* been before. And I had specialized knowledge, knowledge that most people didn't have. But I wasn't sure if I still had those skills. Would I be able to remember the details? The codes?

When the soup was hot, I turned off the burner and then carried the saucepan to the table. The guys sipped their tea while I retrieved the bowls and spoons. Henry had an excuse. After all, he had been shot. I didn't mind taking care of him. But there wasn't anything physically wrong with Reese.

But then I remembered that he had carried in the water jugs and the box of food. Was it enough that he had done the heavy lifting?

I tried to ignore my thoughts as I set out ladling the soup into the bowls.

"Thank you," Henry said when I set a bowl in front of him.

My heart flip-flopped, making me smile and blush.

He reached for me, setting his hand at my lower back. "Sit down."

I nodded and sat down on the chair beside his.

He removed his hand then and picked up his spoon.

I couldn't help wondering what Reese thought of us. But I already knew what he would think of me.

Weak. Submissive. Easy to control. Probably unintelligent.

He didn't know anything about me, but he would assume.

Of course, Henry had warned me of that. How I portrayed myself spoke volumes. But how could you change yourself in a matter of days? You didn't simply become someone else by merely thinking it.

"Are you going to eat?"

Startled from my thoughts, I looked up to find Henry leaning toward me. His voice had been low, but surely Reese had still heard it, judging from the way he was eyeing us again. I could see him in the corner of my eye.

Clearing my throat, I nodded. I wasn't sure if it was really my thoughts that had distracted me from eating or the habit of waiting to be told to eat. I was thankful he hadn't mentioned in front of Reese that I didn't need permission to eat anymore.

"This isn't bad," Henry said, looking over at me. "Thank you."

I shrugged. "I didn't really do anything."

He cocked his head slightly and gave me a weird look, but said nothing more.

"What are your plans for when you feel up to traveling again?" Reese asked. "Where are you going to go?"

Henry finished chewing his spoonful of food and then he washed it down with the tea. After he set the mug on the table, he looked over at Reese. He was silent for a brief moment and then he said, "We are heading to Wilderness."

Reese frowned. "Where is that?"

"DC." When the guy still looked confused, Henry added, slowly, "The District of Columbia."

Reese gave a slight shake of the head. "Of course," he said. "So much has changed in the last twenty years."

"Wilderness wasn't formed, officially, until after the meteor disaster."

The man nodded. "Right." He sighed. "I'm afraid I've lost touch with the goings-on of the world."

Henry and I exchanged a quick look.

"How long have you been living in the area?" Henry asked.

"I moved to Detroit about twenty-one years ago," Reese said. "And when the meteor disaster occurred and everyone was rounded up by the guards, I left to live on my own out here."

"Where had you lived before?"

"Virginia. Southwest of DC, actually."

"And you were a doctor there?"

Reese nodded. "At a children's home."

I thought that was odd. The man was giving me bad vibes and then I learn he used to work with children? That didn't sit right.

"There was a fire that broke out, and unfortunately the building couldn't be saved, so I relocated to Detroit."

I sensed that was a lie, but before I could say anything—not that I had planned on it—Henry touched my leg. Startled again, I jerked my head to look at him.

"We'd like to head out soon." As he spoke, he turned his attention back to Reese. "Maybe tomorrow."

"Stay here as long as you can," the man said. "You need time to heal. Give it a few weeks. You'll be back to normal by then, I'm sure.

"Thanks," Henry replied, "but I want to get us settled. Before the cold weather sets in."

Reese nodded slightly as he lifted his spoon to his mouth. "Well, in case you change your mind…"

CHAPTER 18

LATER THAT AFTERNOON, after Henry and I had excused ourselves and headed back to our room, I closed the door and then pulled back the curtain and peered through the window into the hallway to make sure Reese hadn't followed us.

When I saw that the hallway was empty, I let out a sigh of relief.

"Something's bugging you," Henry said, glancing over his shoulder on his way to the couch.

"He's lying," I said, keeping my voice down. "I can sense it."

He nodded. "I have that feeling, too."

"Why would he lie?"

He shrugged. "Doesn't want anyone to know the truth?"

I rolled my eyes. "That's not what I mean. What doesn't he want us to know?"

"Something happened at the children's home, I would assume. But I don't think we need to know the details. It's not for us to know."

I sighed again. It seemed strange, his lax attitude. Not that he ran off high emotion. He had always been calm, collected, and reserved. But I worried that he wouldn't be able to do anything if we were actually in danger. Not with his injury.

And that worry intensified when he eased himself down onto the couch and sucked in a sharp breath through gritted teeth.

I went to help him, but he waved me off. After he leaned back and rested his head against the cushion with a heavy sigh, he said, "We'll leave in the morning."

He didn't look like he was in any condition to leave. But if I had told him that, it wouldn't have made a difference anyway.

Trying to distract myself, I went into the bathroom and washed my dirty clothes in the sink. I even tried to get the dried blood washed out of Henry's T-shirt.

After I draped the wrung-out shirts over the handrail in the bathtub, I dried my hands on my towel and went back into the room to find Henry lying on the couch, asleep.

He was breathing heavily, but he looked peaceful. Not wanting to disturb him, I slipped out of the room, leaving the door ajar, and wandered down the hallway. I didn't want to hang out with Reese, but I couldn't stay inside the room. I felt too restless.

I breathed a sigh of relief when I found the lounge empty. I cast a quick glance over my shoulder and then I walked in and headed for the collection of magazines scattered on the coffee table by the couches and lounge chairs.

There were magazines for various hobbies, from gardening to woodworking, and technical journals about medicine and psychology. I almost squealed when I found a journal about computer technology. I grabbed it and leafed through the pages as I walked to the table.

When I spotted the date on the magazine cover, I frowned. It was from more than ten years ago. With a shrug, I checked out the table of contents and then turned to the page about nano robots.

With nano robots, a person, or a society for that matter, could achieve just about anything. In fact, the American government had already used them to eradicate cancer cells in the body. The article talked about nano robots as cleaning agents.

It was amazing what could be achieved with technology. After the meteor disaster, the majority of the manufacturing plants had been shut down. We were no longer able to mine for silver, which was a necessary mineral for electronics. The major cities had claimed what little they could from the mines and went scavenging for more to recycle parts.

But I already knew that despite the loss of production, scientists and engineers were still able to make technological advances.

After I finished reading the article, I turned back to the table of contents.

"What are you reading?" Reese asked, taking a seat at the table.

I looked up, a little startled that I hadn't noticed him walk into the room.

He cocked his head and studied the page I was on. "Computer science?" he asked.

I nodded. Then I turned back to my magazine and flipped to the article about computer programming.

"It's been a long time since I've seen a woman."

I lifted my gaze and studied his face. I didn't know what to say. Was he stating a simple fact or was there meaning behind it? Hoping he was merely stating a fact, I gave him a weak smile and then turned back to my magazine again.

"I've been out here by myself for so long. It's been lonely."

"I'm sorry," I said, my voice faint. I shifted my gaze to the door and rose to my feet. "Um. I want to check on Henry."

"I'm sure he's still sleeping. Blood loss and pain wear a person out. He was in pretty rough shape during lunch. I'm sure you noticed."

I nodded and slowly headed to the door, but he grabbed my arm, holding me back. Gasping, I tried to pull my arm away, but his grip was tight.

He pulled me closer.

My stomach twisted as I stared up at him.

"You won't tell him, will you?"

"Henry." My voice came out strangled.

Reese shook his head. "He won't hear you."

I struggled to get free, but my body felt weak. When he forced me against the table, holding me down with a firm hand on my back, I screamed.

As I tried to reach behind me to grab his hand and pull it away, he leaned closer and fumbled with the button of my jeans. When it released, he pulled the zipper down. With a low growl, he tugged at the high waistband, no doubt trying to get the pants down past my hips.

"No," I cried. "Henry!"

Reese removed his hand from my back and then fumbled with my jeans at my hips. When I tried to push myself up, he forced me back down. My arms gave way and I collapsed against the table with a defeated sob.

He released me again, and I thought I heard him gasp.

I craned my head back and stared wide-eyed at the sight of blood spurting from the side of his neck. His eyes were huge and he was clutching his neck.

CHAPTER 19

WHEN REESE FELL to the side, I saw Henry staggering behind me. His blade slipped from his hand and clattered to the tile floor. I whirled around and tried to grab him, but he pulled me to the ground with him when he fell to his knees. I landed on my hip right as he toppled over, crushing me with his weight.

With all my strength, I righted him so that he was leaning back against my chest and then I wrapped my arms around him. He turned his head, craning it back like he was trying to look at me. I smoothed his hair with my palm as I bowed my head against his.

He set his hand on my arm. "Are you okay?" he asked, his voice faint.

I nodded. "Is he dead?"

"Probably."

I looked up and studied Reese's body, looking for movement, but the only thing moving was the pool of blood beneath him. I cringed at the thought of his hands on me.

Sniffling, I clamped my eyes shut and pressed my lips to the top of Henry's head.

He groaned. "This floor is killing me."

I figured it wasn't the best time to remind him that it was the gunshot wound that had nearly killed him. He was lucky we had gotten to the hospital when we did and caught the doctor as he was leaving the building.

"Help me up."

"You shouldn't be walking," I said, hugging him tighter.

"Kallis."

I huffed at the hint of warning in his tone. Did he seriously think he could threaten me given the condition he was in?

"Please." His tone had softened.

With a small sigh, I relented. "Wait here."

His fingers closed around my arm, making me gasp.

"Henry," I said, breathless. "I'm getting the wheelchair."

"All right," he replied, releasing me.

I kissed his temple and then I moved my hands to his back to keep him from leaning backward. He must have been too weak to hold himself in a sitting position and I couldn't hold his weight, so I helped him lie back down instead.

Grimacing, he lifted his arm and pressed his palm to his forehead. His eyes were closed.

Seeing him in pain sent a tingling sensation through my hip and brought fresh tears to my eyes. I had never seen him so vulnerable before. He was always strong. Physically and mentally.

I set my hand on his shoulder. "I'll be right back."

"Okay." The word came out in a gasp.

When I got to my feet, I heard him groan.

"Take my blade."

I shifted my gaze to the blade on the floor. It looked like the blood was starting to dry already. With a trembling hand, I picked it up and then scrunched up my nose as I wiped off the blood on

Reese's pant leg. I had no idea what I was going to do with it. Even if I did run into someone else in the hallway, I didn't know how to use it. And of course, Henry knew that, didn't he?

I staggered out of the lounge, stopping only once to look back at Henry. His eyelids looked closed, but his lips moved into a small smile. I smiled back and then bowed my head and headed for the hospital room. It was a few doors down. Which made me wonder how he had been able to hear me. Had my scream awakened him?

When I returned with the wheelchair, he was already on his knees. I wheeled it to him, locked it in place, and then helped him up.

Well, the best I could.

I doubted I was very effective. He was more than twice my weight. One morning, I had leaned over and looked at the scale when he was standing on it. And then he stepped off and made me get on. I had seen his frown through our reflection in the mirror and then he started making me eat more at dinner. But back before the gangs took over, back when I had been admitted during the first round of sterilizations, I had weighed just under ninety. With no exercise but a healthy appetite, and a high metabolism, I wasn't surprised to see I weighed about the same as three years ago.

"What do we do with him?" I asked, glancing at Reese's body on the floor.

"Leave him. He's not going anywhere."

"Oh."

"What do *you* want to do with him?"

"Um," I stammered, a little puzzled that he was bothering to ask what I wanted. "I don't know. It's creepy having him in the building with us."

"We can close the door. If that would make you feel better."

"Maybe."

"We'd leave if I wasn't dead on my feet."

"I know. It's okay."

I wheeled him out into the hallway and then hurried back into the lounge to snatch my magazine off the table. Henry took it from me and set it on his lap while I closed the door. I wheeled him back to the hospital room, and once inside, I turned the deadbolt, locking us in.

After I wheeled him to the bed, he eased out of the chair and crawled up onto the mattress. Then he held out his hand to me.

Finally, I realized the IV pole was standing beside the bed and that he was unhooked. There was still half a bag of liquid left, so I went around to the other side of the bed and refastened the IV line, screwing it back into place.

"What are we going to do about your meds?" I asked. "I have no clue how much you need."

"I'll be fine."

"Mm hmm," I replied, rolling my eyes as I walked back to his other side. "What about risk of infection?"

"I'm sure there are pills around here," he said, resting his head back against the pillow and closing his eyes. "We'll look after a bit."

I touched his forearm with one hand as I squeezed his hand with the other. He looked a little pale, probably from the exertion of killing the doctor, but his forehead wasn't glistening with sweat, so I took that as a good sign. "Earlier," I said, watching his face. "You heard me?"

He huffed as he opened his eyes. "I could have heard you from anywhere. With as loud as you were. I had no idea you had such a strong set of lungs."

I stared at him, trying to gauge how he meant his comment. Was it a knock or was he just being honest?

"I was already awake. By what, I'm not sure. I awoke in a panic. And you weren't here. I was already out of the bed by the time I heard you scream."

"What do we do now?" I asked. "With Reese dead."

"I'd like to sleep this off."

"You still need medicine. Antibiotics."

"We can look for some later."

"I can look now."

"You think I'm going to let you wander the halls by yourself?"

"Are you seriously going to stop me?"

"Not to bring up the obvious, but you almost got raped by that schmuck."

I looked away.

"If I hadn't shown up…and if it hadn't been for those jeans, I bet. Probably slowed him down."

I looked down.

"I'm glad he didn't try to cut them off."

I lifted my gaze back to his.

"I like them. Even more than those nightgowns I've always made you wear."

I blushed and looked away.

"Come here," he whispered, reaching out and taking my hand. He pulled me closer. When I eased onto the bed, he slid his hand over my lower back to my hip.

I glanced his way and then lay down gently beside him, resting my cheek on his chest.

He sighed heavily. "I hate being this vulnerable."

"It's a real change for you."

He huffed.

"You still protected me."

"That sniveling snake. We're lucky he was too focused on removing your pants, he didn't even sense me behind him."

I shivered at the thought.

"No one else touches you and lives. Ever."

"What about Carl?" I asked, thinking about the other day in the hallway of our apartment building, that first day Henry had taken me to Hopewell.

"He wasn't going to sleep with you. And I was proving a point."

"What point was that?" I asked. "That I was your slave and nothing more?"

"That I am levelheaded enough to determine the difference between an asshole and a real threat." When I craned my head back and met his gaze, he lifted his hand and brushed his thumb over my cheek. "In another city, things would have been different between us."

"How?"

"For one, I wouldn't have allowed you out of the apartment wearing nothing but a mere slip and a sweater."

I felt heat flood my cheeks.

"And you would have been my wife. Not my slave."

I looked away. I didn't know if I wanted that. To be his wife. But if he could treat me the way my father had treated my mom, the way my sister's boyfriend treated her, then I could want it.

"You wouldn't have been terrified of me. And you would have loved me." He rubbed his hand over my back. "And maybe you'd be carrying my child."

My throat tightened as my face flushed. Why did he always have to bring that up?

"Kallis," he said, his voice soft.

When my eyes started to flood with tears, I looked away and stared at the wall behind him. I could feel him watching me. When he took my hand and gave it a gentle squeeze, I gasped.

And then he said, "There's something you need to know."

CHAPTER 20

HENRY BLEW OUT A SLOW breath as I held mine and waited for him to explain.

I couldn't imagine what information he had to share. What could he possibly tell me that would make me feel better? What would justify every time he rubbed the fact that I couldn't have children in my face?

"I was part of the first sterilization group."

"What?" I asked, rearing my head as I looked up at him again.

He gave me a weak smile. "It wasn't just you."

"But…"

"I had no choice. It wasn't until after the first group that the people fully understood what the city was planning." He let out a heavy sigh. "You're the only other person who knows."

I didn't know what to say. I had always thought I was worth less than the average citizen because of my inability to bear children. The gangs made it sound that way. Who would want me when I'd be unable to conceive?

"I never wanted kids anyway, but taking away a person's right to have them is wrong and inhumane."

"I always thought everyone wanted them."

He shook his head. "There are lots of people who don't."

"Is that why you never sold me? Because it didn't matter?"

His frown deepened as he said, "No."

"Then why?"

"I never wanted to give you up." He shifted his gaze back to mine. "And I didn't think you could handle being sold again."

I blinked back tears. I doubted my life would have improved with someone else. And like Henry had said the other day, I was boring. I didn't put up a fight. I didn't make things interesting. I let him do what he wanted so that it would be better for me. I didn't try to get away or cause trouble. There were the few times I had overheard conversations, at least bits and pieces of them, but I did as I was told to avoid getting beaten or punished in some way.

Henry had said I needed to start fighting back. And if I did that, I'd feel better about myself, but I was afraid of the physical results.

"If I had fought back like you said I should, what would you have done to me?"

"I don't know," he said. "What more could I have done?"

I didn't want to think about it. I had so many ideas. I had lived in fear that he would act on those ideas flooding my head.

"Hmm?"

I let out a slow breath. "I can think of a lot of things."

"And I doubt I could have acted out most of them."

"What about last week?"

He was silent for a moment. I thought maybe he was going to refuse to answer. And then he said, "Nothing will excuse what I did. And I'm not trying to justify it. You caught me off guard and I didn't handle it well."

"What if I do it again?"

"I want to believe I would react differently."

I wasn't sure what to think of his response. Was I supposed to appreciate that he was being honest instead of claiming he would never hit me again? No one had ever made that claim, because the guys in Detroit didn't apologize for anything. Not unless they were held at gunpoint and they were pleading for their lives. No one thought women needed or deserved apologies.

"That's why when we get to Wilderness and I make sure you're okay, I'll be leaving."

I sighed. How was it so hard to be kind? Why couldn't he trust himself not to hurt me? And why couldn't he control himself?

"I want you to be safe," he said. "Even if it's without me."

"What if Wilderness is the same?"

He rubbed his hand over my arm. "It's not."

"But you've never been there."

"I've heard about it though. You'll have a job, a place to live. It'll be safe for you inside the city."

Part of me didn't want him to go. He had been a part of my life for the last year. I didn't know what my life would be like without him.

"You could even go to school if you want," he said. "Study computer science again."

I rose onto an elbow and cocked my head. "How do you know that?"

"It was something you said one night. When we were watching a movie. I don't think you intended to let that piece of information slip, because you never talked about it again after that." He lifted his free hand and brushed his knuckle gently over my cheek. "You thought I wasn't listening."

I shook my head. "You never seemed to."

"I was."

I sighed.

He grasped my hand. "You miss it?" When I gave him a questioning look, he added, "The computer work."

I shifted my gaze away as I considered his question. Did I miss it? It had been thrilling, designing programs with code and sneaking into other networks. For the longest time, I thought if I had just broken into the city's network, listened in, I would have discovered their plan to sterilize its citizens. Could I have done something to stop it? Could I have told my father and he could have caused an uproar?

"Hmm?"

I sighed. There wasn't any point to speculating now. It was all too late. Finally, I said, "I just wish people knew I'm more than they think."

"I know that."

"Do you?"

"You're scared. You barely speak to anyone. You usually only speak to me, but certainly not openly. And when you do speak, your voice is so quiet I can barely hear it."

My jaw flexed as he spoke, listing off all my faults.

"Half the time you look like you've checked out."

Bowing my head and staring down at his hand over mine, I said, my voice weak again, "I gave up."

He hummed.

"What was I supposed to do?" My voice cracked.

"You keep fighting."

"I'm powerless."

"No, you're not," he whispered back.

"You would have punished me for fighting back."

"I would have respected you more." He sighed and then said, "Kallis, you command what you want and people respond accordingly."

I raised my eyebrows and stared at him. "So, it's my fault how people treat me?"

"Partly."

"Boy, I didn't know I had that kind of power," I said, sarcasm in my tone. "Carl had made it perfectly clear that I answered to him. And so had all of the guys after him, including you. So, tell me how I was supposed to command the respect."

"It's partly in how you carry yourself."

"Carl murdered my father in front of me," I said, my voice getting louder. "And when he got out of the hospital and recovered from his stab wound, he made me pay for it. You all did."

"I know," he said quietly.

I closed my eyes, but the memory played inside my head. My eyes flooded with tears as I bowed my head.

He rubbed his hand over my back. "Come here," he whispered, coaxing me to lie back down.

I let out a ragged breath as I leaned against him and rested my head against his chest. "I want to forget."

"I know," he said.

The tears were flowing now and my shoulders trembled.

"You're too weak, like I said before. But that doesn't mean you're stupid or mindless. You're beautiful, Kallis. And smart, too. That's what I meant to say."

I sighed at his way with words. Maybe it was the painkiller talking. He did seem so different now. Like he cared about me all of a sudden. Why had he never shown that side of him to me before?

Or had I missed it?

Had I been so focused on how miserable my life had become that I couldn't see the little hints of good in it? With a few exceptions, had he only been so mean because he thought I could handle it? Being rough? I had wanted so much for him to show that he genuinely cared about me. I wanted him to be gentle and affectionate, whisper sweet things in my ear. Let me know that I mattered to him.

"When I was contacted about working on the ammunition project, I jumped at the chance. I wanted the hell out of the city. I guess I could have taken you out without that, but at the time, I had no idea where to go. The closest city isn't for hundreds of miles. Maybe we could have made it on our own. But I don't know. I wasn't thinking. Not to mention, the gangs do monitor who comes and goes."

I shook my head. "We could never have left."

"I would have found a way. If I had thought it was possible. I should have considered it more. I should have made it happen."

"It's over now," I said, closing my eyes.

"That doesn't stop me from having regrets."

I sighed again as I snuggled closer. If he could go back in time, how much would he change? How much would *I* change? If I had stood up for myself, what would have happened to me? Would I have become the thing I feared…a tramp? The kind of girl who sleeps around and thinks nothing of it? Who parades around in skimpy lingerie, showing off her assets?

I wanted to think I was better than that.

But instead of gaining confidence, I had lost what little confidence I had had before. Things had been different back then. Life had been good. I had a family who loved me. Encouraged me.

But then when the city issued the mandatory sterilization, everything had changed.

"I wish I had taken you out of the city a long time ago," he said. "Back before this all started."

I didn't know what to say, so I stayed quiet. What use was it to speculate about the past and how it would have changed things? My dad had once said that was a dangerous game to play. One would never be happy with his own life if he was constantly focused on what could have been.

"I had a chance," he said. "Back then. But I didn't take it."

"It's over now."

"It would have saved you from so many things."

I clamped my eyes shut as my face flushed with heat and my nose got stuffy. "Please stop," I whispered.

He smoothed his hand over my head, pulling my hair away from my face. "I'm sorry."

Unable to stop myself, I started to cry, my shoulders trembling as a sob escaped my lips.

He pressed his chin to the top of my head and shushed me softly.

When I got my breathing under control again, I wiped at my face and then wiped my hand over my jeans. I silently prayed he wouldn't say anything more. I wanted to move on. To not think about the past again. I had to stay focused on the future, on creating a better future.

His hand settled on my shoulder. It had always felt like a possessive gesture before, but now while it still did, there was a comfort in it. It was like now that I was free, I didn't mind being his.

And now that he had changed the way he was treating me, making me feel that he actually cared about me, and maybe even loved me, it felt comforting. I wanted his warmth, his hands on me, guiding me, protecting me. It was hard to explain and it sounded silly as I thought about it.

But that was how I felt.

CHAPTER 21

WHEN I AWOKE, still in Henry's arms and my cheek resting on his chest, sunlight was starting to shine through the window.

He stirred, breathing deeply as he turned his head and pressed his face to my hair. After a moment, he said, "Go get ready. I want to leave soon."

I craned my head back and met his gaze. "Can I shower first?"

He lifted his hand and caressed my cheek with his finger. "Sure."

I eased off the hospital bed, careful not to bump his stomach, and then hurried into the bathroom. I glanced at myself in the mirror. My shirt was wrinkled and my hair desperately needed some conditioner. When I saw the fading bruise on my cheek, I jerked my head, looking away.

As I was raising my foot over the tub ledge to step inside the tub, I heard a noise behind me. Pausing, I looked over my shoulder and saw Henry shuffling into the bathroom.

I shouldn't have felt bashful—he had seen me naked plenty of times—but I curled my shoulders in as I hugged my arms to my chest.

He eyed me with a curious look as he unbuttoned his jeans and pushed them down over his hips. Bracing himself with a hand on the sink ledge, he lifted each foot out of the jeans and then stepped toward me.

My gaze drifted to his arm and spotted the IV still taped in place.

He must have noticed, too, because he looked down and then carefully peeled back the tape and pulled out the needle. Blood began to trickle from the injection site.

My stomach felt queasy and I felt a little lightheaded, but I reached over and pulled a tissue from the box at the back of the toilet and then bunched it up and pressed it to the crook of his arm. When he covered his hand over mine, I craned my head back and met his gaze.

"Thank you," he said.

I smiled and nodded. But with the slight movement, my head whirled. As I swayed to the left, he stepped closer and wrapped his arm around my waist, pulling me back against him. The bloodstained tissue floated to the floor. I clamped my eyes shut and tried to block out the image.

"I hadn't realized you were so squeamish around needles and blood."

I swallowed hard. "I hadn't either."

He brushed my hair aside and tucked it behind my ear. The warmth of his fingertips felt good on my earlobe.

Looking down at his bandaged torso, I asked, "Do you need help with the bandages?"

"I think I can handle it."

"Okay." I couldn't help feeling relieved.

"Go ahead," he said. "It won't take me long."

After I stepped into the tub and under the stream of water, I stood facing the shower tiles as I let the water mat my hair to my head for a minute. Then I moved out from the stream and began shampooing my hair.

When Henry stepped in beside me, I blinked away the water and opened my eyes. His own eyes were closed and his face was scrunched like he was grimacing as he ran his hands over his hair, washing away the grime from the last few days.

My gaze drifted, to the sprinkling of dark curls between his pecs, to the chiseled muscle of his stomach. When I reached the puckered skin where Reese had stitched up the hole from the bullet, my stomach twisted. Quickly, I looked away, lower.

"I never thought a shower could hurt so much."

I almost gasped, like I was getting caught doing something embarrassing—which I had been about to do—but when I looked up, his eyes were still closed. "Oh," was all I could manage to say.

"I wish I could have made him suffer longer. I'm too good a shot."

I hummed. Of course I knew he was referring to Carl, the one who had shot him.

He opened his eyes and glanced at me as he added, "I suppose he's rotting in hell."

I nodded. I picked up the sponge, squeezed out some body wash, and went to lather Henry with it, but he took it from me and turned me around so my back was to him. He glided the sponge over my shoulder and down my arm.

My heart was racing so fast. I kept thinking he intended to use me, but all he did was scrub my body clean. And then he directed me under the stream of water. As I rinsed off, he lathered his hair with the shampoo and his body with the soap.

After we were done showering, I tried to dry him with the towel, but he wouldn't let me do that either. So, I towel-dried myself and got dressed in a clean outfit from the bag. Barefoot, I padded out into the main room.

As I was sitting down to slip on my socks and boots, I saw a shadow moving past the hall window behind the curtain.

CHAPTER 22

I FROZE, my back hunched. Had I really seen a shadow? Or was the stress getting to me? Something, someone, must have been wandering the halls.

Was it Reese? The thought gave me chills, considering I had last seen him lying in his own blood in the lounge.

When Henry walked out of the bathroom, barefoot and wearing jeans and fresh bandages, I went to motion for him to get back inside, but he was rubbing his towel over his head.

Quickly, on the balls of my feet, I darted across the room. Before I could grab his arm and pull him back inside the bathroom, he lowered the towel and frowned at me. "Someone is here," I whispered.

His furrowed brow deepened. And instead of stepping back inside the bathroom, he grabbed my arm and said, his voice quiet, "Put your shoes on."

While he shuffled across the room to the couch, I hurried past him and snatched up my socks and boots.

He tossed the towel on the coffee table and then picked up his firearm and inspected it. Somehow by the time I had my boots laced and tied, he had slipped into a clean shirt and his own boots.

He handed me my sweater and then nodded toward the door. "Which way did they go?"

"Um," I said, trying to remember. Had it been toward the right or the left? I lifted a trembling hand to my forehead. It had happened so fast and I wasn't actually positive now if it had been anything. Had I imagined the shadow?

Finally as my face flushed with heat and tears started to well up at disappointing him, I shook my head. "I'm sorry."

"It's okay," he whispered back. He took my hand, giving it a gentle squeeze, and then pulled me the rest of the way to the door.

I thought maybe I was going crazy, seeing things, hearing things, but then I heard footsteps out in the hallway. When I looked over at Henry, he gave me a slight nod.

Quickly, I pulled my sweater on and then waited for him to make his move. I had no idea what he would do. Would he wait it out and hope the person left the building? Or would he open the door to confront him?

"Come on out," a male voice said from the other side of the door.

Henry moved the window curtain aside and peered out.

I tried to lean over to see, but he was blocking my view.

"I'm here to help," the man said.

Letting the curtain fall back over the window, Henry bowed his head and cursed under his breath. Then with a heavy sigh, he stepped back and opened the door.

CHAPTER 23

I KEPT THINKING, wasn't he going to do anything? Was he really just going to give in? But what choice did he have? He was still in pain from the gunshot wound. He should have been in bed resting, not out walking around like barely anything had happened.

"Who are you?" Henry asked, reaching out his arm behind his back toward me.

I stepped closer, setting my hand on his arm, as I leaned over to see around him.

The man wore a black guard uniform and black boots. He glanced at me and then addressed Henry. "I'm with the Federal Guard of the New United States."

"What do you want?"

"I'm here to take you to the city of Franklin."

"We're not heading that way."

"We can handle your city transfer once you get settled," the man replied.

The muscles in Henry's forearm clenched under my hand. I felt helpless. He wasn't in any condition to attack, and I couldn't help him no matter how hard I tried. I wasn't trained to handle stress. My training, if you could even call it that, had made me weak. And that was the whole point. Weak. Powerless. Easy to control and manipulate.

"She stays with me," Henry said, his voice firm.

The man's gaze shifted to me briefly and then he turned back to Henry. "Very well. You have my word you two will not be separated."

And just like that, after Henry gathered our bag, we followed the guard through the halls to the main door.

When we stepped outside, I shielded my eyes with my free hand. Henry's grip on my hand was tight and I thought I saw the glistening of sweat on his forehead when I looked up at him.

Maybe this was better. Maybe Franklin was our new safe place.

CHAPTER 24

INSIDE THE BLACK VAN that waited by the curb, I scooted closer to Henry. He had his head leaning back against the headrest and his hand clutching his waist. I tucked my right hand around the crook of his arm and set my other hand over his.

He made a soft sound that resembled a sniffle as he turned his head toward me. "I'm sorry I couldn't get us out of this."

I lifted my hand to cup his cheek as I shook my head. "It's okay," I whispered back. "Everything is going to work out."

I almost cringed when I said the words. I didn't honestly believe them. I wanted to, but I didn't feel optimistic enough.

The corners of Henry's lips lifted slightly as he huffed. "Remind me not to use you for motivational speaking." When I giggled, he leaned closer and pressed his forehead to mine.

I ran my palm over his damp hair and then lowered it again to his hand at his waist.

As the van drove on the interstate, weaving around more clusters of vehicles that were parked in the road, I studied our surroundings while Henry slept beside me. He had put up a good fight to stay awake, but eventually the exhaustion had won. Now he was stretched out across the seats with his head resting on my thighs and facing me.

Slowly, gently, I smoothed back his dark hair as I stared out the window.

It only took a couple hours to reach the city. I was a little surprised it was so close by. It wasn't that far from Detroit.

If they were so close by, how could they let the gangs rule the city? Why hadn't they stepped in to help the guards maintain control?

Was Franklin just as bad?

And why wasn't the Federal Guard for the New United States doing anything about the gangs? Had they really just let it happen? Surely, they had the numbers to get the city back in order.

Maybe that was a question I could ask when we got there.

But then again, who was I going to ask? It's not like we were going to visit with the governor or whoever was in charge of the city now. We'd likely be quarantined for a few days, maybe a week.

Back in the day, before the gangs took over, a citizen could transfer to another city, but upon arrival, he was quarantined for a week, and during that time, he was interviewed extensively to ensure he was planning to contribute to his new city. If the guards felt he wasn't going to be a good addition to society, he was sent back to his origin. With my father being one of Detroit's city guards, I had heard stories of people who had tried to transfer and were sent back. It hadn't happened often, but it was a factor.

When the van entered through an open wrought iron gate, I stared in awe at the high-rise buildings. I had never lived anywhere other than Detroit. Traveling across country, or really anywhere outside of our own cities, was heavily discouraged.

There were the occasional trips by certain members of society to South Carolina where the government buildings were located, but the average citizen stayed within the confines of his own city.

We weaved through city streets and finally turned into an empty parking lot of a large building with an expansive awning at its main doors.

When I read the sign of the building, I frowned. "Medical center?"

CHAPTER 25

I STRAIGHTENED UP TALLER in the seat and craned my head to get a better view of the building as I stared out the window.

Henry hummed.

When I looked down, his eyes were still closed and he seemed to be sleeping. I didn't want to wake him, but we were stopping.

"Kallis."

"Um," I stammered, glancing down again. His eyes still hadn't opened. Keeping my voice low, I said, "It looks like they're taking us to the medical center."

Finally, his eyes blinked open as his brows furrowed.

"Why would they do that?" I asked.

"Protocol, probably." He turned his head toward the sliding door and then slowly eased himself to a sitting position as the door glided open.

"Welcome to Franklin," the man said. "Once we get you two checked out, make sure you're medically sound, we will work on the transfer papers."

Henry reached for my hand. Then he rose to his feet, hunching over to avoid bumping his head on the low ceiling of the van, and pulled me to the door. I grabbed our bag from the seat and then hopped out after him.

The man took us inside and led us through the lobby to a set of elevators. We rode to the third floor and then walked down a long, dimly lit hallway, the floral-print carpeting softening our steps.

I thought it was odd the building seemed more like a hotel than a medical center. I had so many questions I wanted to ask, but I kept quiet, holding onto Henry's hand. I couldn't tell if it was my hand or his that was squeezing so hard. And I could sense that he was struggling to stand and stay focused and alert.

Finally, the man gestured for us to pass through an open doorway. We stepped inside and found living quarters, like a hotel room with a main living area and kitchenette. And there were two doors, one to the left and a closed door to the right. When I peeked inside what I had figured was the bathroom, I frowned. There were two narrow cots and a patient's table, like one from a doctor's office.

I turned to Henry to assess his reaction, but he was focused on the main door. As I followed his gaze, a woman, probably in her mid-forties and dressed in a white lab coat, appeared in the doorway.

"This is Nurse Jane," the man said. "She and Dr. Wallace, who you will meet later, will handle your medical examinations over the next few days. Please take this time to relax and get comfortable. Meals will be provided three times a day. If you should need anything, please let Nurse Jane know."

"Thank you," Henry replied.

The guard addressed the nurse. "Keep them together, please."

The woman nodded. "Yes, sir."

When he left, she turned to us and introduced herself again. "I've been told they found you two outside the city, so I'll be getting you checked out to ensure your health is up to our standards."

I stepped closer to Henry. What could they possibly think might be wrong with us? And why were their standards so superior?

"Please make yourselves comfortable while I retrieve some clothes for you."

"Thank you," Henry said again, his voice strained this time.

She bowed politely and then left the room.

"Why do we have to go through this?" I whispered. "What do they think is wrong with us?"

He sighed. "I don't know, Kallis. It's their process." He turned toward the sitting area and eased himself onto the couch.

Hugging my arms to my chest, I paced the floor. I couldn't sit still. The *standards* bit the nurse had said was grating on me. True, I hadn't been to a doctor since I was sixteen, around the time of the random sterilizations. But I felt fine. I didn't need a physical examination to know I was fine.

"Sit down, please," Henry said, reaching out his hand to me. "You're making me nervous."

"You should be," I replied, turning his way. "Why do they bring people here?"

"Kallis, come here." There was warning in his tone. His brows were furrowed, and he was pursing his lips.

I felt a pit forming in my stomach at his reaction. Bowing my head, I closed my eyes, but it only seemed to make the pounding in my ears louder. I could even feel my pulse beating against my neck like it was pounding to be let out. I bit my trembling lip and sat down beside him. "I'm sorry," I whispered.

"Look at me," he said, hooking a finger under my chin and tilting my head back.

Swallowing hard, I opened my eyes and met his gaze.

"You don't have to be sorry. I just need you calm right now."

Before I could reply, he turned his head and looked toward the door.

I followed his gaze and saw the nurse re-enter the room, eyeing us as she closed the door behind her. Quickly, I looked away, averting my eyes.

"Everything all right?" she asked, sounding concerned.

Henry lowered his hand to his thigh. "Everything's fine."

I bowed my head again and stared down at my clasped hands.

If the nurse thought anything of us, she didn't say. Instead, she walked over and handed each of us a folded bundle of fabric. It looked like there was a hospital gown of faded blue and a thick white robe.

"There is a bathroom through the door over here," she said, pointing toward the door to the left. "I would like for you to fast for eight hours, so please, no food after midnight. I will return around eight o'clock tomorrow morning."

She clasped her hands together in front of her. "Do you have any questions? Can I get you anything?"

"Food?" Henry asked.

She nodded. "I will have lunch and dinner brought up at noon and five. If you would like a snack, there are some miscellaneous items in the refrigerator and cupboards. Please help yourself to whatever you would like."

"Thank you," he said.

I couldn't believe he wasn't asking questions. I had so many of them, but I couldn't bring myself to ask them.

When the nurse left the room, Henry set our bundles of clothing on the coffee table and then leaned back against the couch cushions. He let out a heavy sigh as he pressed his hand to his stomach, over his wound.

"Are you okay?" I asked.

"I need painkillers."

I sighed. "Why didn't you ask?"

He turned his head and glared at me.

I bowed my head, looking away from his intense stare. "I'm sorry." I lifted my trembling hand to my forehead. When he cursed under his breath, I clamped my eyes shut. My pulse thumped more against my neck.

"Why don't you go check for food," he said. "Please."

Without looking his way, I rose to my feet and went to the kitchenette, thankful to get some distance between us. I checked all of the cupboards and the mini refrigerator and found packaged protein bars and bottled water. I took a few packages and two bottles into the living room.

As I was setting everything on the coffee table, Henry reached out his hand. With a small sigh, I picked them back up and set them on the couch at his side. Then I backed away and headed for the closed door while he was busy tearing open the packaging.

I opened the door and peered inside to find a large bed and another bathroom. I was about to walk in when Henry said, "Come here."

I closed my eyes and released a quiet breath. Did he always have to control what I did? I couldn't do anything without him cutting in and getting me doing something else.

"Kallis."

With a slight nod, I turned back to face him.

He had his head resting against the back cushion as he chewed his protein bar. Reaching out his hand to me, he said, "Sit down."

I walked around the table and sat down at his other side. My body was still trembling and tense. When he handed me a small piece of his protein bar, I shook my head. "I'm not hungry."

"You need to eat."

I swallowed hard and took the food, careful not to touch his fingers. As I stuck the piece of the bar in my mouth and chewed, he handed me his bottle of water. Flicking my gaze to his, I took the bottle. I couldn't avoid his fingers this time; his pinky finger purposely—or so it seemed—brushed over my hand. My body tensed at his touch.

"We could head farther south," he said, his voice gravelly. "If you don't like Wilderness."

I shrugged.

"South Carolina, maybe. It would be warmer there than in the northeast."

I didn't know what to say. I had never been to either location. And I didn't want to talk to him anyway.

"You like the snow?"

I shook my head.

"South then."

My eyes welled with fresh tears.

Henry sighed.

Sniffling, I lifted my hand and brushed trembling fingers over my temple.

"Come here," he whispered, touching my elbow.

I flinched, shrinking away from him.

He sighed again. "You're upset with me…"

I shook my head.

"Don't lie," he said quietly.

"I'm always afraid of what you'll do to me."

"I can't do anything to you right now. I can barely think straight or stay awake to argue with you."

"You're still mean."

"I just fed you. How mean is that?"

"Before. When you glared…"

"When was that?" he asked, sounding confused.

Shaking my head, I wiped at my face. "Forget it."

"Nah, I think we need to work this out."

"Henry, please," I said, my voice cracking.

He reached out, grasped my wrist, and pulled my hand down. "What's wrong?"

I bit my trembling lip as I stared down at the floor.

"Kallis."

"I always think you're going to punish me. And you look mad. A lot."

"And when did I glare at you?"

I swallowed hard. "When I asked why you didn't get the painkillers."

He sighed. "Come here," he said, releasing my hand and outstretching his arm. His fingers glided over my back.

Relenting, I leaned against him and curled my legs on the couch.

He set his hand on my shoulder as he rested his chin on the top of my head. "I'm sorry," he whispered.

"It's okay."

"No," he replied. "It's not."

I clamped my eyes shut. I felt stupid being so emotional.

"You're scared, I get it." He wrapped his other arm around me, rubbing my back with his palm. "I've made you walk on eggshells, afraid about what I'll do next."

I couldn't believe he was actually admitting to scaring me. The whole time we had been together he made it sound like I had it better being with him instead of one of the other guys.

"You need to learn that sometimes things don't have anything to do with you."

"How will I know which ones do?"

"You won't, unless I tell you. But you need to go about your life and stop worrying about how people will react."

"I can't."

"You need to try. Things are different now."

CHAPTER 26

AS I LISTENED to Henry's steady breathing and his pulse thumping against my ear, I couldn't stop thinking about how I was going to stop reacting to his emotions. Maybe I could do it with other people, but it was ingrained in me to worry about upsetting him. To do anything else seemed strange to me.

When he moaned, the thoughts faded away. His hold around me tightened, like he was afraid I'd leave. I pressed my hand to his chest over his heart and tried to crane my head back. He stirred and lifted his chin from my head as his hand moved to cup my cheek. When I looked up at him, he met my gaze and gave me a weak smile.

I felt a warmth flood inside my chest.

"I need a comfortable bed."

I nodded. Then I sat up and hauled myself to my feet. I walked around the coffee table and headed for the bedroom door.

When I stepped inside, I took a moment to check out the room. There was a huge bed against the far wall, an open door to the right, and a pair of stuffed chairs flanking a small round table beside a floor-to-ceiling window. As I was walking to the bed, Henry came up behind me.

"Oh, thank God," he said, easing his shirt up over his chest as he strode past me. When he raised his arms, he winced, gritting his teeth.

I set my hand gently to his chest.

Giving up, he sat down on the edge of the bed so I could get his shirt over his head.

I tossed the shirt to the foot of the bed and then cupped his cheek with my palm. His stubble had filled in, shadowing his face, and his hair had grown out, longer than we usually let it. Once a week, he had me shave his head with the clippers. It didn't require any skill. He could have done it himself. But we kept it short. I should have trimmed it again the night I found Liana in the bathtub.

But now I realized his hair grew fast. I had never seen it this long. Not that it was growing past his ears, but it looked fuller now. I could even run my fingers through it.

"Daydreaming?" he asked, gliding his hands over my hips.

My cheeks reddened, I was sure.

He smiled. "Come here," he said, slipping his fingertips underneath the hem of my shirt.

I took over, lifting the shirt over my head. His strong hands gripped my sides as I tossed my shirt over with his. "I was just thinking how fast your hair grows."

He huffed as the corners of his mouth curled upward.

"We would have trimmed it by now."

"Do you like it?"

I nodded.

"You don't think I'm too old-looking, do you?"

I shook my head. "How old are you anyway?"

"Twenty-seven." He turned his head to the side as his brows furrowed and his eyes looked toward the ceiling. Then he added, "I think."

"Oh," was all I could manage to say. It sounded old. Eight years older than I was.

"So, now you think I'm too old."

I shrugged. "Does it matter?"

"It's not like you're stuck with me, Kallis," he said. "You can choose someone else. Anyone else."

I shifted my gaze away. I still didn't really think I wanted to be with anyone else. I didn't want to let him go. Maybe every time his grouchiness came out, I had second thoughts. But the way he treated me now...things were different. Right or wrong, it didn't matter.

"When we get to Wilderness..." His thought trailed off.

I closed my eyes as I gave him a slight nod. If his intention was for us to go our separate ways, I wouldn't be able to change his mind. He wasn't so easily swayed once his mind was made up.

His hands glided across my bare skin and splayed over my back as he pressed his forehead to my chest.

Swallowing hard, I hugged him and ran my fingers through his hair.

Finally, he pressed his lips to my chest, between my breasts.

I sucked in a breath as warmth flooded my stomach.

With a sigh, he pulled away. "We need more rest. Or at least I do."

Releasing my hold, I nodded and took a step back.

"Do you want to wear my shirt?"

I hugged my arms to my chest as I shook my head.

He cocked his head and gave me a strange look as the corners of his mouth lifted. But if he thought my response was odd, he didn't mention it. Instead he stood up and unbuttoned his jeans.

I followed suit and then folded our clothes and set them on the nightstand beside the bed.

Once we were tucked in under the covers, he wrapped his arm around me, pulling me against him. I closed my eyes and hugged his arm to my chest.

I couldn't sleep, but lying there with him helped me to relax. We shouldn't have been inside the city, Franklin. We shouldn't have been stuck inside their medical center, waiting for the verdict that would tell us whether or not we measured up to their standards.

But Henry hadn't seemed concerned. I knew part of that was because of the pain he was in, and suffering through because of his stubborn nature, but he also had a better sense of how the rest of the world worked.

I didn't.

I had barely been out of high school by the time the gangs took over Detroit. I hadn't even started my classes at the university yet. I had been living at home with my family—my parents and three younger siblings—when our world changed.

The last time I saw my mother and siblings was the morning my father took me to tour the campus, in the area now called the Creekside district and ruled by Henry's gang.

We were heading back to the truck after the tour when we were ambushed by Carl and his group. It might have turned out okay, at least for my dad, but then they found out he worked for the city guard.

I tried to force the thoughts away. I hated replaying that moment in my mind. I hated replaying the moments that followed, especially after Carl recovered from the stab of my father's blade.

There were so many memories I wanted to forget.

And maybe I *would* need to let Henry go in order for me to do that. He was a constant reminder.

CHAPTER 27

WHEN I HEARD a soft knock at the main door to the suite, I sucked in a breath and held it as I lay frozen, listening for more sounds.

A sharp click sounded and then there were quiet footsteps on tile. Was the nurse bringing our lunch?

I wanted to wake up Henry, but he was breathing deeply. Any moment he could get feeling no pain would help his body heal. And so I listened, unmoving.

After a brief visit, only a matter of seconds, whoever it was left, and then all was quiet again.

I didn't like the idea of random people having access to our room, especially while we were sleeping. But it *was* the middle of the day. And the nurse had knocked first.

But then I realized we had just lost another opportunity to ask for pain medications. I would need to track her down. She hadn't mentioned how we could reach her.

I knew Henry wouldn't want me wandering the halls by myself, and he'd no doubt be upset, but he needed painkillers and antibiotics. Not to mention his wounds needed to be tended. Medicated ointments needed to be applied.

As gently as I could, I lifted his arm from my waist and slipped out from underneath it.

He moaned and tucked his arm in to his chest. For a moment, I studied his face. He looked so vulnerable. And his forehead was glistening with sweat.

Carefully, I pulled back the covers to check his bandage. It was stained with dark red.

I had to find the nurse. Let him be mad. He needed help.

I dressed quickly and then padded out on bare feet into the living room. There was a food tray and a stainless steel teapot sitting on the small dining table. But I didn't bother to lift the lid from the food.

I cast a quick glance over my shoulder to make sure Henry was still sleeping and then I slipped out into the main hallway. I didn't know if the door would lock me out if I latched it, so I pulled it closed until the metal touched the strike plate.

When I turned toward the hallway, looking both ways, I let out a slow breath. The hallway's emptiness and the dim lighting felt eerie, raising goosebumps on my arms.

I wasn't sure which way to go. Was she farther down the hall? The place was so strange. Exactly like a hotel, but with special exam rooms inside.

Finally, I decided to head farther down. After passing a few doors, I came to an intersecting hallway. When I turned right and saw that it opened into a large area with a main desk at the front, I let out a sigh of relief.

Suddenly, the sharp sound of brushing metal and a loud clank from behind me echoed inside the open room, making me flinch. Gasping, I jerked my head and then turned around to see a door opening. I looked over my shoulder, back toward the desk, but no one was there.

As the door opened farther and a dark figure started to appear, I backed away. My heart was racing so fast. I wasn't prepared to be alone. I realized that now. I had no way to defend myself.

A man, dressed in a black guard uniform, strode out into the hallway.

I backed up farther, bumping into the desk.

A look of surprise spread across the man's face as he stopped short. He eyed me for a moment and then his gaze shifted to the open room behind me.

Following his gaze, I jerked my head to look over my shoulder. Still no one.

When he turned his attention back to me and stepped closer, he asked, "Can I help you? You must be lost."

"Um," I stammered, trying to feel my way to the side of the desk.

"Do you need help?"

My throat tightened as I tried to figure out what to say.

"Let me get one of the nurses," he said, heading past me and the desk and giving us a wide berth. He cast a glance my way, giving me a small smile.

I lifted my hand and rubbed my forehead with my fingertips. I felt like such an idiot. The guard must have thought I was daft. But I couldn't think straight. I was expecting to find the nurse, not some random guy.

When he came back with a nurse, a younger one than before, he said, "This is Kelsey. She will take you back to your room and get you whatever you need."

Nodding slightly, I tried to smile. "Thank you," I said, but my voice was barely loud enough for me to hear it and I doubted he was able to.

He eyed me a moment longer and then he turned to the nurse. It looked like he had his hand at her back.

As he leaned down and kissed her cheek, I looked away, trying not to watch their exchange.

"I'll see you tonight," he said.

In my periphery, I could see her smile up at him as she nodded.

Finally, he excused himself and disappeared back through the doorway.

"Is everything all right, miss?" the girl asked.

I shook my head. "My..." My voice trailed off as I tried to figure out how to refer to Henry. We weren't friends. He wasn't a boyfriend, and certainly not my husband. He wasn't my owner anymore; he had made that clear already. Not to mention, that wasn't something I wanted getting out to the rest of the world.

"Is there something wrong with your room?" she asked. She seemed genuinely concerned as she reached out to me but stopped before touching my arm.

"My, um..."

"The man you're here with?" she asked.

I nodded. "He's...sick."

She gestured for me to follow her and then we walked down the hallway back to the room.

At the door, I paused. I still couldn't stop thinking about how he was going to react to me leaving the room by myself. Slowly, I pushed open the door and peered inside. And then I let out a sigh of relief when I saw that Henry was still in bed.

The nurse, Kelsey, gave me a concerned look, but I turned away and hurried into the bedroom.

Henry's forehead still glistened with sweat and he was shivering now.

"Does he have a fever?" the woman asked, stepping past me.

"I don't know," I managed to say.

She sat down on the edge of the bed. She reached out her hand, but must have thought better of it because she pulled her hand back and rose to her feet. "I'll get the doctor. Does he have any injuries?"

I nodded. "He was shot."

Her eyes widened. Then she reached out and set her hand on my arm, giving it a gentle squeeze. "Stay here with him. I'll be right back with the doctor."

"Thank you." I watched her hurry from the room. When I heard the door latching, I turned back and crawled up onto the bed.

Henry stirred as he sucked in a breath.

I studied his face as I smoothed back his fluffy hair. Seeing him so vulnerable still made tears well up in my eyes.

"Kallis," he murmured.

"I'm right here," I replied, my voice cracking. I let out a slow breath and then added, "The nurse is bringing the doctor."

"Thank you."

One of my tears slipped out and landed on the back of my hand. I hadn't expected him to be chill about my leaving the room. But maybe he didn't know I had left. Not yet. Unless he had awakened and realized I was gone.

A couple minutes later, Kelsey came back with a man wearing a white lab coat over a pale-blue dress shirt and black slacks.

As he approached, I eased myself off the bed to give him room.

He sat down on the side of the bed and pressed his hand to Henry's forehead. Then he removed a small pen light from the breast pocket of his coat and shined it at Henry's eyes.

Henry lay motionless as the doctor assessed his condition.

Turning to Kelsey, the doctor said, "Please retrieve a stretcher and two guards."

With a quick nod, she left the room.

I jerked my head when I heard the click of the door latch.

"Nothing to worry about," the doctor was saying.

When I turned back to look at him, he was looking back at me.

"Seems he needs fluids and antibiotics to fight off infection," he said. "The nurse was telling me he suffered a gunshot wound?"

Sniffling, I nodded. "His stomach." My voice cracked.

The doctor hummed softly. Then he pulled back the covers and began inspecting the bandages.

Finally, the nurse returned, accompanied by two guards who were helping her wheel a stretcher into the room. One of the men was the same one I had encountered in the hallway moments earlier.

The doctor instructed the guards to move Henry onto the stretcher and then they wheeled him into the exam room on the other side of the suite.

I hung back, not wanting to get in anyone's way.

Within a matter of minutes, they had him hooked to an IV with antibiotics and pain meds. As the guards were leaving, the doctor removed the bandage and began sterilizing the stitched wounds.

When my stomach protested and my head started to whirl, I looked away. Reaching out, I braced a hand on the doorjamb and closed my eyes.

"Why don't we sit down," the nurse said, touching my arm lightly. She guided me into the living room to the couch.

"Is he going to be okay?" I asked.

"The doctor is making sure of that," she replied.

"He's so stubborn."

She hummed. "I can imagine."

I sucked in a deep breath and then bowed my head in my hands.

She patted my arm. "You did the right thing."

I nodded.

She rose to her feet, and then I heard her footsteps on the tile in the exam room. Soft voices followed, but I couldn't make out the words.

I pressed my hands to my warm face as I sniffled. Somehow I had to get it together. But my emotions kept getting in the way, making me break down in tears with every little thing.

That wasn't a sign of strength.

No wonder people looked at me like I was weak. And how could I cry so much over someone who had made my life miserable? After all he had done to me, how could I want him to recover? I should have taken the opportunity to get away from him.

But yet I couldn't.

And I knew I never would.

CHAPTER 28

WHEN THE DOCTOR and nurse finally walked out of the exam room, I rose to my feet and walked toward them. "How is he?" I asked.

"He's going to be fine, but he needs to stay off his feet and get lots of rest. It seems he's outdone himself," the doctor said.

I nodded. Of course he had. That was how Henry operated. I hadn't expected anything else. I didn't bother to mention he would probably be back on his feet in the next twenty-four hours.

"We will postpone the regular examinations until he's back on his feet. In the meantime, we will keep him heavily sedated so his body can heal."

"Oh," I said, feeling relieved.

"If you need anything at all, there is a phone in the kitchen. Just dial 7 to reach the nurse's station."

"Thank you," I said, my voice weak.

He gave me a reassuring smile. "He'll be all right. Back to new in no time."

Quickly, I nodded.

As the doctor was heading toward the door, Kelsey touched my arm and squeezed it gently. "I'll be back with ointment for your bruise." I must have looked confused because she added, "On your cheek."

"Oh," I said, lifting my hand to my face.

She gave a slight nod and then followed the doctor out into the hallway.

It only took her a few minutes to come back with the ointment. In that time, I had toured the kitchen again, inspecting all of the cabinets and the refrigerator.

She set a small tube on the counter. "This will help with the bruising. Apply it twice a day."

"Thank you."

Her gaze shifted toward the exam room. And then she leaned closer and with her voice low, she asked, "Did he give that to you?"

I didn't know what to say. He had, but everything had changed. Finally, I said, "It's a long story."

She eyed me a moment, looking concerned. But she didn't press the issue. "I'll be back to check on you two. If you need anything, please call the desk and ask for me."

I nodded. "Thanks," I said quietly.

When she left and the door latched, I picked up the tube and turned it around in my hand. My throat tightened as I bowed my head. To be able to apply it, I'd have to face myself in the mirror.

I went into the exam room. Henry's eyes were closed, but when I approached, he opened them and gave me a weak smile. His eyes glistened, bringing tears to my own and making my throat tighten. I reached out and touched his arm. "You try to act so tough," I said.

His throat bobbed. "I seem to remember I tried to get you to leave me behind."

Shaking my head, I looked away. When a tear slipped down my cheek, I wiped it away with my hand.

"Didn't I?"

"I'd never make it on my own."

He sighed as he turned his head and stared out the window.

Trying to change the subject, I said, "The doctor said they'll postpone our exams."

His throat bobbed again as he gave his head a slight nod. "You should go to bed. You look tired."

I glanced over my shoulder, looking toward the living area. With people having access to our room, I didn't want to be in the bedroom alone. I turned back to him, but his eyelids were closed.

With a small sigh, I went into the living room and retrieved the bundle of clothes Nurse Jane had brought earlier. Then I went into the small bathroom inside the exam room to change. It looked similar to the bathroom at the medical center, except there was no shower at the back. Just a toilet and sink against the right side of the narrow room. A small hatch, a mere wooden board with a cupboard door handle, was affixed to the wall off to the left, across from the toilet.

I set the items on the counter and then slowly began to undress. I folded my shirt and jeans and then slipped into the hospital gown and robe. I couldn't bring myself to look at my face in the mirror, so I left the tube of ointment by the sink.

When I walked out of the bathroom, Henry had the back of his hand resting on his forehead. I wanted to ask him if he would put the ointment on my cheek, but for some reason that felt like too much to ask. So, I turned down the lights and then crawled onto one of the cots by the window.

With my back to the wall, I tucked my hands under my cheek and looked at Henry again. It looked like he was staring up at the ceiling.

I wanted to curl up beside him, for him to turn back to me and stretch out his arm, tell me to *come here* as he always did, but he didn't seem to want me around.

How long would he push me away? Did he honestly think I was better off without him?

I didn't want to think about that. Because maybe if I did, I would realize that I *was* better off without him.

CHAPTER 29

OVER THE NEXT two days, while Henry was heavily sedated so he could heal, I slept in the cot in the exam room with him. He didn't want me at his side. But I couldn't leave him.

Kelsey, the nurse, kept asking me to go for a walk with her, at least up and down the hallway, but I didn't feel comfortable being out of the room. So, she came to sit with me during her breaks. I didn't know why she'd do such a thing. She had a boyfriend, someone to keep her occupied already.

"They find people out there all the time, you know," she was saying. "Trackers."

"We don't have trackers," I said.

She shook her head. "You must have been carrying it. On an article of clothing, a shoe... It was on something. They caught the movement. That's how they found you."

I didn't know why she was telling me this. "Is that what happened to you?"

"No. My husband told me."

"Husband?" She didn't look old enough to be married.

"Two years," she said, smiling. "We've been trying to have kids, but it hasn't worked out yet."

I tried to give her an apologetic look. I didn't want to mention that Henry and I had been part of the sterilization plan.

"How about you two?" she asked, glancing over at Henry who appeared to be sleeping. "Any kids?"

I shook my head as I stared down at my clasped hands.

She was silent for a moment. Then she asked, "How did you two meet?"

She probably thought the question would bring a smile to my face, but instead I bowed my head in my hands and fought hard not to cry.

"I'm sorry," she whispered. "I get too nosy."

What story was I supposed to tell people about how Henry and I met? I had never figured I'd ever need to tell a story, so it wasn't something that had crossed my mind before. But now, what was I to say? The truth was too much. But making up a fairytale beginning didn't sound right either.

"It's okay," she said. "We don't have to talk. I didn't mean to make you feel uncomfortable."

I wanted to be able to tell her something. I just didn't know what.

"Do you like movies?" she asked. "I could bring some to help pass the time. The doctor says he'd like to keep Henry sedated for another day or two. Make sure he's not overdoing it before we get him up and walking again. To keep the infection at bay."

I cleared my throat. "I like Turkish films. Romantic dramas."

She smiled. "I'll see what I can find."

After she left the room, I walked over to Henry's bedside.

He rolled his head over the pillow to look at me. His face had regained its color, back to the tanned hue of before.

"Hi," I said, curling my fingers around his.

"That night," he said. "It wasn't the first time we met."

I frowned and looked over my shoulder, toward the door. "What are you talking about?"

"I can still hear everything. I'm not dead."

I felt my cheeks grow red.

"You didn't know what to say about how we met because you don't know the truth."

I thought maybe the medications were affecting him, making him loopy. I honestly didn't know what he was talking about. I had never met him before that night. Not even while Carl was in the hospital recovering from the stab wound.

There had been plenty of other guys though, forcing me to stay at the hospital with Carl. All there to make sure I didn't get away. Kent had been one of them. The gang was a loyal bunch with a moral code of boundaries. They knew not to touch another's girl, and they all figured I'd be Carl's, since he had claimed me.

"You don't know," he said, his voice faint, as he looked away. His eyes drifted closed.

Even if he was making sense, it didn't matter. It wouldn't change anything. And I didn't remember meeting anyone in my earlier life, back when things were normal.

I squeezed his hand gently and ran my fingertips over his hair, straightening a stray tendril that had curled at his temple. I leaned down and kissed his forehead and then I left the room and curled up on the couch.

How much longer was the doctor going to keep him sedated?

I needed him. I needed his strength, guiding me. Watching over me.

And telling me what on earth he had been talking about.

CHAPTER 30

IT WAS ANOTHER DAY until the doctor finally said he was reducing the sedatives and allowing Henry to walk the halls.

He was unstable on his feet after the few days in bed, but it didn't take long for him to get his legs moving. And with the help of the walker for the first two rounds in the hallway, he was able to move.

As I walked with him, I kept thinking about what he had said. I had hoped he would mention it again, but he never did.

And I was afraid to ask.

I thought that maybe it wasn't actually true and he would give me a strange look like I had lost my mind.

But the idea that we had met before offered me hope. And I didn't want to lose that. I wanted desperately to be able to tell a more romantic story of our beginning than the one I remembered.

"How are you feeling?" I asked quietly.

He let out a slow breath. "Better," he said. "Like I might actually live."

My throat tightened at his words and my eyes felt strained. "You're going to be fine." It sounded more forceful than I had intended.

He gave me a weak smile. "Right. I'm taking you to Wilderness. I forgot."

I looked away as tears threatened to spill down my cheeks. Shaking my head, I asked, "How can you be so lax when you tell me I need to fight and figure things out?"

He stopped in the middle of the hallway.

"Everything is going to be fine," I said. It sounded more like I was trying to convince myself of that. "You need to fight, too."

He nodded slightly. "I'm sorry."

It sounded so odd hearing him apologize. I mean, it was nice when it was about him saying something mean, but it was getting to be too much, too often. "Please stop saying that."

He sighed. "What do you want me to say?"

I blinked up at him. "What did you want *me* to say all those times?"

The corners of his mouth turned up a smidge. "All right."

"I just want the confident guy back. The guy who knew what he wanted. Who *took* what he wanted. The guy who didn't wait for permission."

"That guy was an asshole."

I bit my trembling lip.

"You want him back?"

"You can still be nice and confident at the same time."

"Yeah, but the permission thing…"

My face grew hotter and my throat went dry. Clearing my throat, I stared down toward the end of the empty hallway. "You don't need permission." My voice was so faint I wasn't sure if he'd heard me, but then I heard him hum softly.

It felt like the tension between us was thick. But it had to be because of his gunshot wound. The pain, the meds. This wasn't the Henry from before. This was the injured version of him. A much quieter version. More reserved. More apologetic than I thought was necessary. I didn't want him to apologize for everything; I just wanted him to act without having to say he was sorry later.

We walked back to the room in awkward silence. I worried I had said too much. Or maybe I had said the wrong thing.

While he went into the bathroom, I reheated leftovers from dinner the previous night in the microwave: creamy chicken and potato soup and four dinner rolls.

It only took a few minutes to heat, so I kept the food warming in the microwave while I waited for him to get back. I took out two bowls and then when I heard the door open, I poured the soup and then carried the bowls to the dining table.

I tried to busy myself as Henry walked back in, carefully positioning the dinner rolls on a ceramic plate. When he came up behind me and wrapped his arms around me, I gasped. Swallowing hard, I hugged his arms to my chest.

He bowed his head and buried his face in my hair. His soft breath warmed my neck and ear.

I didn't want to ruin the moment, so I said nothing. And he was quiet, too.

Finally, he released me and then pulled out a chair. I thought he meant to sit down, but he moved aside and sat down in the opposite chair. Avoiding eye contact, he reached across the table and picked up a dinner roll and set it on the small plate I had placed beside his bowl.

After I set the glass bowl in the sink to soak with water, I sat down across from him and stared into my soup. I didn't like him being ill.

Everything was uncertain. Nothing meshed. I didn't know what to say. I didn't know how to respond or what to do. He wasn't himself.

"Kallis."

The quiet way he said my name had me feeling confused. "Hmm?" I said as I looked up.

He gestured toward the table. "Are you going to eat?"

"Um," I stammered, looking down at my soup again. I was so used to waiting for him to tell me to eat that I must have been waiting, letting the thoughts fill my mind as I waited for him to say I could eat. Even though he had said I could eat whenever I wanted. "I…"

"It's okay," he said.

I wasn't sure if he was saying it was okay that I had been waiting or that I couldn't come up with an appropriate response.

We ate in silence. He scarfed down his food and then took the last dinner roll from the plate. He pulled it apart in a rough half and handed me the bigger one.

"You can have it," I said.

"I'm offering this to you. Take it." He nodded his head toward the piece of bread. "Please."

I felt my cheeks grow warm. I set my spoon in my bowl and then reached out and took the bread.

He smiled. A weak smile.

"Thank you." I dipped the bread into the rest of my soup.

"I've had a lot of time to think," he said.

I nodded slightly, feeling a little on edge about what he was going to say.

"Maybe we should reconsider where we go from here."

I swallowed hard. "Where do you want to go?"

"Somewhere farther south than Wilderness. Bypass it altogether. Some place warmer. I think you'd like it more."

"You're thinking of me?"

He frowned. "I…" He bit his lip as his brow furrowed. He blinked like he was blinking back tears.

"I'm sorry," I whispered.

"I think about you," he said. "All the time."

A tear slowly trickled down my cheek. I bowed my head and stared down at my soup through the blur of tears.

He cleared his throat. "Finish eating."

I nodded. I thought he was going to say more about his thoughts, but he didn't. Instead, he seemed to stare at the table while I ate the piece of dinner roll he had given me and the rest of my soup.

When I was finished, I got up and carried our dishes to the sink. And after I had rinsed them and set them aside, I turned around to find Henry still sitting at the table. He wasn't paying attention to me though; instead, he was staring at the table's surface. But as I approached and touched his arm, he looked up at me.

"Will you watch a movie with me?" I asked.

With a slight nod, he hauled himself to his feet.

Wheeling his IV pole, I walked beside him and then positioned it by the end of the couch.

He sat down, put his bare feet up on the coffee table, and then outstretched his arm to me. When I sat beside him, tucking myself up against him, careful not to bump his wound, he rested his chin on the top of my head.

It was like old times. Whenever we watched movies together, he let me cuddle with him. He seemed to like it. I mean, he had to, otherwise he wouldn't have been the one to initiate it every time.

When a soft knock came at the door about halfway into the movie, we both groaned. I was about to get up when the door opened and Nurse Jane peeked her head in.

"I'm sorry to bother you," she said, stepping hesitantly into the room.

"It's okay," Henry replied, his voice weak.

"We will be starting your medical examinations tomorrow. I will return around nine o'clock in the morning."

Henry nodded.

"Is it all right if I swap out your bag of fluids?"

"Sure," he replied.

With a slight nod, she turned toward the hallway for a brief moment and then stepped inside the room carrying a full IV bag. While she made the switch, she asked, "Do you two need anything else? Food? Any supplies?"

He turned his head to look at me as if asking if I needed anything and then he shook his head. "I think we're fine. Thanks."

The nurse bowed slightly. "Very well. We will be running some tests, so please no food after midnight." She took the empty bag and headed for the door. Then she turned back to us and said, "I'll see you tomorrow."

When she was gone and the door was latched, I let out a heavy sigh.

Henry wrapped his other arm around me and rubbed my shoulder with his palm. "Why are you so worried? Everything is fine."

"I don't like hospitals or doctors."

"They serve their purpose."

"Sterilizing the population?" I asked.

"That was in Detroit. And by the directive of the city government."

"The nurses still carried out the order."

He lifted his hand and caressed my cheek with his thumb. "It bothers you."

My throat tightened at his quiet words. I nodded. "My life isn't my own. I can't make my own decisions. They took away my right to choose."

"Would you rather have three kids with another on the way, all by different fathers? Because that would be your life right now."

"But the people wouldn't have fought back."

He shook his head. "The gangs still would have taken over. The sterilization plan just gave them the ammunition to get it done quicker."

"So…"

He gave me a sad smile as he brushed a tear from my cheek with his knuckle. "Sometimes things really do work out for the best. All things considered."

CHAPTER 31

THE NEXT MORNING, there was a knock on the door as Henry and I were getting out of bed. Slipping into the robe and wrapping it tightly around my waist, I walked to the door. I opened it and peered out to find Nurse Jane standing in the hallway.

"Good morning," she said with a warm smile.

I opened the door the rest of the way and let her come through. As I backed up, I felt Henry's presence behind me.

"I will need urine samples from both of you." She handed us each a plastic cup with a black line around the middle. "Please collect a urine sample to the black line. You can set them inside the little window on the back wall inside the bathroom."

"Do you have any questions?"

"No," Henry replied.

"If you do, just let me know. I'll give you a few minutes."

When the door was closed again, Henry said, "You can go first."

I nodded. With defeat, I dragged myself across the room to the bathroom door. After I collected the urine sample and set the cup in the window, I quickly pulled the robe back on.

When I stepped out of the bathroom and into the main living area, Henry looked up. He was sitting at the table. His gaze seemed to track down toward my bare feet and then back up.

I felt my cheeks flush as I headed back across the room.

Slowly, he got to his feet. He set his hand at my lower back for just a moment and then headed for the bathroom.

While he was gone, I sat at the table with my hands tucked under my arms.

A few minutes later, the nurse walked back in and gave me a warm smile. "We can get started on your blood work while he's finishing up in there," she said, nodding toward the bathroom.

I cleared my throat. "Blood work?"

"Yes. We will take a small blood sample to test for any diseases and nutrient deficiencies."

I eyed the bathroom door, hoping Henry would hurry up and come back out. Finally, I stood up and stepped closer.

"Over here, dear," she said. "We'll have you sit on the table."

As she spoke, I approached the patient's table.

"Are you okay around needles?"

I shook my head.

"Well, it will go by fast. Won't take more than a couple of minutes."

Casting a nervous glance toward the bathroom door, I stepped up onto the pull-out step and then sat on the edge of the cushioned seat.

As I was about to hug my arms to my chest again, she reached out with both hands and touched my left arm. Gently, she outstretched my arm and pushed up the sleeve of the robe and then examined my wrist and the crook of my elbow.

With a soft hum, she released me and then she turned toward a panel by the door. I couldn't tell what she was doing, but when she turned back to me, she said, "I'm just turning up the heat in here to get your veins to pop."

"Oh," was all I could manage to say.

"We may need to wait a little while. There's no sense trying it now and sticking you more than necessary."

Finally, Henry came out of the bathroom. It had felt like an eternity that he was in there, but I knew it had only been a few minutes. His absence weighed heavily on me.

"Oh, good," the nurse said, addressing Henry. "We'll start with you to give us time for the room to warm up."

He walked over, eyeing the tray of packaged needles and tubes. When I hopped off the table to allow him to sit down, he caught me around the waist. "Go sit down," he said, his voice low.

I searched his eyes, trying to figure out if he was saying that to order me around again.

But it didn't really matter.

Finally, I nodded. When I caught the nurse eyeing us, I bowed my head and pulled away. Henry had made a habit of telling me what to do. It was like I wouldn't be able to decide things for myself without him. But he always seemed to know what to say. He knew that I could pass out on the floor if I watched the nurse...

I shook the image from my mind. Just the thought of what she was about to do was making me feel queasy.

Keeping my eyes averted, I sat on the cot and tried to think about something else, anything else. Computers and technology. I could think about that without feeling queasy.

It actually made me feel sad though. That part of my life was gone.

But maybe Henry was right. Maybe I could go to school and study for a degree in computer science. Maybe I could work for the Federal Guard in the security and surveillance department.

By the time the nurse was done with Henry, the room was so warm I itched to take the robe off.

"Good lord," Henry said, sounding annoyed. "Do we need it so hot in here?"

"It's just to make her veins pop."

"Come here," he said, stretching his arm out to me.

I got to my feet and walked to him.

He steered me back to the patient's table and once I was seated, he pushed up the sleeve of my robe and closed his hand around my wrist.

His warmth relaxed me, and I caught myself starting to lean against him.

When he removed his hand, the nurse inspected my arm and said, "Well, that works beautifully, doesn't it?"

While she swabbed the side of my wrist with cold alcohol, I clamped my eyes shut and then grimaced as the needle pierced my skin. Oh my God, was she fishing around for the vein? It felt like it took forever, and I was starting to feel lightheaded.

There was firm pressure at the side of my wrist and then she was saying, "All done. You did great."

I felt a strong hand—Henry's—close over my wrist again. All of this made me feel so weak. My ears were ringing. And I couldn't stomach seeing blood. I nearly cried getting pricked with a needle. I knew I needed to toughen up, but I didn't know how to do it.

"You're okay," Henry whispered, smoothing his hand over the back of my head.

I tried to nod.

"Just breathe."

Blinking my eyes open, I craned my head back and gazed up at him.

He frowned as he caressed my cheek with his thumb. Slowly, he released my wrist and then leaned over and set a bloodied cotton ball on the tray.

The nurse suddenly reappeared and handed a small cup to Henry. "Give her this."

As he took it, he asked, "What is this?"

"It's a little juice to help with the lightheadedness from the blood draw."

I didn't need her to tell me what it was though. I could smell the sweet, sickening scent of apple juice. When Henry held it for me to take, I shook my head. "I can't stand apple juice."

"Just take it."

I shook my head again.

"Kallis," he said, his voice firm, staring into my eyes.

With a defeated sigh, I took the little cup from him and raised it to my lips. I wasn't in charge of my life even now. I couldn't make my own decisions; he made them for me.

Holding my breath, I sipped a little bit of the juice and then handed it back to him. I ran my tongue over my teeth and tried to suck out the rest of the flavor from my mouth and quickly swallow it down.

"You are such a baby," he said, eyeing me. "Drink the rest."

"No." My voice came out strangled. I shouldn't have expected anything else. I wasn't used to speaking my mind. I had done that days ago, but that was when he was in the most pain and I knew he wasn't going to hurt me. Now I felt like he could punish me if he wanted. But I had to try sticking up for myself like he had said I needed to.

His eyebrows lifted. "What was that?"

Shaking my head, I cleared my throat and said, "No," this time a little louder.

The corners of his mouth curled upward. He took the small cup from my fingers and drank the juice himself. Then he tossed the paper cup into a small trash can beside the counter. When he turned back to me, he lifted his hand toward me.

I sucked in a breath, bracing myself for the punishment of defying him.

He stopped, his hand suspended.

My heart was racing so fast.

His expression softened, turning to worry. Then he hooked his finger under my chin.

I swallowed hard. "You would have hit me before."

He hummed as his gaze drifted. His throat bobbed. "I'm sorry."

"I still have the bruise you gave me," I said, looking away.

"Why do you say that like it's a surprise to you?"

I couldn't bring myself to look at him, and I didn't know how to respond.

"That was only a week ago. Of course you still have it."

How could I tell him I couldn't bring myself to look in the mirror? If I did, it was only for a second or two. I couldn't meet my own eyes in the reflection.

My eyes started to flood with tears and then my nose started to run. Sniffling, I pressed my hand to my face.

He wrapped his arms around me and smoothed his hand over my hair at my back.

It was weird. To be comforted by the same person who had hurt me. Who had contributed to my hating myself. He had been there from the beginning, forcing himself on me when I had never been with anyone before, but he wasn't the only one in the last three years who had made me hate myself and my life.

When I heard a soft knock at the door, I pulled away.

"We should get started on the next part of the examination," the nurse said, approaching. Speaking to Henry, she said, "You may be seated. Dr. Wallace will be in shortly to finish your examination."

He gave her a slight nod and then squeezed my hand gently.

I glanced up at him and tried to smile.

When he had sat down on the cot at the far end of the room, the nurse turned to me. "Do you wish to do this in private?" the nurse asked, keeping her voice low, probably so Henry wouldn't hear her.

I shook my head.

"Okay," she said softly. "I just want to make sure you feel safe."

I swallowed hard. She was no doubt referring to the bruises on my cheek and neck and probably coming to her own conclusions about them. Which were probably true.

I cleared my throat. "I'm okay."

She set her warm hand on my arm as she gave me a comforting smile.

I knew she was trying to look out for me, but what she didn't know was that things were better now. We were out of Detroit.

"Part of our medical evaluation includes a vaginal and pelvic exam," she said, lifting her hand and setting it gently on my shoulder. "So, I'll need you to lie back and put your heels into these stirrups."

"Um, what?" I stammered, my eyes widening.

"It's simple procedure," she replied. "It'll be over in a few short minutes."

"No," I said, shaking my head. I hopped off the patient's table and headed across the room.

Henry frowned and rose to his feet. "What's going on?" he asked, catching me around the waist. After the nurse explained the procedure, he gave her a slight nod and then turned to me. "Kallis, you need to let her do this. It's a standard procedure for women."

He spoke softly as he brushed my hair from my face with his fingertips. Already I was feeling more relaxed.

"Come on," he said, leading me back to the nurse.

Relenting, I let him help me up onto the cushioned table.

He supported my back as he pressed his other hand to my chest, coaxing me to lie back.

"I take it women's reproductive health is a lower priority where you're from," the nurse said.

"We do things differently in Detroit."

She gave a slight nod. "I've heard."

I let out a ragged breath and turned my head to stare at the blue fabric of Henry's hospital gown. He kept his palm on my chest, the warmth and weight of it somehow relaxing me as the nurse gently placed my heels in the stirrups. When I blinked up at his face, he was watching the nurse.

"When was your last menstrual cycle?" the nurse asked. I could see her looking up at me in my periphery. And then her gaze shifted to Henry.

"I think it's been years," Henry said, speaking for me. He looked down and studied my face as he whispered, "Right?"

My throat was tight again, and I was fighting the tears. His thumb caressed my skin while he held his palm to my chest. I bit my lip and blinked tears away as I gave him a small nod.

"I heard about what Detroit did to their people," the nurse said, her voice soft. "I'm sorry."

"Yeah, well..." Henry replied. It looked like he wanted to say more, but he didn't.

I closed my eyes and tried to zone out again, but it only intensified my other senses, making me restless and want to haul myself off the table and run out the door.

But I couldn't.

Henry wouldn't allow it.

The nurse hummed softly. And then she said, "There's a way to reverse it."

CHAPTER 32

LIFTING MY HEAD off the pillow, I stared at the nurse. "What?" I found myself saying before I realized it.

"From what I heard," she added, glancing my way. "But I don't know how it works. You two should ask the doctor. He might know more."

Laying my head back with a sigh, I focused my gaze on the ceiling. If there was a chance to reverse the sterilization, would I even take it? Would I want that? Henry had said things would be much different if I hadn't been included in that first round. I'd be a mother, most likely. I didn't think I wanted to be. Ever. But I also didn't want my decisions made for me.

"We'll do that," Henry said.

While the nurse performed the examination, she explained the whole thing, but I wasn't really listening. I zoned out, focusing on Henry's hand pressed firmly on my chest and contemplating my options. With him there, things would be okay. He wouldn't let the nurse, or anyone, hurt me. He saved that for himself.

Or at least he *had* in the past.

Everything was different now.

When he moved his hand away and began lowering my feet, I turned my head and gazed up at him.

With a frown, he pulled me to a sitting position and then guided me across the room as the nurse left, closing the door behind her.

My inner thighs were wet and sticky with lubricant. I wanted to go into the bathroom, but Henry was draping the thick, white robe over my shoulders and guiding me in the other direction. I shoved my arms through the sleeves and hugged them to my chest.

He steered me to his cot and then tucked me under the covers. He didn't ask why I was so upset about something that should have been second nature to me after three years of being used. Instead, he set his palm on my head and brushed my tears away with his thumb. "Get some rest," he said, his voice soft.

Sniffling, I turned my face toward the pillow and closed my eyes.

He tucked the covers tighter around me and then I heard his feet on the floor and the rustling sound of fabric.

Just then another knock came at the door. I peeked my eyes open and saw Dr. Wallace entering the room.

While Henry started the rest of his exam, I buried my face in the pillow again. It didn't feel right for me to watch. I could hear their soft voices from across the room. The doctor asking him questions he probably didn't want me to hear.

But he knew everything about me. Every detail. Things he shouldn't have known because they hadn't involved him. Things that should have been kept private.

If only I could go back and change the past...

But I didn't know how far back I'd go.

Just to the day of my campus tour?

Maybe then my father would still be alive.

The night before my sterilization?

But what would I do then? How would I fight back? If I had run away, the guards would have caught me anyway. Or worse, the gangs would have found me, and I'd still end up in the same position.

Or back even further?

I could have done something. I could have dug deeper into the city's network. I could have learned about the plan and alerted the people. I could have told my father and maybe we could have done something to stop the city. We could have convinced them that mass sterilization wasn't the answer.

All the speculating made me feel helpless. Because in reality, I couldn't do anything. I was weak. I'd never be able to raise an army of fighters. I'd never be able to get a city to listen. I'd never be able to change the world.

It was what it was. All the terrible stuff would just keep happening, and I'd never be able to stop it.

I wasn't sure how long Henry's examination took or how long he let me sleep. But sometime later, the nurse returned and let Henry know our test results came back fine, with the exception of a nutrient deficiency for me.

"Does that explain her mood?" he asked. I could tell he was trying to keep his voice low, but I could still hear him. "She's tired all the time. Depressed. More so than normal."

"It's a good possibility," Nurse Jane replied. "Vitamin D helps with many things, including mood."

"I'll make sure she takes them."

That didn't surprise me. Of course he'd make sure of it. But I honestly didn't think the pills would help.

When she left, I kept pretending to be asleep. I wasn't ready to get up. I didn't want to face him.

"You know I've watched you sleep before," he said, his voice cutting through the silence and raising the hairs on my arms. "I can tell when you're faking it."

I sighed as I rolled my head back against the pillow and looked at him. I heard the soft clink of the pills inside the bottle when he leaned against the patient's table and folded his arms over his chest. The short sleeve of his white T-shirt stretched tight around his arm, showing the bulge and definition of muscle. When he cleared his throat, I realized my gaze had drifted.

His eyebrows narrowed. "How much did you hear?"

"All of it."

He hummed.

"Why did you tell her?"

"Tell her what?"

"You think I'm depressed? *More so than normal?*'"

"Aren't you?" When I didn't reply, he added, "I think that's the same as checking out. Don't you?"

With another sigh, I looked away. My throat felt tight. How was I supposed to feel? My life had changed the day the gangs took over the city.

He walked over to the small sink and filled a paper cup with water. Then he opened the bottle and tapped a pill into his palm. As he padded barefoot across the floor, he said, "We should get out for some fresh air. After you take this."

When he knelt on the tile in front of me, I forced myself to a sitting position and draped my legs over the side of the cot. "Will they let us out?"

He shrugged as he held out his palm. "We're just going to the roof. It's not like we're escaping."

I stared down at the pill. "What if I start spending more time in the sun? Do I still have to take this?"

His eyebrows lifted and his lips pursed.

"Isn't that what I need? Sunshine?"

"You can take it now, and when you start feeling better, I'll consider it."

"I thought you weren't the boss of me anymore."

"Is that what you called it?"

"You know what I mean."

"If that's what you thought, why would you ask permission?"

"What?" I asked, confused.

"Why wouldn't you just refuse to take the pill instead of asking me if it was okay if you don't?"

I felt my shoulders drop as I sighed again. "That's not what I was asking."

"There is value in words."

"Yeah, well, I can't help that you read into things." I bowed my head and massaged my temple with my fingertips. "I meant, can I get the same effect from the sun as I can from the pill?"

"Why didn't you just say that?"

I clamped my eyes shut. I was starting to need more than a Vitamin D tablet. Something for a growing ache in my forehead.

"That's not at all what you said."

"Forget it," I said, opening my eyes and plucking the pill from his hand. I took the cup from him, too, and then washed the pill down with water.

He hummed, looking thoughtful as he studied me.

"What?" I asked.

"One little sign of conflict and you cave."

"It's easier this way."

"Life isn't easy."

"Well, this is."

"You don't get what you want by caving."

"It's not a big deal. It's fine."

"You have to fight for what you want."

"Please, just stop." My voice trembled.

"Kallis."

"I trust you, okay? I just didn't want to say it." When he set his hand on my arm, I flinched.

"I know you do," he said quietly. "When you're not mad at me or afraid of me."

I blinked back tears as I looked away.

"Sometimes I think you're not mad often enough."

"I shouldn't be *at all*."

He closed his fingers around my hand and then lifted it to his lips. When he kissed my knuckles, warmth flooded inside my stomach.

I bowed my head and watched as a tear dripped onto my lap and soaked into the soft fuzz of my robe.

"I'm sorry," he whispered.

Letting out a slow breath, I dried my face with my sleeve.

"Come on," he said, rising to his feet and pulling me with him. "We're going outside."

"In this?" I asked, looking down at my clothes as he led me toward the door.

He glanced over his shoulder at me and shrugged. When we stepped out into the empty hallway, he said, "It's so quiet here. They must not find many people outside of the city."

I nodded.

"Makes me wonder how they found us."

"They tracked us." When he turned to stare at me, I added, "That's what Kelsey said."

"We don't—"

"It was on a piece of clothing or something." I swallowed hard as he continued to stare at me. "It's likely a tiny chip that manufacturers used to sew into the fabric to prevent theft."

He cursed under his breath as he ran his hand over his head.

I studied his face, trying to figure out what he was thinking. His eyes were drawn in and his jaw was clenched.

Finally, he asked, his voice hushed, "How is that possible?"

"They act as beacons on the right tracking device." I tried to keep the explanation simple, so he'd understand. Technology wasn't in his realm of extensive knowledge.

He sighed. "I guess it doesn't matter. They'll be sending us on our way soon."

I nodded. The fact that he looked defeated and helpless had me worried. But I knew there wasn't anything we could do. We just had to stick it out and let Franklin handle our transfer to Wilderness.

When we reached the open area at the end of the hall, Kelsey looked up from the front desk and smiled.

"We're just heading to the roof," Henry said, reaching for the door handle. "This has access, right?"

She nodded. "You'll find an open lounge on the fifth floor. The next level up."

He thanked her and then guided me into the stairwell. When the door closed, he said, "At least we're not prisoners here."

I hummed in agreement, but it wasn't like we could leave the building. I didn't think they'd allow us out on the street.

We followed Kelsey's directions and found an outdoor sitting area with numerous chairs, chaise lounges, and tables. There was a swimming pool, too, but it had been drained and covered. Judging from the condition of the place—the black mold and debris—it wasn't maintained.

There was a slight chill in the air, but the sun was warm on my face and feet.

Henry took my hand and led me to a lounge chair designed for two people. He pressed his free hand to his stomach and winced as he sat down on the cushioned seat and leaned back.

"When are they going to let us go?"

"It shouldn't be much longer," he said, squinting up at me. "We passed their medical examination."

I sighed as I sat beside him. I knew he needed more time to heal. If they didn't force us to stay until he was able to get back to a normal life, he'd end up hurting himself again. Ripping a stitch or pulling open newly healed flesh.

"It'll be soon."

"*Too* soon."

"You think we should stay?"

"I think you need more time to heal."

"I'll be fine."

I bowed my head before he could catch me rolling my eyes. I could feel his gaze on me, so I busied myself with smoothing my robe out over my legs. When I chanced a glance his way, he had his eyes closed and his face turned up to the sun.

I leaned back and closed my eyes, too. I tried to just lie there, but my mind kept racing. Worrying about what would happen if Henry's condition worsened again. When we left, we'd be out on our own again. I doubted the guards would escort us across the country to the east coast.

And then I started thinking about Detroit.

If the Federal Guard of the New United States was able to capture people on the outside, couldn't they also take back the city from the gangs?

Why wouldn't they do it? They probably had the manpower to handle it.

Or was this guard outfit a joke? This Federal Guard...did it even exist?

No one knew how many survivors there were. Each city could easily claim they were part of the federal government to make themselves appear more powerful. And no one, none of the survivors, would realize they were lying.

"What?" When I turned my head and gave Henry a puzzled look, he said, "You're humming."

"Oh," I said, looking away again. How could I tell him what I was thinking? He was already furious about our situation. Having been shot, having been forced out of Hopewell. The capture by the guards. The helplessness.

"Something's bothering you."

I sighed. I couldn't keep anything from him. "The Federal Guard. Do you think it exists? That that guy was telling us the truth?"

"I've wondered the same thing."

"So, you're not mad?"

He cocked his head, looking confused.

"Never mind," I said before he could say anything. I hoped he would forget that I was referring to his reaction to my question. It didn't really matter if he was mad at me for bringing it up anyway. "If it doesn't exist, then clearly I can't work for them."

"I guess not," he replied. I was expecting him to say more, like ask me if I had really wanted to do that or why I had even considered it in the first place, but he played along.

"But why would he lie?"

"Any number of reasons."

"But you're not mad about it?"

He turned his head against the cushion. "Do I look happy to you?"

Quickly, I shook my head at the bite in his tone.

"I'm beyond furious," he said. "But there isn't anything I can do about it."

I swallowed the growing lump in my throat as I stared out at a small white cloud. When he felt better physically, would he return to his usual self? The verbally abrasive one?

He sighed. "That probably came out harsher than I intended."

I grazed my teeth over my bottom lip, trying to get it to stop trembling.

"I didn't mean to snap at you. I'm sorry."

"You've been saying that an awful lot."

"I mean it though. Probably more than you ever have."

I turned my head and blinked against the bright light as I met his gaze. I cleared my throat. "Probably."

I didn't see the point in arguing. And he was probably right. I said I was sorry to avoid being punished, not because I genuinely meant it.

He gave me a weak smile as he turned back to stare out across the city.

Far off in the distance I thought I could see Lake Erie. If we stayed out long enough, we'd probably even see the lights from Detroit. Not that the city was lit up well. The districts knew enough to conserve the energy from the solar panels.

That made me wonder if a person could see the city lights of Franklin from across the water. I had never thought about it before. It was dangerous to consider the world outside of Detroit.

"I feel like a heavy burden has been lifted," Henry was saying, sounding relieved. "We don't have to fight to survive anymore."

I turned my head to meet his gaze again. But I couldn't bring myself to agree with him. Not even to help him ease his mind. I already knew life could always get worse.

CHAPTER 33

WHEN THE SUN DRIFTED behind the next building over, taking the warmth with it, I cinched my robe tighter and hugged my arms to my chest.

Henry leaned forward and moved his legs over the side of the lounge chair. Looking back at me, he said, "I guess it's time to go. We've been out here for hours."

I rose to my feet and moved around the chair to help him, but he was already pushing himself up.

Pressing a hand to his stomach, he blew out a slow breath. "I'd like to do this more. But with any luck, we'll be on our way to Wilderness tomorrow."

I nodded slightly as I watched him walk. The way he was grimacing with each step, I didn't think it'd be wise to leave yet. He needed more time to heal. But without a doctor keeping him sedated, he wouldn't listen to reason.

And he certainly wouldn't listen to me.

As he reached for the door handle, he glanced at me. "I wish I had made him suffer for this."

I knew he was talking about Carl. "Why did he do it? He wasn't on your side?"

Henry huffed. "He wasn't on anyone's side but his own."

"I don't understand."

"He was working a deal with one of the other gangs. Get the ammo, get special access into other parts of the city."

"For what purpose?"

"So they could take down the gangs in the other districts. Gain control of the entire city that way. And by keeping the ammo from reaching DC, they'd have an upper hand against the organization that actually runs this country."

I was so confused. So much had happened since the city officials and guards were killed. Had I really missed that much? "How do you know all this?"

"I have friends in higher places."

I was too tired to bother pursuing *that* topic. Like, how did he even know these people? Was he referring to the people who had hired him to produce the ammunition? And how did *they* know about it? Did they really have a controlling interest in the country? Instead, I said, "But why would Carl shoot you?"

"Probably thought he could kill me and get you back."

The thought raised the hairs at the back of my neck and sent a shiver down my spine. I didn't want to think about that possibility. No doubt he would have sold me to the other gang.

"It's a good thing he's dead," he said, holding open the door. "For both of us."

I nodded slightly as I stared out toward the north. Toward Detroit.

"I should have done it a long time ago."

I shifted my gaze to his. "But you didn't," I said, my voice quiet.

"I would have protected you."

Looking away, I closed my eyes and bit down hard on my lip. I couldn't keep thinking about all the things that would have made my life turn out differently. It only made me sad. And angry.

"I'm sorry," he whispered. Letting the door close, he took my hand and interlaced his fingers with mine. "I know this doesn't help. It won't change anything."

I swallowed hard and nodded.

Gently, he tilted my head back with a hooked finger under my chin. When I blinked my eyes open and looked up at him, he gave me a sad smile.

I silently prayed he wouldn't say anything else. No other sweet words about how he could have saved me from all the terrible things that had happened. About how he would have treated me differently because Carl wouldn't have been there to set the rules. I didn't need that. I needed him to help me forget. To take away the power it had over me.

He searched my eyes as he caressed my chin with his thumb. And then he bowed his head and kissed me.

My body melted against him as I kissed him back.

He released my hand and set his own on my upper arm as he slid the fingers of his other hand through my hair to cradle the back of my head.

If he had only done this before, things would have been so much different.

When he winced and his fingers circled my wrist, gripping it tight, I realized I had touched his wound. "Sorry," I said, panicking. "I didn't do it on purpose. I swear."

He let out a heavy breath as he loosened his grip on my wrist. "I know you didn't."

"I…"

"Kallis," he said firmly. "Do you honestly think I never pay attention? To how your body responds. To all of your little moans. To where you put your hands…"

I felt my face grow warm despite the chill in the air.

"*I'm* the one who should be more careful." He sighed again. "Besides, you can't hurt anyone on purpose. That's not you."

I knew that wasn't true; I could hurt someone. But I didn't bother arguing. Instead, I asked, "Why did you never kiss me before?"

He looked away. His throat bobbed as his jaw clenched.

I waited for him to say something, afraid that if I spoke first, he would push me away and tell me to forget it.

"I couldn't have you getting the wrong idea."

"About what?"

"About us. About the arrangement."

I was so confused.

"I couldn't have you falling in love with me. We don't do that in Detroit. Women are…"

Slowly, I nodded as his voice trailed off. Of course I knew exactly what he meant. He didn't have to explain.

"It's not rainbows and unicorns there. No one gets their happily ever after. There's no room for that."

"You could have at least been nice."

He shook his head. "No, Kallis. I needed you to fear me."

"You could have explained it then."

He huffed. "You don't get it."

With a sigh, I bowed my head and stared down at our bare feet. In all the times we had showered together, in the whole year we had been together, I hadn't noticed the tiny hairs on his toes. I had gotten used to seeing without really seeing. Not in detail, anyway. Details hadn't mattered. No detail would have gotten me out of there. It was better not to pay attention. Not to see.

But now…

Maybe details mattered now.

"What's so funny?"

I felt a pit in my stomach as I jerked my head and looked up at him.

He sighed as he reached out and cupped my cheek with his palm. "Don't look so scared. Things are different now."

I nodded. "I know. I just…" How was I supposed to tell him I was amused by his little hairs? It sounded so silly, especially when we had just been talking about why he could never kiss me before.

"Tell me why you look terrified."

"Um," I stammered. He was never one to let anything go. Before, he would have made a justification or comparison. I wasn't quite sure what he would say now.

"Well?"

Finally, I said, "I've never really looked at your toes before."

He gave me the strangest look, like I had lost my mind. "How is that scary?" he asked, his voice a soft whisper.

"*You* are scary," I said. "The hair on your toes…*that's* funny."

He frowned.

"I guess I was worried about what you would say."

His frown deepened, and then he was saying, "Come here," as he pulled me into his arms. He rested his chin on the top of my head and sighed.

I hadn't expected this. I had expected him to say something. But instead he held me in a tight embrace.

After a moment, he pulled back and then rubbed his hands up and down my arms as he said, "We should go. You're shivering."

As we walked slowly down the stairs to our level, I thought about what he had said about Carl. Why hadn't Carl just waited until Henry and I got back that night? Why drive out to Hopewell? Did he not know where the ammo was stashed? I was about to ask Henry when he held up his hand, gesturing for me to stop.

He leaned closer to the door and pressed his ear to the metal. When I came up beside him, he wrapped his arm around my waist.

My heart was racing so fast I didn't think I'd be able to hear anything over the sound of my booming pulse, but then I heard faint voices on the other side of the door.

"What should I tell them, sir?" It sounded like Kelsey, but I wasn't sure.

A male voice spoke. "Tell them we are preparing for their transfer."

"But—"

"Just do it. I will collect them when they return."

"Yes, sir."

Henry's arm tightened around me and then he was pulling me away from the door, back into the shadows. I felt a small jolt as I heard him suck in a breath. His back must have made contact with the wall. He wrapped his other arm around me, holding me tight against his chest.

When the door opened, I held my breath.

A man dressed in a guard uniform appeared. It looked like the same guy who had taken us from the hospital. He didn't even seem to notice us as he rushed past us and hurried down the stairs.

I listened to his footsteps and then finally one of the doors below us opened and slammed shut.

As soon as the man left the stairwell, Henry released me and then took my hand and pulled me toward the door. Quietly, he opened it and nudged me through.

When we stepped into the open area, Kelsey looked up at us from the front desk. Her eyes widened and then she was rushing toward us. "You have to leave."

"Why? What's going on?" Henry asked.

"They are taking you to other facilities," she said, ushering us down the hallway back to our room. "They will separate you."

"For how long?"

"Indefinitely."

I felt sick to my stomach as I cast a worried glance at Henry.

"They have no intention of transferring you to that other city. They never did."

CHAPTER 34

I COULDN'T BELIEVE what Kelsey was saying. The guy had said they'd handle our transfer after our medical evaluations. And that we wouldn't be separated. I thought this city would be different, and that people would actually do the right things. But it was clear this was just like Detroit. Well, not just like it, but similar in that I couldn't trust them any more than I could the gangs.

"You need to leave before David comes back," Kelsey said, her voice hushed, as she opened the door to our rooms.

"How are we getting out?" Henry asked. "They'll just catch us again."

"There's a man, my husband," she said, glancing at me. "He will be waiting for you inside the parking garage. Downstairs. He'll take you away."

"How can we trust you? I don't know this guy."

Kelsey nodded her head toward me. "She does."

Henry and I exchanged a quick look. I must have seemed convincing enough—though I wasn't trying to be anything—because he sighed and said, "All right."

"Don't take more than a few minutes. Then head down this hallway, take two lefts, then a right, and take the stairs to the parking garage. Evan will meet you there."

Everything was happening so fast. After Kelsey left, Henry hurried into the room and retrieved our bag. When he came back, he set the bag on the kitchen table.

"Get dressed," he whispered, pulling out my clothes and setting them on the table. Before I could do anything, he was pulling my robe open and pushing it off my shoulders. He was moving so fast, faster than I could have, and within about twenty seconds—at least it must have only been that long—I was standing naked in front of him. He reached down and picked up my clothes. He shoved the shirt at me and after I took it, he shook out my pants.

When he bent down and grasped my ankle, I gasped. "Henry?"

With a soft hum, he turned up his head to look at me.

"I need my underwear."

"Skip them," he said, resuming his work of pulling my jeans on. "We need to get moving before they come back."

With a sigh, I braced a hand on his shoulder and lifted my other foot. "I don't understand what's going on."

"They're going to separate us," he said, pulling my pants up my legs.

"I know, but why?"

He turned his head and glanced up at me as he reached my thighs. "I think you know why."

As I took over and pulled the jeans over my hips, I thought about Kelsey. Had she said something? About the bruises? And my inability to answer her simple questions?

But she was helping us. If she had said something, she couldn't have intended for them to separate us.

While I pulled on the shirt, Henry hurried through the other room and retrieved my boots.

I wasn't sure how he was moving so fast and getting things done so quickly, but I felt groggy. And I hadn't slept well in days. If we ever found a place where we could settle in, I'd probably sleep for a good twelve hours.

After I finally had my boots laced and my sweater on, he took my hand and dragged me to the door. He had the strap of our bag slung over his shoulder and the gun in his holster at his hip.

Slowly, he opened the door and peered out into the hallway.

It was driving me nuts not knowing what was going to happen. Why were they taking us to another facility? Were we in danger? I supposed we must have been since Kelsey was ordering us to go.

But where were we going to go? Would we be able to walk out of the city unnoticed, undetected? And what would happen if we got caught?

And did he even know how to get out of the city? I hadn't been paying enough attention to think I'd be able to make it out. At least not without a little backtracking. And I knew *he* hadn't been paying attention; his eyes had been closed.

But then recently he had been hounding me to pay attention. Was that something that came naturally to him? Could he make it out without knowing the way first? Was that even possible? All we had to do was travel in the same direction, right?

When we reached an intersecting hallway, Henry pressed his forefinger to his lips and peered around the corner. Then he pulled me after him into the hallway.

"Did she really say to take two lefts?" I whispered. "Won't that take us back behind the nurses' station?"

He hushed me as he cast a quick glance at me over his shoulder.

We hurried down the hall as quietly as we could and rounded the corner down another dimly lit hallway.

"How do we know she's not leading us into a trap?" I whispered.

He glanced over his shoulder and gave me a strange look but didn't say anything.

When we finally took a right, I spotted signs for the exit. At the end of the hall, Henry eased the door open. Sure enough, it was a stairwell. Pale red lights lit the way in both directions.

We tiptoed down to the lowest level and stepped inside a dark parking garage. It was packed with vehicles. But there was a dead look to the whole place, like the cars had been abandoned years ago. My guess was that whoever owned them had been caught unaware when the meteor disaster occurred. Being the daughter of a city guard had afforded me the luxury of the underground protection. I had always considered that to be a good thing. Up until Carl killed my father and took me to be his slave.

"What does this guy look like?" Henry whispered, bowing his head toward mine as he pulled me up against an SUV.

I shrugged as I tried to remember. "That was days ago." I caught a glimpse of his annoyed expression before he turned away and peered around the passenger door into the dark garage.

I was about to say we should head toward the exit when a vehicle engine roared to life. Then I saw movement toward the end of the row of parked vehicles.

Henry pulled me back behind the vehicle again and to my knees, making me wince. I wanted to peer around the car, but he was blocking me in.

I could hear the vehicle approaching, but no lights shone out past us. Its lights were clearly out. When it stopped beside us, with its passenger side window rolled down, a male voice said, "Get in."

CHAPTER 35

HENRY ROSE TO HIS FEET, pulling me with him. With a hand at the holster on his hip, he approached the guard vehicle. "Are you Evan?"

I peered through the side window at the driver. It looked like the guard I had seen with Kelsey.

"Yes, Kelsey's husband," he replied. "Hurry. We don't have much time."

Henry looked over his shoulder at me and then he opened the back passenger door and helped me get in. He hauled himself up after me and closed the door.

"Keep your heads down, in case we get stopped," Evan said.

Keeping our heads down wasn't hard; there weren't any seats in the back. I crawled across the open space to sit behind the driver's seat. Oddly enough, the floor was padded and made with a thick, waterproof leathery material. It reminded me of the thick pads we had used in gym class back in high school.

Henry sat beside me, against the side wall. He pulled his legs in and rested his elbows on his knees as he bowed his head in his hands.

When the van started to move, I clamped my eyes shut. What if we got caught? Outcomes were always worse when a person was caught.

And what if Evan and Kelsey were punished for helping us? What would happen to them? If anything bad happened to them, it would be our fault.

When Henry set his hand on my thigh, I looked up, startled.

"You seem a little tense," he whispered.

"I'm scared."

"Everything's going to be fine."

"What if we get caught?"

"What if you just sabotaged our efforts by thinking the worst?"

I reared my head back. "So, it'll be my fault then if we get caught?"

"I didn't say that."

"Isn't that what you meant?"

"No," he said with a sigh. "Never mind. Forget I said anything."

"Sure. Like all the other things you've said to me…"

"Kallis."

I swallowed hard. "I hate the way you say my name." I was on a roll, waiting for him to say more so I could say more, but all he did was stare at me. Finally, averting my gaze, I bowed my head and clasped my hands together, trying to get them to stop trembling. "I'm sorry," I said.

He hummed.

His hand was still on my thigh. I wanted to push it off. It was just another way to control me. Keep me from speaking up.

When a tear slipped down my face, I brushed it away with my hand. And then my nose started to run. I tried to sniffle as quietly as I could, but I wasn't stupid to think he couldn't hear it.

Evan could probably even hear it from the driver's seat. He had probably heard our whole conversation.

"Where are you taking us?" Henry asked, his voice loud as he lifted his gaze over my head.

"There's an abandoned train station not far from here. Another ten miles. I'll drop you off there. You can follow the tracks most of the way to Wilderness."

"All right," was all Henry said.

I wanted to ask about the trackers. If a microchip had been the only reason that David guy had found us at the hospital, we needed to make sure we weren't still carrying one. I wasn't wearing the same clothes as that day, but we still had our bag and who knew what else was in it.

Maybe Henry would mention it.

But then I got to thinking about what would happen if he didn't and I didn't either. I had thought about the trackers, so wasn't I obligated to ask?

Wasn't that a rule from psychology? Just because you thought someone else would bring up an issue or call the police, didn't mean you shouldn't also do it. Because you never knew. What if everyone was thinking the same thing and not a single person called? I couldn't live with myself if I knew I could have said something but didn't.

"What's wrong?"

I turned my head to look at Henry.

His eyebrows were furrowed and he was staring at me. When I said, "The microchips," he lifted his head in a slight nod.

"Kelsey mentioned them. She said that's why we were caught."

He nodded again. "I remember you said that." He gave me a weak smile as he squeezed my thigh gently. "I'll ask him."

I let my gaze drift. How would I get through life if I needed him to speak for me? But I didn't feel comfortable with anyone else. I barely felt comfortable with him, and only because he and Liana had been the only two people I ever talked to. Hector didn't count; he had only been occasionally and only because I had to.

When the vehicle slowed to a crawl and then made a tight right turn, I sat up straight and peered out the side window. Evan had just pulled into a huge parking lot overgrown with weeds coming up through cracks in the pavement.

"This is the place," Evan said, stopping beside the curb at the terminal.

I rolled onto my knees and crawled to the door. Before I could reach out and touch the handle, Henry appeared from behind me and opened the door, sliding it out of the way. He stepped down and then reached up and helped me out, his hands gripping my sides. He wasn't supposed to be lifting any weight, but I couldn't remind him of that. He wouldn't listen to me anyway.

He slid his hand down my arm and then grasped my hand firmly.

Evan hurried around the hood and guided us inside the building.

Since he hadn't used a key to unlock the door, I couldn't help wondering if we would find other people inside. But I pushed that thought away.

"Kelsey had mentioned tracking devices inside the clothing," Henry said, glancing my way. "How do we make sure we don't get caught again?"

"That's what this is for," Evan replied, holding up a device that looked like a penlight. "It's an EMP emitter. It will fry any electronic device in a ten-foot area. It should take care of any hidden chip you might be carrying."

Henry and I exchanged a quick glance. I wasn't sure if he knew about EMP emitters or how they worked. If he had questions, he wasn't voicing them.

When Evan held up the device and pressed a button on one end, a tiny red light came on. Then he said, "I'll check the sensors when I get back to the truck to make sure it's not picking up any devices. If I don't come back in five minutes, everything worked."

Henry nodded.

"Follow the tracks toward the southeast."

"Okay."

Suddenly, he dug into his jacket pocket and pulled out two white pill bottles and a small tube. "I almost forgot. Kelsey wanted me to give these to you. Pain meds, antibiotics, and an ointment. Instructions are on the bottles."

"Thank you," Henry said, taking the bottles. "We are grateful. For you both."

Evan nodded slightly. Then he looked to me and gave me a small smile before turning back to Henry. "Good luck out there."

I wanted to tell him to say goodbye to Kelsey for me and to thank her for helping us, but I didn't.

And then he was heading back outside.

When the door closed, Henry asked, "How do we really know if his device worked?"

"He'll come back if it didn't."

"You trust him?" When I nodded, he sighed. "Okay."

"I wish I had said goodbye. To Kelsey."

He lifted our clasped hands over my head and then pulled me back against his chest. His arm tightened around me as he bowed his head and pressed his stubbled cheek to my temple. "I'm sure she understands," he said.

I closed my eyes and leaned my head back against his chest. A few minutes later, I heard the sounds of the guard vehicle driving away. I turned my head to look up at Henry. "I guess that means we're clear."

He released me and then took my hand again. Then we walked through the terminal to the other end.

I kept thinking about Kelsey and Evan. How they had risked their lives to get us out of there. What would have happened to us if we had stayed? What had the city been planning? I thought Detroit was the only place I had to worry about. But were other cities the same? Did they have strange rules? Were we safe anywhere?

When Henry pushed open the door and waited for me to step through, I stopped and gazed up at him. It felt strange that it was just the two of us again. But I couldn't imagine being separated from him. I didn't want to know what it'd be like without him.

"We should hurry," he said. "We're too close to Franklin. They could still find us."

With a small nod, I brushed past him and stepped outside onto the wide walkway that lined the tracks. The sun was sinking into the horizon to the right.

He hopped down onto the gravel alongside the tracks and then held out his hand for me to take.

"You're not supposed to lift anything," I said, eyeing him as I crouched down onto the walkway and eased myself over the edge onto the gravel.

"I forgot." He shoved his hands in the pockets of his jeans. "Old habit, I guess."

With the sun to our backs, we walked along the tracks.

"I'd like to find a vehicle. If we can. Otherwise it will take us weeks to get there. And if we run into winter which could be any day now, we'll need to stop until spring."

"What if we don't go to Wilderness?" I asked. "What if we just stay here?"

He stopped and turned to face me. "Live out here on our own?"

I nodded.

"What about all the stuff you want to do?"

I shrugged.

"We need to find a city for that. Not Detroit. And sure as hell not this place. But somewhere else."

"I don't need it."

He sighed as he looked away and stared off into the trees. "I don't know."

"What if every place is just like this one?" I asked. "Then what? We'll be running away again."

"We'll think about it."

We walked in silence for the next hour or so. With our slow pace, I doubted we had traveled more than a few miles. Five at the most.

Finally, Henry said, "We should get off the tracks. And we need to find a warm place to stay for the night."

I looked around at the trees that surrounded us. It didn't look like there would be any houses or buildings nearby. We probably had another few miles before we'd reach anything.

"A little farther," he said.

I followed him along the tracks. I couldn't tell if he had slowed down because of me or if he was getting tired. The sun had slipped past the horizon and the air was cooling.

Finally, around a bend, I saw an office or business building up ahead. It was only about twenty feet off the tracks.

When Henry outstretched his hand to me, I took it and let him guide me off the tracks and down the slight embankment. It looked like we had reached a small town. I could see more buildings through the trees north of the tracks.

We walked underneath an awning and peered into the row of windows that spanned the entire length of the building to find tables of various sizes and chairs inside.

"We'll stop here for the night, and head back out early tomorrow."

I nodded.

But as we rounded the corner of the building, I saw a man walking toward us from the street. He couldn't have been any older than mid-twenties and he was dressed in outdoor gear rather than a guard uniform.

"You have got to be kidding," Henry said.

"You guys have been hard to track," the man called out. "Are you Henry Winden?"

CHAPTER 36

I COULDN'T FOR THE life of me figure out how the guy knew Henry's name. And Winden? Was that Henry's last name? I honestly couldn't remember ever hearing the last name before.

And where had this guy come from? Was he from Franklin?

"Who's asking?" Henry replied.

"A friend of Donovan's."

Henry cursed under his breath.

"What's going on?" I whispered, stepping closer. "Do you know this guy?"

"No," Henry replied, bowing his head toward me. "But I know who he works for."

I had so many questions that I wanted to ask him, but the guy was already approaching.

"So, what happened to driving to DC and dropping off the ammo supply?"

"What's your name?" Henry asked, taking a small, slow step in front of me.

"Eric. I'm working with Donovan. I believe you know him."

Henry was quiet for a moment, no doubt staring the man down and assessing the level of threat. Finally, he said, "We got attacked. Had to get out of there."

When I stepped out from behind Henry, Eric's gaze shifted to me and then Henry was wrapping his arm around my waist and drawing me against him.

I could tell by the way Eric was eyeing us that he had suspicions, like he didn't believe the story. And then he asked, "Where is the ammo now?"

"Near Detroit. At the warehouse we were working in."

"Take me there."

"I'm not taking Kallis back to Detroit."

Eric glanced at me as he said, "She can stay here."

"I won't leave her behind either."

"I need to obtain the ammunition, and I need your help. And since you already agreed to help us…"

"Why were you sent alone?"

"Limited resources."

Henry cursed under his breath, but it was loud enough for me to hear.

"We have to go back," I said, keeping my voice down so only he could hear me. "I can help."

He huffed. "Doing what? I'm sure as hell not letting you drive again."

I frowned and looked away as I blinked back fresh tears. Was it totally impossible for him not to cut me down? Not to mention, he had survived. I had driven him out of Detroit. Wild ride and all.

With a sigh, he cupped my cheek with his palm. "I'm sorry. I'll let you drive. Whatever. We'll think of something."

I didn't want to make a scene, so I refrained from telling him how I really felt. Save that for later. Instead, I nodded. "So, we'll go?"

"I guess we have no choice. I had already agreed."

I lifted my gaze back to his. Keeping my voice down, I said, "How are we getting the ammo then? And what if they moved it?"

"I think we should talk inside," Eric said, cutting in.

I turned my attention back to him and saw him glancing up at the sky. I followed his gaze. There were rolling dark clouds rapidly approaching from the west and the wind had started to pick up. I could hear thunder from a few miles away.

Henry led the way inside the building. We walked around tables and chairs and found a casual seating area with stuffed chairs and couches behind the restaurant's dining room. With his hand at the small of my back, he led me to the sofa that lined the back wall.

I sat down and hugged my arms to my chest as I watched Eric sit across from us on one of the armed chairs.

He leaned forward and rested his elbows on his thighs. "So, what happened in Detroit?"

Henry shrugged out of his long-sleeved shirt and draped it over my shoulders. Then he sat down beside me and wrapped his arm around my waist, setting his hand against my hip. "We were planning to work through the last batch of shells that day. Kallis and I arrived in Hopewell, but I knew something was up. I was hoping to wait it out and get away with the ammo later, but we were attacked. We managed to get away, obviously."

I eyed him, wondering if he was going to mention the part about him getting shot and me driving him out of the city. Maybe it was up to me to provide those details. But I wasn't sure if Henry would want me to do that, so I stayed quiet. Not that I would have said anything anyway.

He glanced at me and gave my hand a gentle squeeze. "If it hadn't been for Kallis, I wouldn't have made it out of there alive."

My eyes felt strained as I gave him a weak smile.

"She even insisted on getting me to the hospital for antibiotics."

"Gunshot wound?" Eric asked.

Henry nodded.

"Did you find someone out there then? A doctor?"

"Yes."

"And where is he now?"

I looked up at Henry.

"He's dead." There was no hesitation. No change in expression. "He attacked Kallis." As he spoke, his arm tightened around me.

"I see," Eric replied, shifting his gaze to me briefly. "But you were able to get treatment at least?"

Henry nodded. "There, and at the medical center in Franklin."

"How long ago was the attack?"

"A few days," he replied, turning to look at me. He must have seen my frown because he asked, "How long was I out?"

I cast a quick glance at Eric and then I said, my voice quiet, "We were in Franklin for five days."

"Oh." He looked a little disappointed. "About a week then."

Eric gave a slight nod.

I didn't understand what was with all of the questions. It was almost like he was testing us to make sure our story lined up.

"Do you live in Wilderness?" Henry asked.

"No," Eric replied. "I'm part of a small group that has been managing on our own since the roundup."

"Why live on your own?"

"We like our freedoms."

I wanted to know what Henry thought of that information, but he remained quiet. Would he still want to leave me in Wilderness on my own? Was that even possible?

"Is it safe there in the city?"

Eric shrugged. "I suppose it is. Most people don't have a reason to be scared. I take it Donovan mentioned it to you?"

"Yes."

"I have two brothers there. I haven't seen them since the roundup, but I hear they're doing well."

When his gaze shifted to me, I looked away, glancing up at Henry and then at the window to stare out at the dark sky. I could feel Eric's eyes studying me for that brief moment before he returned his attention to Henry. His expression always remained blank, if not a little curious, so it was hard to tell what he was thinking.

He probably thought I was weak, timid. All the things Henry had said about me.

I hadn't thought about that before. What other people, people who didn't live in Detroit, would think about me. Being out in the rest of the world was what I had always wanted, but now that I was, I was afraid people would judge me only for my outer appearance. They would see a weak girl. I wasn't weak. I just didn't feel comfortable around anyone.

When Henry rubbed his hand over my arm, I jerked out of my daze and looked up at him.

"Do you want to go lie down?" he asked, his voice low as he searched my eyes. "You looked tired."

I shook my head as I tried to give him a small smile.

He frowned, eyeing me a moment longer. Then he sighed and turned back to Eric. "The ammunition is packed and locked inside the meat locker of the warehouse across the street from the manufacturing facility. As long as no one has broken inside, it should all be where I left it."

"And where's the truck?"

"Inside the warehouse," Henry said. "Hopefully."

Eric gave a slight nod. "I'd like to leave in a few hours, if that's fine with you. It's best to travel at night, undetected. That'll get us there around two in the morning, so we can get in and get out. Hopefully without getting caught."

"Fine."

"Get some rest. We'll leave soon."

"Sure." Henry pulled me to my feet and then set his hand at the small of my back. He guided me to the staircase behind the main desk. Once upstairs, we found several bedrooms and a shared bathroom.

We went into the first room. After Henry closed the door, he pulled me into his arms and bowed his head against mine. His warm hand cradled the back of my head as I closed my eyes.

"What's wrong, baby?" he said, his voice low.

I shook my head against his chest. "I'm fine."

He hummed. "You don't look fine."

My eyes felt strained and my throat tightened. Finally, I said, "I'm worried what he thinks of me."

"Why do you care?"

"I don't want him to think I'm, um…" I stopped mid-sentence when I realized how ridiculous my statement was about to sound. Of course Eric would think I was weak, because I *was* weak. And that's exactly what Henry would say.

"Hmm?" he asked.

I pushed away from him and turned toward the bed as I said, "It's stupid. Forget it."

He caught me by the arm, stopping me. "What's stupid?"

"I said, 'forget it.'"

"So, you're just going to let it bug you then?"

"Henry," I said with a sigh.

"You think he'll think you're weak."

I bit my trembling lip as I stared at the bed.

"He'll think that because you look it."

I blinked back tears as I lifted my head and met his gaze. Why did he always have to say these things out loud?

"You're stronger than you give yourself credit for. And a hell of a lot stronger than you look," he said. "Did you know that?"

"Is that supposed to make me feel better?"

"It should, yeah."

I sighed.

"You have to prove yourself, Kallis," he said. "Everyone is going to judge you by your outward appearance."

"You make it sound so easy."

"Why do you think I've been such an asshole to you?"

I lifted my eyebrows.

"Because that's what men do in Detroit to show that we can lead."

"The gangs do that. It wasn't like that before."

"Being a leader opened up this opportunity. We couldn't have left the city otherwise."

"That doesn't justify anything."

"I know," he said quietly. He sighed and then reached for me again.

I stepped back into his arms and pressed my cheek to his chest as I wrapped my arms around his waist.

He rubbed his hand over my back. "Why does it bother you so much what other people think? What does it matter what they say?"

I sighed again. Did he really not understand? My whole life was about whether or not I measured up. Whether or not I pleased someone else. It shouldn't have bothered me, but it did. A lot.

"You're not inadequate, Kallis," he said, taking my hand and giving it a gentle squeeze. "Besides, you shouldn't concern yourself with people who don't even care about you."

I frowned. "Why do you say things like that?"

His brows lifted. "The truth?"

I chewed on my lip as I tried to explain why the truth wasn't something I wanted to hear.

"It's not healthy for people to live in a world of deception," he said. "You have people who care about you. Well, one person, anyway. And your family, if they're all still alive."

I bowed my head and clamped my eyes shut. The way he spoke, the words he used, made me cringe. I didn't think I'd ever see my mother or my sisters again. I had no idea where they had ended up. And now that we were outside of the city, it's not like I was ever going back.

"Most of my family is dead," he said, his voice soft. "I have an uncle in Wilderness. That's it."

I blew out a slow breath.

"All that matters is the people who care about you. Sure, you'll meet people along the way, and because we're human, we'll care about them, but not to the extent that we should. So, you shouldn't get hung up on what people think. As much as it hurts to think about it, they're not thinking about you. And they're not thinking about me either."

I pressed my palm to my forehead as I considered what he was saying.

"*I* care about you. I know that doesn't mean much to you, after everything I've done." When I lifted my head and looked up at him, he interlaced his fingers with mine and said, "But I do."

I didn't think he was capable of lying. Everything he ever said had at least some truth to it, whether I wanted to hear it or not. If he said he cared about me, he at least cared in his own way, whatever that meant.

"We should try to get some sleep," he said, lifting his hand and brushing a tendril of hair from my face and tucking it behind my ear.

I sucked in a breath as his fingertips brushed over my earlobe.

When I closed my eyes, he pulled me back into his arms and let out a heavy breath.

I pressed my face into the crook of his neck. I could have stayed standing there all night, in his arms—it felt so good—but he reached past me and pulled back the covers.

After I slipped out of my boots, he helped me up onto the high mattress, and when I crawled under the covers, he pulled them over me, tucking me in.

"Aren't you getting in?"

"I'll sleep on the floor."

"You'll get cold."

He smiled a little. "I'll be fine."

I watched him back away and then lower himself to the floor. I curled onto my side and pressed my face into the pillow and closed my eyes. When he groaned, I imagined him lying out on the hard floor.

"Henry?" I whispered.

"Hmm?"

"Will you cuddle with me?" I was confident he would take me up on the offer after stretching out on the floor.

"No, baby. Get some sleep."

I sighed. So much for asking. I didn't understand why he was avoiding me. Why now after all this time?

As I lay there, alone, I listened to his breathing. It sounded labored, like lying on the floor was painful. But I doubted he would change his mind.

CHAPTER 37

A FEW HOURS LATER, we headed out. I thought we'd be walking on the tracks again, but Eric led us in the other direction. When I saw the truck, I sighed with relief. It would have taken us several days or more to get back to Hopewell traveling by foot.

"We won't drive the whole way," he said, opening the driver's side door. "It will be easier to avoid detection by sneaking in on foot."

"Fine with me," Henry replied.

As we hauled ourselves into the truck and got settled in the front seat, with me in the middle and Henry on my right, I couldn't help worrying about getting caught again. We had just lucked out in Franklin. Now we were heading back to Hopewell and driving past that city in the process. I kept wondering about what Kelsey had said about the trackers. If the guards could find us because of a tiny tracker inside a piece of clothing, what hope did we have of avoiding capture this time?

And if the Federal Guard was out scouting and looking for survivors again, we'd get caught.

Guaranteed.

I highly doubted Evan would help us a second time.

The fact that Hopewell was located outside of Detroit and a couple hours from Franklin did improve our odds of not getting detected. That was a small comfort.

"How do we make sure we're not going to get caught out here when cities have tracking sensors?" Henry asked.

"I've been told there's a blocker installed in this truck." When Henry cursed under his breath and turned back to the side window, Eric added, "Sorry. I wish I could tell you how it works, but I have no idea. I'm not a techie."

When I looked over at him as he spoke, he shifted his gaze to me, but then turned back to focusing on the road.

"My uncle is behind all this, right?"

Eric nodded. "Donovan doesn't mess around."

Henry seemed to relax beside me. I knew he still wasn't at his best physically. He was still in pain and would be for who knew how long. Weeks, maybe. He would put up a front. Make it look like he was doing fine.

But I knew better. Not that I was going to tell anyone. I'd keep my mouth shut.

With only a few more miles left to Hopewell, Henry started to appear anxious. But I knew there wasn't anything I could say to make him feel better.

When we reached a small tech center on the south end of Hopewell, Henry said, "Stop here."

Eric pulled up to the curb alongside a large building.

Henry opened the passenger door and stepped out. Then he outstretched his hand to me and helped me out.

"Why are we stopping?" I asked, bracing myself with my hands on his arms.

He gestured toward the building we had stopped at. "You will wait here."

I let out a defeated sigh as I looked at the main door. The etching on the glass suggested it was an office building, the firm's specialty apparently having to do with communications equipment.

I cast a quick glance at Eric, hoping he'd interject on my behalf. But he stayed out of it. And there was no point arguing. Henry always got his way.

With a gentle hand at the small of my back, he led me inside the building.

I paused at the entry to take in our surroundings. The main entrance had dumped us out into a lobby with a tightly woven carpeted floor and a long desk that rose to my chest.

"We should be back in about an hour," Henry said, glancing over his shoulder at me as he walked across the lobby.

I sighed. "Okay." I didn't want to ask what I should do if they failed to return. But knowing Henry, he wouldn't even consider that to be a possible outcome.

He opened the door behind the desk and peered into the darkness for a few seconds. Then he closed it.

I almost let out a sigh of relief that he hadn't said I was to stay inside the dark room.

"I guess you can hang out behind the desk."

"And look pretty," I mumbled.

"What was that?" he asked, walking back to me.

I swallowed hard and shook my head as I avoided his gaze. "Nothing."

He reached out and tilted my head back with his fingertip. He searched my eyes for a moment. Then he said, his voice low, "I don't care what you look like when I'm not here."

I nodded, unable to think of anything of value to say in response.

"You will be here when I get back."

It wasn't a question, but I nodded again. "Of course."

He eyed me for a moment like maybe he didn't believe me.

"I'm safer with you. Remember?" My heart raced as his thumb traced the column of my throat.

He bowed his head and pressed his lips to mine.

Closing my eyes, I pressed my hand to his chest as I rose onto my toes and returned his kiss.

His hand went to my back and drew me closer.

When I realized Eric was in the lobby with us, I turned my head away and pressed my forehead to Henry's chest. My face was burning despite the chill in the air.

"You'll be all right by yourself?" he asked, sounding more concerned than demanding this time.

"Let me go with you."

He pulled back and cupped my cheek with his palm. "That doesn't answer my question."

He hadn't said it with the usual sharp tone. He seemed genuinely concerned about leaving me behind. And in that moment, as I searched his eyes as he held my gaze, I thought it was strange that I could look in *his* eyes, but not my own.

"Hmm?" He caressed my chin with his thumb, sending little shivers down my neck and making me forget what he had asked me. "You'll be all right?"

He wasn't going to change his mind, so I just nodded.

He lowered his hand and then grasped mine. It felt like this was goodbye. That he would walk out the door and I'd never see him again. But if he was anything, he was true to his word. If he said he'd be back, he'd be back.

I tried not to make it obvious that I was blinking back tears. But somehow I knew he saw right through me. Maybe it was the way his brows furrowed even more. He didn't look angry or upset. He seemed worried. Anxious.

And then he released my hand and headed out the door.

Letting out a slow breath, I watched him and Eric disappear from view as they walked along the sidewalk outside past the lobby's floor-to-ceiling window and back to the truck.

I turned toward the front desk. Henry hadn't needed to tell me to stay out of sight. I didn't want to get caught by someone who was scoping out the city. Years ago, it would have been city guards looking for people who were surviving outside of the city's boundaries. But now, aside from the Federal Guard, it would be gang members conducting the searches, if they even still did them. Getting caught by the gang was the last thing I wanted to do.

I had no idea how long they would be gone. It would likely be hours. We were still a mile or so from the warehouse, so they would need to stash Eric's truck and walk the rest of the way. Then they would load the truck Henry had planned to use and drive it out of town.

Theoretically, it should have only taken an hour. Maybe two. But what was I going to do in that time? I should have been out there with them. Surely, I could have been of some help. But then again, who was I kidding? I would just get in the way.

As I wandered down the hall, I wasn't sure what I was going to find. It was a communications building, which should have actually excited me, but I was more into hands-on stuff. Not office junk. I needed a computer to dig into. A network to hack.

Everything was dead inside the building. Abandoned offices and server rooms. Even with all of the equipment still inside, I couldn't have gotten online if I had wanted to.

Finally, after about an hour of looking around and trying to keep my mind occupied, I made my way back to the lobby. They should have returned already. But I hadn't heard anyone enter the building, and surely they would have called out for me.

There wasn't any point to continuing my search. My search for something to do was about as fruitful as an attempt out of the apartment. I knew something had been beyond that locked room. Maybe some form of escape Henry had been hiding from me. But with the camera directed right at that door, I had never bothered attempting to get inside. And neither had Liana.

When I approached the lobby, I heard a sound, a soft clomp of rubber sole on tile. And then when I saw a dark figure standing inside the main doorway, I froze.

CHAPTER 38

IT ONLY TOOK A FEW seconds for me to get moving again. I stumbled backward, bumping into the wall, and ran down the hallway. I thought I would hear running footsteps behind me. But it was quiet. Maybe the pounding of blood pulsing through my veins that flooded my ears was blocking out all other sounds.

"Stop running or I'll shoot!"

I glanced over my shoulder to see Hector standing by the desk, his gun down at his side.

"Kallis!"

I let out a defeated whimper as I drew to a stop. I hung my head as I turned to face him. I knew I couldn't outrun him. And I was pretty sure he would actually shoot me if I kept running.

"There's nowhere for you to run. I'll hunt you down wherever you go."

With a sigh, I closed my eyes. A tear slipped down my cheek as I bit my trembling lip. The nearest door was still ten feet away.

His footsteps got closer, one slow step at a time.

My heart was racing so fast. I sniffled and wiped at my face as I lifted my head to look at him. When he stretched out his hand to touch my face, I jerked my head from his reach.

He clucked his tongue against the roof of his mouth.

"Don't touch me," I said, my voice barely a whisper.

He stepped closer and grabbed me by the arm, making me gasp. "Since when do you have a say on what a man can do?"

My throat tightened as my lip trembled.

"Well?"

"I'm sorry," I whispered, bowing my head and closing my eyes. There was no point to fighting him. Fighting him would only provoke him and make things worse for me. I was used to caving, never standing up for myself. I had started to with Henry, but he had made it clear that was what I needed to do, at least around him.

Not to mention he had been injured and too distracted with pain to punish me. And he was getting me to see that I could speak my mind without consequence now.

But I knew Hector wouldn't understand that. He had never been anything other than controlling toward Liana.

"Where's Henry?"

I shook my head. "I don't know." It was true. I didn't know his exact location. Was he on his way back yet?

He dragged me down the hallway to the main entrance and then outside. The chill in the air made me suck in a breath. I tried to keep my footing as he hauled me across the cracked street, but my feet kept catching on cracks and upheaved pavement.

He held me up, his hand gripping my arm like a vise and pinching my skin beneath my sweater. When he dragged me to the side of a truck and opened the door, I tried to jerk my arm free. I finally slipped from his grasp, but he quickly recovered, grabbing me again, and then he started to shove me inside the truck.

My shin rammed into the metal door frame. Crying out, I hunched over and grabbed my leg.

"What's the problem?" Hector asked, gripping me by the waist and hoisting me up.

I tumbled onto the seat in an embarrassing heap, smacking my face against the cushioned bench. I tried to push myself back up, but I couldn't muster up the energy to do that. My arms felt too weak.

He grabbed my arm and righted me and then slammed the door closed.

While he walked around the hood, I turned to the door and frantically grasped at the handle. My fingers slipped on the plastic, forcing back the nail of my middle finger.

Gritting my teeth in pain, I fumbled with the handle again. But before I could lift it all the way, the locks clicked into place.

I let out a defeated sigh as I dropped my hands in my lap.

With another click of the automatic locks, the driver's door opened and Hector hopped inside. Turning his head to look at me, he said, "You're wasting your efforts. You're stuck with me."

I swallowed hard. "What do you want from me?"

"Leverage."

"For what?"

"You don't think I know Henry would fight to get you back?"

I closed my eyes. "Why would he do that?"

He laughed. "I'm not an idiot, Kallis. I've seen the way he looks at you."

I shook my head. Two weeks ago, Henry hadn't looked at me the way I had wanted him to. And surely Hector had seen the same thing.

"Why do you think he volunteered to handle the ammunition project?"

I sniffled and pressed my trembling hand to my cheek.

The truck engine revved to life and then we were moving.

"Put your seat belt on," Hector said.

I opened my eyes and stared out the side window as I leaned my head back against the seat rest. I reached up with a trembling hand for the buckle and then pulled it down and clicked it into place.

"Henry's been plotting to get you out of the city since Carl killed your father."

I lifted my head and stared at him. "How do you know this?"

He glanced over, his eyes raking over me. "You caught his eye. Did you know that?"

Why was he tormenting me? Why was he suggesting Henry could have saved me the two years of misery with the others?

"At the medical center. Before the people fought back."

My breath caught in my throat and my eyes welled with tears. I bowed my head.

"Did Henry never tell you?"

A tear slipped down my cheek when I closed my eyes.

"I guess that's a *no*."

My lip trembled as I wiped my face dry with my fingertips.

"It's too bad it took him so long though. He could have saved you from so much. Being taken as a slave has got to be a pretty bad blow."

I leaned my head back against the seat rest and stared out the window again. He couldn't really say anything else that would make me feel worse about my life and situation. I always wondered if being a guard's daughter meant I'd be treated worse. It certainly hadn't seemed to have helped my cause.

We rode in silence, clearly back to the city. And it seemed to take forever. I kept glancing at the digital clock on the dashboard. A mere twenty minutes was feeling like an hour.

When he drove into a dark underground parking garage, I shifted in my seat and glanced his way. The place didn't look familiar. But then again, I had barely been outside in the last three years. And even the other day, Henry had taken me to a parking lot across from our apartment building.

After Hector drove to the back of the garage and then parked beside a concrete wall, he said, "Get out."

I unbuckled my seat belt and then pushed the door open. The truck was so tall, I couldn't get my foot down without using the door as support. But Hector appeared from around the back and grabbed me around the waist.

Without bothering to set me down, he slammed the door shut with his free hand and then walked through an open doorway into a stairwell. It seemed he thought it was easier just to haul me over his shoulder than drag me up the stairs.

On Level 3, four floors up from the garage, he pushed through into a familiar looking hallway.

I groaned. He had brought me back to the apartment.

CHAPTER 39

THROUGH THE BLUR OF TEARS, I tried to ignore the stares and jokes about my return. About Henry tiring of me and selling me after all. About servicing the guys because if I could keep a guy happy for over a year, clearly I must be good at my work. Hector had laughed along with them. He hadn't agreed, thank God, but he hadn't flat-out declined either.

Inside the apartment, he closed the door and then set me on my feet. "Go change," he said, turning me around by the shoulders. "Slip into something more relaxing. You're going to be here a while."

This was exactly like being sold to someone else. I just hadn't realized it would be Hector.

Slowly, I made my way across the living room and down the hallway. When I stepped inside Henry's room, I paused at the door. It felt strange being there without him. Would he know where to look for me? How long would it take before he realized I was gone? And would he think I had been taken or would he assume I had run on my own? Away from him? Would he even bother looking for me?

Fresh tears flooded my eyes. I had finally made it out of Detroit and now here I was back inside that godforsaken city once again.

Everything had gone all wrong. If we hadn't run into Eric, would we still be in Franklin? Would the federal guards have found us a second time?

Wiping my face dry, I stumbled to the dresser and pulled open the top drawer, the one with all of my gowns. Had Hector really meant a gown? I didn't actually have anything else. Other than Henry's clothes which were all too big for me. And all of the clothes he had packed in his bag must have come from somewhere else.

I pulled out a gown, one of the less sheer ones, from the drawer and went inside the bathroom to change. I kept expecting Hector to return, to see what was taking me so long, but he never did.

When I finally stepped out into the hallway, dressed in the gown, my thickest remaining sweater, and my tall boots, I found Hector coming out of the extra room, the one they had always kept secured with a padlock.

He turned toward the door and pulled it closed. Then he set the padlock in place.

I looked away before he turned around again, trying to make it look like I wasn't paying attention. I could hear him move again, and I thought it was odd that the bolt hadn't clicked into place like all the times before.

When his footsteps approached, I held my breath.

"That's better," he said, reaching out and gliding his hand over my hip.

I bit my trembling lip. My heart was racing so fast.

He grasped my chin, his fingers digging into my skin, and forced my head back against the wall. "I've been waiting a long time for this."

I tried to shake my head.

"You're mine now."

My vision blurred with tears.

"I don't really care if you cry," he said, his voice low. "I kind of like it."

When I blinked, tears slipped down my face. My legs shook so badly I thought they were going to give out.

Holding my chin firmly in his hand, he removed his other hand from my hip.

When I heard the tinging sound of metal, I clamped my eyes shut. I tried to suck in a breath, but my nose was too stuffy and I couldn't breathe. Gasping as my body tensed, I pressed my hands to his chest and tried to push him away. But it didn't do any good.

He leaned down and slid both hands down my backside and then lifted me, forcing my thighs apart to straddle his hips. He wasn't as strong as Henry and his movements weren't as fluid either.

But still, I wasn't strong enough to fight him.

As he pressed against me, pinning me to the wall, a loud rap came at the door.

I jerked my head and saw Kent walking through the open doorway of the apartment.

"That's a little premature, don't you think?" he asked calmly, walking across the living room.

"You come to watch?"

"Henry's not at the warehouse."

Hector groaned.

When he set me back down and released me, my legs gave out and I slid down the wall to the floor. Bowing my head, I tucked my knees in close as I hugged my arms to my chest.

Hector started to walk away, but Kent approached and hauled me to my feet with a tight grip around my arm and a hand at my waist.

I knew it was too good to be true that he would help me. But at least he had stopped whatever Hector had planned.

He looked toward the living room and then he lifted his shirt and pulled out a holstered blade.

I gasped and tried to take a step back, but his grip on my arm was firm.

He released my arm but then grasped my wrist, stopping me as I tried to shrink back. His fingers curled mine around the hilt of the blade.

"What am I supposed to do with this?" I whispered, my voice strained.

He leaned closer, his stubbled cheek brushing over my hair. "Slip it inside your boot."

I looked down the hall. Hector must have been in the kitchen. Quickly, I dropped to a knee and shoved the sheathed blade inside my boot, nearly all the way down to my ankle.

Kent grabbed me by the arm again and hauled me back to my feet. "Go make dinner, yeah?"

Sniffling, I wiped at my face and then nodded. I took a step but would have collapsed to my knees if he hadn't been holding me up. My shoulder ached from the jolt of my weight. I reached out with my free hand and grasped his sweater.

He plucked my hand off his shirt, digging his thumb against my palm, and then he grasped both my wrists as he wrapped his arms across my chest.

"You really think Henry won't make good on his threat?" he called out, his warm breath blowing over my head.

Hector appeared in the hallway again and glanced back at us as he huffed. "I don't think he'll care when he's dead."

"He's smart," Kent said, pushing and supporting me out of the hallway. "How'd he know something was up anyway?"

If he was referring to the attack in Hopewell, I knew why, but I wasn't going to mention it.

"Got tipped off, obviously," Hector replied. "I don't know how."

Kent sat down at the table and pulled me onto his lap like I was a kid. If his plan was to protect me from Hector, I had gotten lucky. He set his hand on my thigh, his warmth seeping through the thin fabric of my nightgown. It reminded me of those few short months when I was his.

"Kallis," Kent said, his voice sounding harsher than before.

I jerked my head, clearing away the thoughts.

"I said, 'What do you know about Henry's work?'"

"Um," I replied, trying to gather my thoughts and figure out what he meant and then what I should say. "Not really anything."

"He took you with him. What'd you do?"

I bowed my head as my mind replayed the bathroom scene where I had collapsed to my knees and thrown up. And then when Henry had made me drink the whiskey. "Nothing," I said quietly. "He wouldn't let me do anything."

"So, you didn't overhear anything? See anything?"

"If I did, I can't remember." I lifted my gaze, but only long enough to see him narrow his eyes like he didn't believe me. I squeezed my hands together, trying to get them to stop shaking. "He had me drinking whiskey."

"Good lord," Hector said from the kitchen.

"And you don't know where he is right now?"

I shook my head.

"What you should do, Hector, is take her back and wait it out. That's what you should have done in the first place."

As he spoke, I looked up at him, hoping he wasn't planning on leaving me alone with Hector.

"Yeah, right. He'd kill me. At least here, I have backup."

I had been about to relax, but then I heard Hector say *backup* and I almost groaned out loud. Maybe Kent was trying to tip the odds into Henry's favor. Hector wouldn't stand a chance against Henry, at least not alone. And he must have known that.

Hector gestured toward me as he said, "She going to make breakfast or what?"

My cheeks grew warm as I bowed my head. Kent gripped my waist and helped me up off his lap. Folding my arms over my chest, I stumbled into the kitchen and set about preparing a meal, one of the things I did best.

When Hector started talking again, I looked up thinking he was talking to me, but he was holding a walkie-talkie up to his mouth and asking about the status of the recipient's search.

"He's not here. And the ammo is gone," a male voice replied through the speaker.

I tried to make it look like I wasn't listening. My hands shook so badly, I was going to end up with dehydrated food pieces all over the floor if I wasn't careful. I bowed my head and tried to focus on my work. But I couldn't stop thinking about Henry and the ammunition. If it was gone, that meant he and Eric had found it, right?

I tried to listen to their conversation without being too obvious. It was almost like they thought I wasn't there, the things they were saying, details they were trusting me with.

To think Hector was involved with taking Henry down, that made me hate him even more. I had finally ended up with someone who claimed he had no plans to sell me to someone else. I had thought that maybe I could count on that, on never having to be with any other guy. And now these two were threatening to end all that. I didn't want to be with anyone else. I didn't want to sleep with yet another guy. I wanted to feel safe and secure, and I wanted to be able to rely on a sense of normalcy.

"How long do you think it'll take for Henry to show up?" Kent asked, catching my eye as he spoke.

"Another few hours, maybe."

"You really want to keep her that long?"

"Sure. I have some plans after we eat."

I clamped my eyes shut. My hand trembled as I stirred the contents of the saucepan. I didn't want to think about what he was planning. I knew what he wanted. I considered myself lucky he hadn't taken what he wanted already.

"If you want to stay and watch, be my guest."

The ladle slipped from my hand as I went to set it down on the holder. It bounced on the counter and then somehow propelled off and clattered to the floor, leaving a mess of soup down the cupboard door and all over the tile. With trembling legs, I knelt down and began to clean it up with the kitchen towel.

"She's such a spaz, I don't know how Henry handled her," I heard Hector say.

Bowing my head, I closed my eyes again. I didn't know if I could wait for Henry to find me. Hector seemed confident Henry would be back. He would come for me. But I couldn't stand the thought of being alone with Hector for another few hours. Would Kent watch over me? Could I trust him? Or would he sit back and let Hector do whatever he wanted? And why had he given me a blade when he probably knew I didn't have the skills to use it?

I didn't have a reason to trust him. He had sold me after a few months. If he really cared, he would have kept me longer. But then again, he had sold me to Henry. So, maybe he had been looking out for me back then, too.

I let out a ragged breath and shook my head as I tried to shake away the thoughts. I was just justifying their behavior. I was trying to make it sound honorable when it wasn't.

Back on my feet, I washed the ladle with the liquid dish soap and then stuck it back in the pot to stir the soup. I kept wondering where the girl was, the one who had come to the apartment the night Hector carried Liana away. What had happened to her? Had she stayed with him long? Had Hector sold her off already?

I opened the cupboard above the counter and took out three bowls. After retrieving three spoons from the drawer, I carried the items to the table. Staying closer to Kent's side of the table, I set a bowl and spoon in front of Hector.

He looked up and stared at me.

Keeping my eyes downcast, I set out the other bowls and spoons. I couldn't stop thinking about the blade that was tucked inside my boot. What if Hector found out? *How* would he find out?

And then I had the thought that Kent was going to tell him. Surely, he wouldn't do that. I shook that idea from my mind as quickly as it had popped in. I needed something, someone, I could rely on.

At least until Henry arrived.

I just had to make it until then.

CHAPTER 40

WHILE WE WERE EATING, Hector received another call over the walkie-talkie, the static and then the voice cutting off his casual conversation with Kent.

"Give me good news," Hector said into the speaker.

"We can't find him," the male voice said.

Hector cursed out loud as he got to his feet, sending his chair crashing to the floor behind him with a bang.

I flinched, dropping my spoon. It clattered against the ceramic bowl, flicking liquid to the table around me. I caught Kent giving me a sidelong look.

"Check it again. I want him brought to me."

"We've scoured the place, Hector. He's not here."

"Tell the guys to keep their eyes and ears open for when he shows up. I'm going to need reinforcements." He slipped the walkie-talkie into his back pocket and started pacing the floor. His eyes narrowed at me. "We checked the warehouse. Tell me where Henry is."

My lip trembled as I closed my eyes. "I don't know. If he's not there, he's looking for me." I refused to tell him about the building across the street, the one that was supposed to store the truck. It seemed clear he didn't know about that.

He sighed. "Why did you two come back? I thought you were gone for good."

I stayed silent. He didn't need to know the details. And I was smart enough to know that Eric wouldn't want me to mention he was there. Not to mention Henry would be furious with me.

"Come on," Hector said, smacking his hand on the table and making me jump. "Give up the information."

I swallowed hard as I shook my head and lifted my gaze to blink up at him. "I don't know anything."

With a huff, he pushed himself from the table. Crossing his arms over his chest, he said, "I'm not that stupid. I know he was telling you details."

"What do you think I know?"

"Why did he leave you behind?"

"He thought it was safer for me to stay out of the city."

"By yourself?" he asked, raising his eyebrows.

"We weren't expecting you to find me."

He smirked.

"What were you doing?" I asked. "Out there." It had been almost a week. It didn't make sense. Why now? And Henry had been gone for several hours. How had Hector found me? And inside a building, no less. Had he been watching? And if so, why hadn't he stopped Henry and Eric? He knew about Eric. And he was waiting for me to mention it. He knew I knew. How long would he allow me to deny it?

His smirk deepened. He seemed to be enjoying watching me put the pieces together.

"Kallis, I think it's time to stop playing the naïve girl and just tell us where Henry is."

Shaking my head, I looked up and met Kent's gaze. "I don't know where." I had to figure that Hector had followed us, to know where I was, but then he had lost the guys somewhere along the way. That's how it had taken an hour for him to come back. Had he been waiting for Henry to return? And had finally decided to take me instead? "You were following us," I said, turning to look at Hector.

He pursed his lips as he cast a glance at Kent.

I swallowed hard. "How'd you lose them?"

His eyes narrowed when I said *them*. For a panicked moment, I thought I had made a mistake. But then he said, "Who's the other guy? Is he from DC?"

I nodded. It was close enough.

"They got away. Made a turn and I lost them."

The simple fact that Henry hadn't returned suggested to me that he hadn't known he was being followed. Surely, he would have gone back for me if he had known. Or maybe he figured he had gotten far enough away from me before he was followed. Or maybe he figured there was no way Hector would find me inside the building.

I also had to trust that Henry would show up any minute. He had to know where I was. He had to know that Hector would take me back to the apartment.

I tried to will the information to him, but the minutes ticked by and it seemed I was being hopeful for nothing. He wasn't coming. He'd have no clue where I was. He'd have no clue that Hector had found me. It didn't make sense. He wouldn't even consider it.

The more time that went by, the more I realized I was on my own. I'd have to use the blade Kent had given me.

But then again, what was I thinking? I didn't know how to use it. I'd more likely lose it to Hector and have it used on me instead.

It was a stupid idea.

I was weak. It took strength to use one. And then if I didn't aim right, I could end up jabbing it into rib bone. If that happened, he'd smack me so fast, send me hurtling to the floor. It would make him mad.

Kent rose to his feet and pushed in his chair—Henry's chair. "I need to head out. To make sure the perimeter is secure."

I stared into the kitchen. There wasn't anything I could say to make him stay. And I couldn't make it obvious that he had tried to help.

"Remember what I said, Hector. He'll kill you if you lay a hand on her."

Hector pursed his lips and gave a slight nod as he cast a glance my way.

"We'll let you know if we hear anything." With that, Kent strode out of the apartment.

When Kent disappeared in the hallway, Hector said, "Looks like it's just the two of us now."

I nodded slightly as I lowered my gaze to the table. I could see him staring at me. He was probably wondering if I would actually speak again. Now that Kent was gone, I didn't know how we were going to pass the time.

"Why don't you clean this up?" Hector said, backing away from the table.

I rose to my feet, my knees shaking uncontrollably, and then gathered up the empty bowls and silverware. I hugged the bowls in my arms and carried them into the kitchen. Carefully, I set them on the counter and then turned on the faucet. I could feel Hector's stare on me, watching my every move.

After I washed the bowls and set them out to dry on a towel by the sink, I began wiping down the counters. I tried to ignore Hector as he approached. My heart raced when he stepped around the island and stopped two feet away.

"If Henry doesn't get here soon, you're sleeping in my bed tonight."

My stomach twisted, making me groan. I pressed my hand to my mouth and clamped my eyes shut as I silently prayed that I wouldn't throw up my meal.

"Stomach hurt again?"

I nodded quickly without thinking. And then I remembered he had offered me a muscle relaxer last time.

Before I could tell him I was fine, that I didn't need any medication for it, he had left the kitchen.

With a helpless sob, I slid against the sink cabinet to the floor. I couldn't do this. I couldn't stay with him, but there was no way I could leave. Even with the knife Kent had given me, what was I supposed to do once I got out into the hallway? Cross that threshold and I'd be fair game.

When I heard footsteps, I lifted my head. Tears had streaked down my face. I pressed the back of my head against the cabinet.

He rounded the corner and stopped short when he saw me. Then he strode into the kitchen, reached down, and grabbed me by the arm and hauled me to my feet. "Here. Take this," he said, setting a single pill on the counter. "It's a muscle relaxer. Same as before."

I couldn't stop staring at it. Finally, I shook my head. "I'm okay."

"Take it."

"Hector, please."

"Take it or I'll shove it down your throat."

My eyes widened.

"What do you think of that?" he asked.

Quickly, I shook my head and picked up the pill between my thumb and forefinger. The last one had made me feel tired and sluggish. It would probably be the same this time around. And maybe the side effects would be reduced after the soup I had just eaten.

He took a glass from the cupboard, filled it with cold water from the faucet, and then held it out to me.

Seeing no way out of it, I set the pill on my tongue and washed it down with the water. I couldn't bring myself to throw it back up. I just hoped he was being honest about what it was. At least it looked like the same thing as before.

He grabbed me by the arm again and ushered me to the table. When he released me, I sank down on the chair and held the back of my hand to my mouth as I bowed my head.

"It shouldn't take too long for the pill to work."

"Thank you," I said, my voice faint. I wasn't grateful for his help, but he didn't need to know that. And I remembered what Henry had said, about Hector not helping me.

Maybe it wasn't that bad. Maybe he was trying to do a good thing.

I also couldn't stop thinking about Liana and what she had said about throwing up the pill. But I couldn't do it. I couldn't shove my finger down my throat and intentionally make myself gag. It just wasn't going to happen.

"I'm surprised you still have a weak stomach," he said. "I figured you'd have acclimated by now. With all the guys you've been with… What's one more?"

I lifted my chin and glared at him.

"What? You don't think I'm right?"

I bowed my head and sucked in a ragged breath through my gritted teeth. How could he not realize that I wanted to be appreciated for other things?

Sniffling, I wiped the fresh tears from my face and then wiped my hand dry on my sweater.

"You know that girl they sent to replace Liana?" he said, shaking his head. "She was really something."

I felt my jaw clench. "What happened?"

He shrugged. "I didn't like her."

I raised my eyebrows. "I can't imagine that. And no replacement?"

"Just you." He smiled. "I'm really looking forward to it. I've been feeling left out. Nearly everyone else in this building—"

"You asshole," I said under my breath.

His head leaned forward as his eyes widened. "Excuse me?"

I glared at him.

"You know what?" he asked, reaching across the table and yanking me to my feet by the arm. "I don't feel like waiting."

CHAPTER 41

MY EYES WIDENED and then I was struggling against him and trying to get my arm free. His grip was tight and wouldn't let go as he dragged me toward the hallway.

When I clawed at his arm, he growled and pried my hand away, gripping my wrist. And then when we reached the nearest wall, he slammed me against it, forcing air from my lungs.

Despite the onset of fogginess from the pill, my heart was racing frantically inside my chest.

"There's no one here to save you now," he said, out of breath.

"Why are you doing this?"

"I can get what I want, too, you know."

He released my wrist and moved his hand down my side.

My body quivered at his touch and my stomach twisted, making me feel like I was going to throw up.

I had to get the knife.

But I couldn't reach down to grab it, not with him holding my arm.

I raised my knee, going for his groin, but he stopped it with a strong hand and then forced it aside as he lifted me off my feet.

He leaned into me, trapping me against the wall. And then he released my upper arm and lifted his hand to my neck. His fingers dug into my tender skin, pinching it.

The muscles in my thigh screamed as I fumbled with the hilt of Kent's blade. My hands felt so weak, and Hector was slowly cutting off my air.

My head whirled.

I tried to go limp and calm my panic. All of those times Henry had gripped my throat had actually prepared me for something.

Staring Hector in the face, I circled my fingers around the hilt and pulled it from its holster. I closed my eyes, hoping he would sense that I was losing consciousness, and then with all the force I could muster, I plunged the blade into his side.

He grunted and released his hold on me.

When my feet touched the floor, my knees folded, dropping me to the carpet.

Dragging in a breath, I grasped my neck and watched him look down at the blade still stuck in his side.

With a growl, he grabbed me by the arm and hauled me up. Then he struck out his arm and backhanded me, sending me crumpling back to the floor.

I landed on my knees again. Casting a quick glance over my shoulder, I saw Hector pull out the blade and drop it to the floor. Blood was soaking his T-shirt, but he didn't seem fazed by it.

He stumbled toward me, his breathing heavy and his lips curled up and exposing his teeth.

I collapsed onto my hip as I pressed my palm to my cheek. My watery eyes blurred my vision. When he bent down and swung his arm toward me, I tried to scramble out of his reach, but he caught me by the arm again. His fingers pinched my skin, making me cry out in pain.

He yanked me to my feet and then slammed me back against the wall.

My head bounced.

I struck out with my fists, catching him in the side where the blade had gone.

Yelping, he stepped back as he clutched his waist.

I charged past him and scrambled to the discarded blade. I could hear his heavy footfalls right behind me. I closed my fingers around the hilt and then slashed out as I rolled onto my back. The sharp edge connected, slicing a deep line across his forearm.

He screamed as he grabbed his arm. Blood oozed between his fingers.

"Hector, stop," I pleaded, my voice trembling and my throat raw. My hand shook. My stomach twisted and it felt like I was going to throw up any second.

He lifted his head, baring his teeth again. His jaw was clenched and he was heaving.

I held up the bloodied knife and tried to scoot away.

"Don't you fucking move," a voice warned from the doorway.

CHAPTER 42

I LOOKED UP and saw Henry stepping into the room with his gun aimed at Hector. I scrambled to my knees and crawled away, getting as much distance from Hector as I could.

But he wasn't going anywhere. He glared at Henry. "Go ahead. Shoot me."

Henry huffed. "I want you to suffer. For laying a hand on Kallis."

"For doing the things you have done? That's noble of you. What changed?"

"I never tried to kill her."

"She stabbed me."

"You expect me to believe she didn't have reason to do so?"

"Where'd she get the blade anyway? You give it to her?"

"I think the more interesting question is, why did you stab me in the back? I thought we were in this together."

Hector grunted. "You think the gangs were going to let us walk out of this city?"

"So, you sold me out? Let me take the fall?"

Hector shrugged. "It was a foolhardy plan."

"Who paid you off?"

"Wouldn't you like to know."

"You son of a bitch."

"You think those people in DC can stop all this?" Hector asked, his voice wheezing now. "They can't."

"You're wrong," Henry replied. He nodded his head toward Eric. "If he moves, kill him."

"What about taking me to a doctor?"

"You're on your own. I don't save traitors."

"That's funny because you're the biggest traitor of them all."

Henry huffed as he turned back to address Hector. "How do you figure that?"

"Remember your father?"

"My father deserved his fate." He raised his firearm, aiming it at Hector again. "As do you for touching Kallis."

"What's one more?"

"Do you not remember what I said?"

"I didn't figure you meant it," he replied. "Not for a whore."

Henry huffed again. "I keep my promises. You of all people should know that."

Hector would probably have bled out, from the wound that I had given him, but Henry didn't take the chance. With the sound of the muted gunshot, Hector's head slumped forward.

When Henry crouched down in front of me, he reached out and touched my arm.

I released my grip on the blade as I tilted my head back and fought hard to keep my eyes open.

His brows furrowed with worry and then his eyes widened. "Baby, what did he give you?"

I bowed my head again and stared down at my hands. "Is it true?"

He lifted his hand to my neck. "Is *what* true, Kallis?"

I bit my trembling lip as I looked up at him.

His thumb grazed my throat.

"Hector said..." My voice trailed off when he sighed and bowed his head. It was clear he didn't like it when Hector tried to rule over me. "He said you saw me."

He cocked his head. "Saw you? Where? I need a little bit more information to understand what you're saying."

When a fresh tear slid down my face, I clamped my eyes shut and wiped away the tear with my hand.

"Kallis, there's no time for this right now," he said. "We need to leave."

I nodded. As I dropped onto my hip to roll onto my knees and pressed my palms to the floor, he grasped my waist and hauled me to my feet.

I braced myself with my hands against his chest. When I looked up, he cupped my cheek with his palm, sliding his fingers through my hair.

"It's another muscle relaxer, isn't it?"

I nodded but I wasn't really paying attention. My mind was too preoccupied, trying to remember when I was at the medical center that day three years ago, trying to place him. But I had been so scared I hadn't noticed anything. I couldn't remember anything other than sitting on the patient's table and clasping my hands tight in my lap. I had looked in the nurse's face, trying to gauge if she felt bad for me or not. Her face was expressionless and in fact she even seemed to avoid my gaze.

"We need to go," he whispered, brushing his thumb over my cheekbone and wiping away a fresh tear.

With another nod, I cocked my head and put my hand over his. When I sniffled, he pulled me into his arms and rested his chin on the top of my head.

After a brief moment, he slowly released me and then took my hand and pulled me toward the door. He guided me down the hallway to the staircase.

"We can't go back down this way," Eric said, running toward us. "There are guys coming up the staircase."

Henry cursed under his breath.

"Unless you want to take them out."

Henry sighed. "There's another way out of here." He led us back inside the apartment. Glancing over his shoulder at Eric, he said, "Lock the door."

He pulled me down the hall to his room and then released my hand. He flung open the bottom drawer of the dresser and brushed aside a small stack of folded white T-shirts.

"No, no, no," he groaned.

"What are you looking for?"

Ignoring my question, he started shaking out all of the clothes and then dropping them to the floor. He turned his head to stare at me. "Kallis, where is it?"

"What? I don't—"

"There was a key," he said, pulling out the drawer and looking inside. "For the padlock to the other room."

"It didn't latch," I said, barely hearing my own words.

"What?" he asked, narrowing his eyes.

I cleared my throat and tried to speak up. "Hector. He was in there."

He raised his eyebrows.

"When he came back out, the lock...it didn't latch."

As I spoke, he got to his feet and then hurried out of the room. When he got to the door, he reached out and closed his hand gingerly around the padlock. It was almost like he was handling a bomb, careful not to do the wrong thing and mess everything up. He yanked his hand down, releasing the bolt. He let out a ragged breath. "How did you know it didn't lock?"

"I can hear everything, too."

The furrow of his brow deepened as he eyed me a moment longer and then swung the door open. I wasn't sure what to expect inside the room. All this time, I had wondered what was inside.

But to find it empty...

I thought that was odd. And why had Hector gone inside an empty room?

"It doesn't make sense," I heard myself saying.

"What?" Henry asked, turning his head to look at me.

I tried to point into the room, but I could only lift my arm halfway. "Why would Hector go in there?"

He narrowed his eyes as he stared at me.

Averting my gaze, I tried to figure it out. What was the point of going inside an empty room? What was he hiding inside?

It had to be a trap.

He hadn't been in the room long, just a couple of minutes. But Henry and I had been gone for several days. Hector would have had time to go in there during our absence.

"That son of a bitch," Henry said finally, pointing into the room. He stepped inside and walked to the window. "He screwed the windows shut."

CHAPTER 43

I COULD HEAR GUYS walking in the main hallway. They wouldn't have a clue that Hector was dead. Sprawled out on the living room floor. How long would it take for them to realize he was missing? Would they figure out something was up with the door being closed?

"If we break the window, the noise will alert the guys within a whole city block," Henry was saying.

"Hold on," Eric said, reaching into his jacket pocket. He walked across the room as he pulled out a metal object. He extended a tiny piece of it and then used it to remove the screws that fastened the window.

With the screws out, he slipped the tool back into his pocket and then slid the window up, opening it and letting in a cold draft of air. He hoisted himself up onto the window ledge and then stepped out onto the platform of the fire escape. He reached out his arms as Henry gripped my waist and nudged me to the window.

Eric grasped my arm, supporting me as I crawled up onto the ledge. When my feet stamped down onto the landing, he held on a moment longer like he was making sure I wasn't going to fall over.

"All right?" he asked.

Keeping my head bowed and my eyes downcast, I nodded. Silently, I prayed he'd release me. It was strange to be touched by someone else.

Slowly, he let go and then helped Henry.

We traveled down the stairs, with Eric leading the way. When we reached the final landing, an entire story above street level, I peered over the railing.

"There's a ladder on the side," Henry said.

Eric nodded and reached up to grasp the bottom rung of a straight ladder. It didn't look tall enough to reach the street.

And I was right. It stopped about seven feet above ground.

"How are we—"

"We'll have to jump down," Henry said, cutting me off.

Eric stepped down onto the first rung. After he landed on the street, Henry nudged me across the platform.

"You go first," I said, panicking.

He forced me to the edge and set my hand on the railing, curling my fingers around the metal. "I can't support your weight, Kallis. You need to do this on your own."

"But—"

"Go!" He sounded irritated now.

I bit my trembling lip and grasped the railing tighter as I set my foot on the rung. I didn't know how I was going to get down the rest of the way. I didn't want Eric touching me again. I didn't want him gazing up my nightgown either. But I knew I didn't have a choice. They would make it for me.

When my feet touched the last rung, I pressed my forehead to the metal to catch my breath. My whole body was trembling. I didn't think I could hold on with just my hands. I wasn't strong enough.

"Keep moving," Henry said, his voice hushed.

Blowing out a slow breath, I eased myself down into a crouch, with my feet still on the bottom rung.

"You need to lower your legs," Eric said, reaching up and touching the heels of my boots with his fingertips. "You're almost there."

"I can't," I said, shaking my head.

I could hear Henry sigh above me. And then he was grasping my wrist and saying, "Let go."

With a gasp, I uncurled my fingers, trusting him to hold me by the arm. Slowly, I lowered one foot, extending my leg.

"Kallis, I swear, if you don't hurry it up…"

I clamped my eyes shut and tried to lower myself down nice and easy, but my arm gave out, dropping me so my arm was extended. Henry's grip on my other wrist tightened.

And then Eric was grasping me by the waist and lowering me to the street.

My gown rode up as he set me down. Quickly, I straightened the hem and then hugged my arms to my chest in an effort to fend off the cold air and warm up my freezing hands.

"Which way do we go?" Eric asked.

"We'll need to head around to the next block over. There should be nothing that way," Henry said, wrapping his arm around my shoulders and then rubbing my arm with his hand.

My throat tightened and I fought hard not to let the tears fall.

He pressed his free hand to his stomach and groaned, a quiet exhale of breath. Before I had a chance to question him, he slid his hand down my side to my hip and then guided me down the street.

We skirted the building across the street from our apartment building. But when we reached the next corner, Eric jerked back, pressing himself against the brick. He turned his head toward us and whispered, "We have to go back. They're trapping us in."

CHAPTER 44

I SLUMPED AGAINST HENRY as he cursed under his breath. I knew it was too good to be true. The gang would corner us, take us back to the apartment where they would kill Henry for his betrayal, maybe even make me watch, and then sell me to another member of the gang. It was anyone's guess what they would do with Eric.

"Come on," Eric said, interrupting the terrible thoughts that were running through my mind. His voice was low as he steered us around, back toward our building.

My head whirled as I closed my eyes and pressed my forehead to Henry's chest.

"Kallis," he whispered. "You need to walk."

"It's over," I heard myself saying. "I can't."

He let out an annoyed groan.

"I'll take her," Eric said, grasping my forearm.

I opened my eyes and tried to jerk out of the way, but it was too late. He was already wrapping his arm around my back and gripping my waist. I thought I heard a soft hum when the portion of sweater underneath his hand slipped against the silk of my gown. He brushed my sweater aside and set his hand directly to the silk at my rib cage.

"We have to get across that street," Henry said, releasing his hold on me. "It's the only way out."

"We'll find another way," Eric replied, glancing at him over my head.

"The parking garage."

Henry turned to me as he asked, "What?"

I flicked my gaze to his as I swallowed hard. "Hector's truck."

"Do you have the key?" he asked, sounding irritated. "Because I don't."

"It's under the seat."

He narrowed his eyes as he stared at me. It was like he didn't believe me. Or maybe he didn't think Hector would actually do that. Finally, he said, "How are we getting out of the garage unnoticed?"

"What if we wait it out?" Eric said. "The ammo is safe for now."

Henry pursed his lips as he shook his head. I couldn't tell if he disagreed with Eric or if he was just disgusted with the potential outcomes. But I couldn't imagine he wanted us staying inside the city any longer than we had to.

"They'll just keep searching for us," I said quietly.

Henry sighed. "I know." He turned back to Eric. "We can't stay here. Whatever we do, it has to involve us getting out."

"Leaving *now*? That's dangerous."

"But so is staying."

"I don't have any backup," Eric said, leaning closer and keeping his voice down. "There's no one who can help us in here."

"We'll make it."

Eric released my arm and then withdrew his holstered gun at his hip.

When his other hand glided forward like he was going to hug me, I craned my head up. I still felt lightheaded and probably would for another few hours.

"Sorry," he whispered, meeting my gaze. He dropped the gun's magazine into his hand to inspect it and then he clicked it back into place and reholstered the gun, jostling me slightly as he moved.

After he put his hands back, one at my side and the other gripping my arm, he lifted his gaze to Henry and frowned. "You realize you don't look so hot, right?"

"I'll be fine."

Eric didn't seem convinced.

When I looked back at Henry, I wasn't convinced either, but I'd never be able to change his mind anyway. It would be a waste of time and effort to try.

"We can get to the garage through a tunnel," he said. "That will buy us some time. Give us a few minutes to catch our breath."

"Fine. Let's go."

As we hurried back toward the apartment, I was acutely aware of Eric's index finger pressing against the swell of my breast. But I knew the way he was touching me was different. It wasn't meant for anything other than to help. He was supporting my weight. Nothing more.

I fought hard to keep my feet moving and to clear the fog and dizziness from the muscle relaxer. I didn't understand why I was feeling worse side effects than before. The pill had looked the same. Had Hector lied about what he had given me?

I didn't put it past him. If he had given me a stronger drug, he could have done whatever he wanted with me. That thought made me shudder. It was bad enough being helpless while conscious. To be incapable of fighting back...that thought scared me.

When we reached an alleyway in between our building and the next one, we headed north. Then Henry led us down another alleyway and then up a small flight of stairs. He took out a key from his jacket pocket and slid it into the keyhole.

I wanted to ask him why he had a key for the building next door, but I knew now wasn't the time.

We hurried inside and secured the door. Then Henry took my hand and pulled me into a dark stairwell. I held onto his arm with my other hand and tried to keep my eyes open and my feet moving.

When we headed down, Eric asked, "Why would they put a tunnel down here if it goes to the parking garage of another building?"

"Easy access? I don't know," Henry replied with a shrug. "There is a parking garage under this building, so the tunnel connects the two."

"Do we need to grab the key now? Maybe scope out the place first?"

"We should be fine. No one usually goes in that garage. I'm actually wondering why Hector did."

He led us inside a large storage room in the basement. There were bankers' boxes lining what appeared to be several rows of floor-to-ceiling metal shelves.

"How long you want to wait? Ten, fifteen minutes?" Eric asked, looking around the room.

"I just need a minute."

I watched Eric wander around the room and shine his flashlight at the boxes. I heard Henry clear his throat, a subtle sound no doubt meant to get my attention. When I looked up at him, he was watching me. My cheeks flushed as I bowed my head, but I didn't think he'd be able to see my reddened face in the poor lighting.

"Are you okay?"

I nodded. I wasn't okay. I was worried we'd get caught. I was worried I'd be sold again. I was worried I'd never see him again.

He wrapped his arm around my waist and pulled me into a tight embrace. "I'm sorry," he whispered. "I shouldn't have left you by yourself."

Sniffling, I shook my head as I clamped my eyes shut. "It's my fault."

"What are you talking about?"

"You didn't have a choice. You *had* to leave me."

He sighed. "I should have taken you with us. I shouldn't have let you out of my sight."

Slowly, I tilted my head back to look at him. "Why do you care so much?"

His frown deepened.

"About me."

He lifted his hand and pressed his palm to my cheek as he brushed a fresh tear away.

"He said you saw me at the medical center." I stopped to clear my throat. "Back before the people revolted."

His throat bobbed as his gaze drifted. Then he nodded. "It's stupid," he said, pulling his hand away and then rubbing it over his head. "I had a fleeting plan that never would have worked. They had every exit heavily guarded. In case anyone tried to escape."

I looked away.

"I was walking past your exam room. You were alone, waiting for the nurse to get back with your vaccines." He blew out a slow breath. "I had already passed an unattended exit, a window of opportunity. And for a few seconds, I thought I could make it work.

Maybe I could have. But I chickened out. Didn't want to take the risk."

"Why didn't you buy me sooner?"

"I couldn't. I didn't have the money. Carl wanted an insane amount anyway. Especially after that night. It wasn't until I agreed to the ammo project that I finally had the funds to cover his cut. He wouldn't let anyone else sell you without making his own profit."

I shook my head, disgusted and angry with Carl.

"I shouldn't have said the things I did, Kallis," Henry said, setting his hand on my shoulder. "It wasn't anything you did. The guys sold you to get their money back."

"What about you?"

"I don't want it back."

"So, you did all of this for me?"

He sucked in part of his bottom lip and nodded.

"Am I worth it?" I asked, my voice a mere whisper.

"Kallis."

I bowed my head and closed my eyes. "How much did you spend?"

He lifted his hand again and hooked a finger under my chin as he said, "Look at me." His thumb grazed my chin, sending a warmth inside my chest. When I met his gaze, he searched my eyes. "No price would ever be too high."

My throat tightened. "I don't understand why you think that."

"You think far too little of yourself, and that needs to change."

I closed my eyes as I bowed my head. "How much?" I asked again, my voice quiet.

"Why does it matter?"

"Please tell me."

"Kallis."

"Ten thousand?" I had no idea what a good rate was for a slave.

"More."

I blew out a slow breath. "Twenty?" When he didn't reply, I looked up at him. "More than that?" I couldn't believe anyone would even sell a person for that price.

Still, he said nothing.

"Please tell me it's not more than that."

He leaned his head back against the wall and stared out into the room, at all the shelves.

It didn't take a genius to realize by his lack of response that he had paid more. But how much more?

"A hundred thousand," he said finally.

I felt my eyes bug out at the number. I couldn't fathom it. I had never seen that much money all in one place at one time.

"Kent covered the rest."

I frowned. "What?"

He cleared his throat. "All of it went to pay Carl's share."

I didn't know what to say. How could anyone spend that much for someone?

"Like I said, it's not about the money." He closed his hand over mine. "There's no price too high. Don't you know that?"

I shrugged as I bit my trembling lip and fought back fresh tears. I tried to take a step back, but his arms tightened around me, closing me in as he buried his face in my hair.

"I'm so sorry for everything."

I clamped my eyes shut as I clung to him. How was it he had been the one I feared the most? I had hated him. I had never known what to expect with him. From him. My body had trembled as I waited for him to get back from work every night. And now here he was apologizing and trying to convince me that I was worth something.

I so much wanted to believe him.

If he was saying it, it had to be true. But what about all the other things he had said? Had those not also been true? But then he had a way of saying what was true, even if it was hurtful. So, how much of all of that had been a lie?

And then another realization occurred to me. "So, we're in this mess because of me."

"What do you mean?"

"You needed the money to pay for me, so you took on the ammo job."

"That's not exactly how it happened."

"Oh."

"I would have taken the job anyway. I just bargained for the money so I could buy you."

"But if I was so valuable to you, why did you treat me the way you did?"

"I was one of the leaders, Kallis. I couldn't do anything else."

I was too confused to reply. It didn't make sense.

He lifted his hand and brushed my hair off my shoulder. "Maybe someday you'll understand," he said. "Sometimes we're forced to do things because of our connection with the world around us rather than our own personal goals."

CHAPTER 45

I THOUGHT ABOUT WHAT Henry had said. That the world could dictate our actions, no matter what they meant to someone else. I wanted to tell him he was wrong. That I could never treat someone horribly because of a job. And I could never choose a job over someone I cared about. Even if it meant survival.

If I were being honest, I wasn't afraid of dying. In the messed-up world of Detroit, dying was better.

Sometimes I wished I had died. Not enough to act on it on my own. But if one of my owners had taken things too far...

"Kallis."

The sound of Henry's whisper startled me, making me jerk my head.

"We should go," he whispered. "Get the hell out of here. The sooner we get out of Detroit again, the better."

I nodded.

"So, what's the plan?" Eric asked, walking back toward us. "Head through the tunnel, get to the truck, drive away. And plow through anyone who stands in our path?"

Henry nodded. "That about sums it up. Make sure we're not being followed before getting back to the ammo."

"All right," Eric replied, gesturing toward the door. "Lead the way."

When Henry took my hand, interlacing our fingers, and pulled me gently toward the door, I gripped his arm with my free hand. I tried to ignore the urge to rest my head against him and close my eyes. I had to stay alert. I probably needed more food to help metabolize the drugs from the muscle relaxer. If Hector hadn't given me the pill... Damn him.

Or damn myself for telling him I wasn't feeling well. I should have known better. I should have known he'd give me drugs.

My head kept whirling and it felt loose on my shoulders, like it was too heavy for my neck to keep it upright.

"Hey," Henry said, his voice hushed.

I blinked my eyes and opened them wide to try to wake myself up. He was facing me now and his arm was around my waist, holding me up.

He leaned down and cupped my cheek with his hand. "Kallis." He searched my eyes for a moment and then he cast a worried glance at Eric who was standing at my side and staring at me now, too.

"There's no way this is from a simple muscle relaxer," Eric said as he squeezed my wrist. "What else would Hector give her?"

Henry's jaw clenched and his brows furrowed as he looked away.

"Slowed breathing and heart rate. Bloodshot eyes."

Henry cursed under his breath. "That son of a bitch gave her Rohypnol."

My eyes watered with tears as the air seemed to thicken. I couldn't keep going. My legs felt like jelly, and my head wouldn't stop whirling as Henry's words played over and over in my mind.

Don't ever take what he gives you.

I remembered what Liana had said, too.

He bowed his head and pressed his forehead to mine. "Kallis, what did I tell you about Hector?"

I clamped my eyes shut. "I'm sorry," I said, my voice cracking. "She tried to warn me. But I couldn't do it. I can't." The words had sounded so clear in my head, but it felt they like were stumbling out of my mouth as I spoke them.

"What's she talking about?" I heard Eric whisper.

"Liana," Henry replied. "The girl who was living with us before we left."

"We need to induce vomiting," Eric said. "It'll help. Get it out of her system sooner."

I tried to shake my head. I couldn't do it. I couldn't make myself throw up.

"Let me take her," Eric said. He lifted me in his arms as Henry stepped back.

I couldn't move. I was totally helpless. If they hadn't come back for me, I'd be lying on Hector's bed.

Eric knelt on the floor inside the storage room and laid me down on the cold concrete. Then he rolled me onto my side.

"Are you sure we need to do this?" Henry asked, crouching behind me and setting his hand on my arm.

"It's either this or let her system handle it on its own. It could take twelve hours or more for her body to recover that way."

"All right." Henry lifted me to a sitting position and then held me with his arm tight across my chest and my arms trapped at my sides.

"Have you ever done this before?" Eric asked.

"Once," he replied. "With my dad."

Before I knew it, I was tasting gunpowder and oil on my tongue as he stuck his fingers down my throat. I tried to fight him off, but his hold was too strong, and it didn't seem like my muscles were cooperating anyway. As he held me up, keeping me from collapsing to the floor, I felt a rush of burning heat in my throat and then I was coughing and gagging.

It felt like forever until my stomach finally settled. My eyes were wet with tears and my throat burned.

He smoothed back my hair and then rested his warm hand on my shoulder. He hushed me gently as he rocked me back and forth.

"We'll have to stay a little while," he said. "I can't carry her."

It was all my fault. If I hadn't complained about not feeling well, if I had just pushed through instead of giving up on getting free again, none of this would have happened. And if I had just stayed out of the way, maybe Hector wouldn't have found me at the communications building. We could have gotten halfway to Wilderness in all the time I had wasted.

"Maybe they'll think we've escaped by now," Eric replied. "They won't think to check this building, right? Being so close to your apartment."

"I don't think so."

"How is it you have a key to this place?"

"It was a safety measure," Henry said. "I like planning ahead."

"A damn lucky one then. I guess it runs in your family."

I was barely registering what they were saying. I still felt dizzy, my body felt like deadweight, my throat was raw, and grit from the floor was digging into my bare thigh. Not to mention the cold concrete was numbing my leg.

Henry tilted my head back, and then water trickled down my tongue and over my chin. When it hit my throat, I gagged, coughing it back out. He held me, keeping me from collapsing to the floor, as he patted my back.

Finally, the coughing subsided. I pressed my hand to the concrete, but my arm began to tremble under the weight.

"Try some more," he said.

I tried to shake my head, but the movement made me dizzy. A small sob escaped my lips as I clamped my eyes shut and let my head roll against his arm.

He leaned back, pulling me with him. And then he was tilting my head back again.

We went through the process until I was able to keep the water down. My gown and sweater were cold and wet, but not soaked. He pressed a damp cloth to my face and then to my chest.

"Help me get her up," he said, rising to his knee and taking his warmth away and letting in the cold.

I felt hands on me and then I was being hauled to my feet. Before I collapsed back to the floor, Eric lifted me in his arms. I heard Henry sucking in a breath through gritted teeth behind me.

"Is there another part of the building to hang out?" Eric asked. "A lunchroom with chairs, perhaps."

"This is the safest place. The roof on the east side collapsed years ago."

I cringed at the sound of cardboard scraping across concrete.

"Here. Set her down," Henry said, out of breath.

It felt like I was being handed off to someone else, and then Henry's arms were circling my waist and hugging me to his chest. My cheek rested against his collar bone. He brushed hair from my face and over my shoulder. I hated feeling so helpless, but the drug Hector had given me wasn't letting up. Not yet.

"It could take a while for the side effects to wear off," Eric said. "A couple hours. Even with the vomiting."

I swallowed hard. It was my fault. I had gotten us into this mess.

Henry shushed me. "Everything's going to be fine. It's not your fault."

I hadn't realized I had said anything out loud.

His hand smoothed over my hair and settled at my back as he pressed his cheek to the top of my head.

His shirt was soaked. From sweat, maybe, and my tears.

Despite my vulnerable state and aside from the possibility that we could still get caught, I felt safe. In Henry's arms, I felt safe.

"Why don't you try to sleep?" Eric said. "I'll keep watch."

"All right," Henry replied.

I heard quiet footsteps and then a door opening and closing.

With a sigh, Henry lifted his head from mine and removed his hand from my back. The chill in the air swept in and chased off the warmth.

CHAPTER 46

THE SOUND OF FOOTSTEPS snapped me from sleep. I held my breath and listened for more sounds as I regained a sense of my surroundings and allowed my eyes to adjust to the dim lighting.

"It's just Eric," Henry said. He gave my hand a gentle squeeze.

For a few seconds, my mind scrambled to figure out who he was talking about. And then I remembered. I relaxed and exhaled slowly.

He lifted my hand to his lips and kissed my knuckles. "How are you feeling?"

"Good," I whispered back. "Right here." I didn't mention the warm feeling that had flooded my stomach from his gentle kiss.

"What's your name?"

I huffed and snuggled my face against his neck.

"Hmm?"

"Kallis," I said. "You're Henry. And we're stuck in Detroit again because of me."

He hummed. "Your first *two* answers are right."

"So is the other one."

He sighed.

"You warned me. Liana warned me. I shouldn't have taken it."

"I know you didn't have a choice," he said. "Not a good one anyway."

I didn't want to know what Hector would have done to me if I had refused. He had said he'd cram it down my throat, but what else would he do? And to think what he was planning later after the drug had gone into effect...

Henry tucked my hair behind my ear and glided his fingers through it to cradle the back of my head. "I'm sorry I didn't get to you sooner."

I nodded against his chest.

"We were heading back with the ammo when I saw Hector's truck on the road."

"I didn't see you."

"You wouldn't have. Eric has a sensor device that alerts him whenever anyone is nearby. We were able to get off the road and travel back on foot to see who it was."

"Why would you do that? Go back to see."

"I was worried about you, and the gangs don't usually travel outside of the city. For anyone to be out, there had to be a reason. And when I saw Hector's truck, I knew he had found you."

"If you hadn't seen us..."

"It just would have taken me longer to get to you."

I nodded, but I couldn't figure out how they had gotten inside the apartment in the first place. Wouldn't they have been stopped by the other guys?

Or had they all been out looking for Henry?

I was afraid to ask, but I needed to know.

Finally, I asked, "What happened to all the others? Weren't they inside the apartment building?"

"The place was virtually empty when we arrived."

"So…"

"We took care of them."

"I didn't hear anything in the hallway."

"Apparently, you don't hear everything."

I felt my eyebrows scrunch together as my lips pursed.

He shrugged. "You were busy fighting with Hector at the time."

I tried to process what he meant by *took care of*, but my mind filled with too many bloody images that I forced the thoughts out.

His warm hand settled at the back of my neck and he leaned his head closer. "Are you okay?" he whispered.

Biting my trembling lip, I searched his eyes as I shook my head.

He pressed his lips to my forehead as he slid his hand over my shoulder and down my arm.

"I didn't think Hector would actually try to hurt me."

He sighed. "I told you he wasn't helping you."

"But…" My voice trailed off. I didn't have the energy to argue.

"Everything's okay now," Henry said.

"Is it?" I asked, flicking my gaze to his before looking away again.

"Yes."

I wanted to believe him. I wanted to know that he had cleared the way for us to leave the city again.

But I wasn't so sure.

I couldn't help having doubts. Especially when I had thought I was safe inside the communications building. I hadn't expected Hector to find me. How had he found me?

That made me wonder how that was possible. There's no way it should have been possible. There was no way he should have been in Hopewell to begin with. Why would he be there? And almost a week after Henry and I left?

That still didn't make any sense to me.

Did he know someone outside of the city? Someone who could tell him that we had come back. That was the only way the whole thing made sense to me.

It was too bad Hector was dead. We could have asked him how he knew. I had asked, but he hadn't indulged the information.

Maybe we would never know.

CHAPTER 47

THE THOUGHT THAT SOMEONE on the outside was watching our every move scared me. Was that how the Federal Guard had found us? Had Kelsey or Evan lied about the tracker? Was Evan's tool even what he said it was?

I hadn't learned much about electromagnetic pulse emitters before the gangs took over Detroit, so my knowledge was limited. Not to mention my memory was a bit fuzzy going that far back.

"Are you okay?" Henry asked, sounding concerned. "You seem distracted."

I shook my head as I said, "No."

"It's all going to work out."

"What if it doesn't?"

He sighed. "I can't have you sabotaging our efforts. We need the hell out of this city."

"But what about after that?" I pushed against his chest and sat up so I could look at him. "What if Evan lied about the trackers to distract us from what's really going on?"

Henry frowned. "I'm not sure I'm following."

"If we're not concerned anymore about trackers because Evan used an emitter to fry them, we won't be worried about getting caught any other way."

"Um…"

"How did Hector know we were back?" I asked, trying to get more to the point. "We had been gone for, what, five days? So, who informed him that we were back?"

He nodded slightly. "I've been wondering the same thing."

It should have made me feel relieved that he was thinking about it, too, but the looming questions overrode every bit of that feeling. "Someone on the outside would have to be watching. But who?"

"And why Hector?" he added. "He sold us out to Creekside, but who was he working for? And why were they working with *him*?"

"Exactly."

He sighed again. "It doesn't really matter," he said. "We have to be cautious, but we can't let that stop us from leaving."

"How many times do you want back inside Detroit?"

"None."

I cringed a little at the bite in his tone. "Okay. But what if it's Franklin again?"

He pursed his lips like he was annoyed. "I know you can't trust anyone, but I need you to stop worrying. Your anxiety is going to create problems and get us killed."

"I'm just being realistic."

"I don't care."

"So, you want me to act like everything is fine?"

"Yes."

I sighed. Did he seriously not get it? How did he explain the attack on my father and me at the university? Or all the parts after that? Bad things happened whether I wanted them to or not. And nothing I did ever made a difference.

"It's great that you're thinking about the what-ifs, but I need you to envision us getting out of Detroit again and getting to Wilderness."

I swallowed hard as I looked away. "Fine."

He lifted his hand to my cheek and turned my head so I could look at him again. His dark eyes bored into mine. "I get that it's hard for you to do that, and I'm sorry. It's my fault, and I can't excuse the things I've done. But we got out of Detroit the first time because I saw it and I acted on it."

Tears slipped down my face. He was ruling my life even now. I couldn't get away from it. He was saying that he had acted on it, but those actions included hurting me. I knew he couldn't take me out of the apartment with me looking like I loved him. He needed me to fear him for the sake of pretenses. There was a reason for everything he did, whether I agreed with it or not.

"I don't expect you to ever forgive me, and I don't think I'll ever forgive myself."

I wiped at my face with a hand and then ran my palm over my sweater. I thought I had already forgiven him, but deep down, I knew forgiveness required more grace than I possessed. I would tell myself that I had so we could carry on like normal, but that wasn't forgiveness. That was acceptance. And settling for what I clearly thought I deserved.

"Please tell me you're feeling okay, so we can get out of here," he said.

Sniffling, I looked down at my thigh and then eased my leg off his lap and set my foot on the floor.

Henry sat forward and grasped my arm with one hand and supported my back with his other.

Once I was on both of my feet, I took a small step. My legs trembled the slightest amount, but I didn't think that would keep me from walking. "I think I'll be fine," I said, glancing up at Henry as he rose to his feet beside me.

My skin tingled as he slid his hand down my arm.

"Come on," he said softly, giving my hand a light squeeze.

He led us through the underground tunnel and to the door leading to the parking garage of our building. "Ready?" he asked, glancing at me before directing his attention to Eric.

Eric gave him a curt nod and brushed past us to take the lead. Slowly, he opened the door and peered out into the dimly lit space. He looked over his shoulder and cocked his head toward the door.

After we slipped out into the parking garage, Henry closed the door quietly behind us.

I scanned the area, peering around concrete pillars until I spotted Hector's truck still sitting by itself at the other end of the garage. When I cast a quick glance at Henry to make sure he saw it, he glanced back at me and nodded.

Everything seemed too good to be true. It couldn't be this easy, could it? Why wasn't someone there to stop us? But what if Hector was the only one who cared? What if the other guys really weren't blocking us in, but just happened to be around the corner when we got there? What if they would have let us go?

I kept my thoughts to myself. I knew what Henry would say anyway. He'd tell me to knock it off, stop thinking like that. Stop tossing up ideas. Focus on us escaping.

"Wait!"

CHAPTER 48

THE HAIRS AT THE BACK of my neck rose on end at the sound of the deep, male voice.

I knew it. We'd never be able to leave. Not again. We had been lucky the first time. But a second time… Forget it.

I slumped against a pillar and closed my eyes as soft footsteps approached.

"I've been looking all over for you."

Finally, I recognized the voice. Well, barely. It was the guy Henry had worked with on the ammo project before the attack. When I looked up, he was halfway across the parking garage.

"What are you doing here, Rick?" Henry asked. "I thought you were dead."

"Nah. I managed to slip away when Carl walked in looking for you. I've been on the run ever since."

I wanted to ask how he had gotten back inside the city without getting caught. Surely the guys would have wanted him dead. Or at least alive to tell where the ammo was stored. Maybe that was why the ammo had been moved. Was he on our side or was he a traitor? I had no idea. Although I had my suspicions. To be honest, I was suspicious of everyone. No one was good in my eyes.

I eyed Henry, trying to gauge his reaction. Was he just as suspicious?

"I saw you get away last week. That was some escape! Especially with *her* driving. I bet you won't let that happen again." He laughed like it was some big joke.

I bowed my head as I bit down hard on my bottom lip.

Henry squeezed my hand gently. "She saved my life."

"Shocker, considering."

"So, you saw us drive off then?"

As Henry spoke, I lifted my gaze and studied the guy's reaction.

He opened his mouth to speak and then closed it as he looked away.

"There's only one way you could know about that," Henry said.

The guy nodded slightly, clearly realizing he had just given away his hand. He rubbed the top of his head with his fingertips.

I scanned the parking garage, looking for movement of any kind. All was quiet. Was he working alone? Or were there more guys we needed to worry about?

"Where's the truck, Henry?"

"I'm not sure which truck you're referring to."

The guy pulled out a gun and aimed it at Henry as he yelled, "The one with the ammo in it!"

"Oh, *that* one. I'll have to show you. I don't remember the name of the street we left it on."

It was so odd the way he spoke. Calmly… as if it didn't matter to him in the slightest that he had a gun aimed at his chest. So calm that his voice relaxed even me. But it didn't have the same effect on Rick. It only served to agitate him more.

Rick's lips curled back in a silent snarl.

"Put the gun down, Rick. I don't want any trouble."

"You think I'll let you walk out of here now?"

Henry sighed. "I thought we were friends."

Rick pursed his lips as he shrugged. "Just a means to an end."

"Why do you want the ammo anyway? What are you going to do with it?"

"Sell it to the highest bidder."

"You're a bigger fool than I thought," Henry replied. "No one will pay you for it. They will just kill you and take it."

"I figure I'm worth as much as her," Rick said, pointing at me.

"You should have taken the money from Carl. If you wanted it so bad." Henry turned his head and searched my eyes. We looked away at the same time, as he added, "Last I heard, he hadn't spent a penny of the money."

"I heard that, too, but it was already gone by the time I got there."

Henry nodded slightly.

I was hoping he was thinking the same thing I was. That Rick had said he was in hiding after the warehouse attack. What was the truth, and what was a lie?

"So… about that truck."

"I'll take you to it, but you have to get us out of here."

Rick huffed. "You know, you could have just walked out of here. No one else cares. They would have let you leave."

"You could still do the same thing. And nothing is stopping you from making more ammunition."

He shook his head. "I've done enough hard work. And for what? A good cause? Give me a break."

"You want the truck or not?" Henry asked.

Rick nodded his head to the side, toward the other end of the parking garage where Hector's truck was located. He kept a wide berth, with his gun aimed at us, as we walked.

I kept waiting for Henry to take his shot. Why wasn't he eliminating the threat? Surely, he was capable of doing it. Was he making sure Rick would get us out of the city? If there was any trouble, surely Rick would smooth it over.

When we reached the truck, Rick turned his aim on me as he said, "Give me your gun first."

I held my breath, waiting for Henry to make his move. I knew he could do it. He was quick. Obviously skilled. And surely he was quicker than Rick was.

"Leave her out of this," Henry said, his voice calm. "This is between you and me."

Rick smirked. "You don't think I'll take advantage of an opportunity for leverage?"

"Fine," Henry replied, setting his hand on his gun. Slowly, with just his thumb and forefinger, he removed it from his holster.

"Set it on the backseat."

Henry opened the back passenger door, set down his gun, and then backed away with both of his hands raised.

Motioning to Henry with the barrel of his gun, Rick said, "You drive. Your friend stays here. And she'll sit in the back with me. If you try anything, she dies."

Henry turned to me then. I knew that look. Hard eyes, slightly narrowed. Squared jaw. He was ticked. And if I put up a fight, I'd regret it.

When he stepped toward me, I sucked in a breath. But then I remembered our situation. His anger probably wasn't directed toward me.

His expression softened as he cupped my cheek and brushed his thumb gently over my skin. "Come on," he whispered, lowering his hand and gliding it gently over my back. He nudged me toward the back door on the driver's side.

Before we reached the truck door, Rick, with his gun aimed at Henry, moved past us and hopped into the backseat, swiping Henry's gun off the seat as he went.

After Henry helped me up, I sat down and smoothed the gown back over my legs. I tried to ignore the gun aimed in my direction, but my legs wouldn't stop trembling.

He reached over my lap and clicked the seat belt into the lock. He glanced up at me as he moved his warm hand over my knee. And then he stepped back and closed the door.

I blew out a slow breath. If I could calm my nerves enough, I could reach into my boot and pull out the knife. Hopefully take the guy by surprise long enough to slice into his arm and then his gut, but I knew I'd never be able to pull it off. He'd likely shoot me in the face or turn his aim and kill Henry.

I had to wait it out. I had to let Henry handle it. I just didn't know how long that would be. Was he planning to kill Rick when we got to where they had stashed the truck? Before then?

Surely, he wasn't planning on crashing Hector's truck. That thought terrified me. Quickly, I shook the thought away and focused on the windshield. When we got outside, the sunlight glinted off the metal of Rick's gun, catching me in the corner of my eye.

Squinting against the bright light, I turned my head and glanced at Rick.

He eyed me and then glanced out the back window, back toward the parking garage as he asked, "Have you done that guy yet?"

"What?" I asked, confused.

He laughed. "I bet you have. You've slept with nearly every other guy in your building."

My jaw dropped as I turned my head to stare at Rick.

"Leave her alone," Henry warned.

"Just a question."

"What do *you* care?"

"I'm playin', man. Chill out."

I bit my trembling lip and looked away. If Henry didn't kill this guy, I would. I didn't know how to do that, but I had injured Hector. I had that going for me.

But then I remembered I didn't have the blade anymore. The sheath was still tucked in my boot, but I hadn't picked up the knife and put it back. I was completely powerless yet again.

"Who is that guy anyway?"

"Just a guy we met on the road."

They kept talking, but I zoned out. I stared out the side window instead. Henry wasn't driving the way we had taken to Hopewell the prior week. It looked like he was taking side streets through a heavily damaged part of the city.

When he stopped the truck, I looked over at Rick and then out the windshield. Up ahead there was a huge hole in the pavement, making the road impassable by vehicle.

"What the hell is this? Why are we stopping here?"

"We have to walk the rest of the way," Henry replied, turning off the engine. "It's not much farther."

I glanced at Rick. He looked upset. I thought he would argue. Surely there were other routes we could take. We were in a section of city that had been hit in a terrorist attack in the early eighties. Most of the roads were torn up or covered with building debris from the bomb strikes.

When Henry opened the door and stepped out onto the pavement, Rick called out, "Try anything and she dies. Remember that."

I didn't know him well enough to know if he would actually kill me if Henry made a move.

But I knew Henry well enough to know he wouldn't try anything unless he was certain it would get him the result he wanted. The gang hadn't made him a leader for nothing.

Before he bought me, back before I had been with Kent, I had seen him interact. The way he carried himself, stayed calm and observed his surroundings with quiet reserve, spoke matter-of-factly like he took life seriously, it had given me chills. He didn't let emotions, if he had any, interfere with how he interacted with others.

Cool, calm, collected, aside from various facial expressions. But as for emotionally charged verbal or physical outbursts... that wasn't Henry's way.

I knew I could trust him in that.

That didn't stop my heart from racing though.

Casting a cautious glance Rick's way, I slowly reached for the buckle. My hand trembled so badly I couldn't get the heel of my thumb pressed down hard enough to release the latch. I blew out a slow breath, hoping it would calm my nerves.

But then Henry was opening the door and reaching inside. His fingers grazed mine as he unbuckled my seat belt and then carefully moved it aside. He stepped back, giving me room to get out.

Rick watched us with mild curiosity. I kept telling myself he just wanted the truck. He wasn't planning to kill us.

Gripping the door handle, I lowered myself to the pavement.

Henry guided me away from the truck as Rick moved across the seat and hopped out, keeping his gun aimed in our direction.

"Lead the way," Rick said, waving his gun at Henry as he outstretched his free hand and grasped my arm.

With a slight nod, Henry stepped away. His jaw clenched when Rick turned his aim on me, but he stayed quiet and began leading us across the broken pavement and around huge piles of debris.

I was unsteady on my feet. And still feeling sluggish from the Rohypnol Hector had given me earlier.

Henry kept glancing my way. It looked like he wanted to help me, but with Rick holding his gun at my chest, he wasn't going to risk it.

When we came to a huge hole the size of a large crater in the road, Henry sat down on the pavement with his legs dangling over the edge.

"I thought you said the truck wasn't far."

"It's not," Henry replied, glancing over his shoulder. "Another couple of blocks." He eased himself over the edge and then dropped down onto a flat piece of concrete.

Rick stared down into the hole and then shook his head. "We'll go around."

I looked in both directions. Our other options weren't much better.

"It's easier getting up on the other side."

Rick sighed. "Fine."

I honestly couldn't believe this guy was accepting Henry's idea of going into a huge hole as an option. But if this gave us an opportunity to gain the upper hand…

But I just knew he would eventually kill Henry. And he would sell me to the highest bidder. He was after money. He wasn't Henry's friend. Probably never was.

"Kallis," Henry said, his voice quiet but enough to stir my attention. When I looked his way, he was holding out his hand to me.

I cast a quick glance at Rick and then lowered myself onto the pavement, sucking in a breath when the backs of my thighs pressed to the cold, debris-covered surface. Slowly, I eased myself over the edge and dropped down in front of Henry. When my head whirled, I outstretched my hands for balance.

Henry caught me around the waist. He pulled me against him. "We should stop for a while," he said, wrapping his arms around me as Rick hopped down not far from us. "She's working off the side effects of the drug Hector gave her."

"No," Rick replied, waving his gun at Henry and motioning for him to step away. "We can keep going."

"She's not steady enough on her feet."

"It's okay," I said, pushing away. "We're almost there, right?"

He cupped my cheek with his palm and studied my face for a moment. It looked like he wanted to say something, but he simply nodded. Then with a small sigh, he stepped away.

Rick reached out and grabbed me by the arm, yanking me toward him and farther away from Henry.

Somehow I managed to stay on my feet—and do it without catching a toe on upheaved pavement—but my head whirled. With a groan, I waved out my hand, catching it on Rick's shirt. I inhaled slowly and tried to clear the fog in my head.

Henry stepped over a crack in the pavement to another small section of relatively flat asphalt. Then he dropped down onto the dirt-covered bottom of the hole.

When Rick tugged my arm, I sucked in a breath. Quickly, I studied our pathway down and then took a small step. My legs trembled as I picked my way to the bottom. It didn't help that Rick's grasp on my arm kept jostling me around. As I took the final step, my knee folded, sending me tumbling to the ground.

With a yelp, Rick released his grip on my arm and thudded to the hard-packed dirt beside me.

For a moment I lay there, too stunned to move. But then Rick was grabbing my arm again and yanking me back to my feet.

I pressed my free hand over my forehead, trying to get grounded. But when I stumbled once more, his grip released and then I was crashing back to the ground again. Dirt kicked up in my face and over my head. On hands and knees, I looked up, squinting against the plume of dust, right as Henry swung his arm and smacked Rick in the jaw with his fist.

I scrambled to get out of their way as they fought, each taking swings and punches. When they crashed to the ground, I cringed and looked away. And then I spotted the glint of metal in the dirt.

Rick's gun.

Casting a quick glance at the guys to make sure they were still occupied, I hurried across the dirt and snatched up the gun. Its cold steel sent a shiver through my veins.

I lifted it and adjusted my grip, getting a feel for its weight.

But that didn't help.

The gun wavered in my hand; I couldn't keep it steady.

But I needed to do something. Henry and Rick were back on their feet again. With Henry recovering from a gunshot wound to his stomach, he wouldn't be able to hold out for long. Not when Rick didn't seem to let up.

So, I aimed the gun at Rick's back and braced myself for the recoil as I squeezed my finger against the trigger.

Only the trigger pull was too stiff.

Gritting my teeth and squinting my eyes, I squeezed harder. The blast stunned me, making me jerk my head back. The recoil was more than I had experienced before.

Rick jerked his head, too, giving Henry the upper hand. With one final punch, Henry had him dropping to the ground.

"Did you just close your eyes?" Henry asked, sounding panicked, as he jerked his head to look down at his arm. His fingers pulled away, looking like they were coated with a gloss of blood.

I scrunched up my face as I shook my head.

He strode across the open space as he said, "You could have killed me. You know that, right?"

"I'm sorry," I croaked. I didn't know what else to say. He needed my help.

"Don't *ever* close your eyes when you're firing a gun!"

I swallowed hard. "I didn't." My breath caught in my throat the way he was stalking toward me. He looked so mad I feared what he would do to me.

Movement behind him caught my eye and then I saw Rick rising to his feet and lifting his arm. I thought it was odd that his arm looked so long and then I realized he was holding Henry's gun.

With a gasp, I raised the gun in my hands and pulled the trigger. If Henry had cursed out loud—I was confident he had—I hadn't heard it. Instead, all I could hear was the ringing in my ears from the gun blast.

Rick looked down as he dropped the gun. With a stagger, he pressed a hand to his chest, covering the darkness that had begun to spread across his shirt. Then he collapsed to his knees on the ground.

When I looked away, I caught Henry's bewildered look as he stared at Rick.

It didn't take Henry long to recover. A matter of seconds, really.

"Give me that," he said, reaching out and grasping my wrist. He pried my fingers off the gun. "Remind me to give you a lesson in target practice."

My eyes felt strained, pressure building up in my forehead. I swallowed hard. "I don't need practice."

"You could have fooled me." He hurried over to Rick and picked up his own gun from the ground.

"It's my hands."

"Uh huh," he replied, eyeing me as he released the magazine of Rick's gun into his palm. His bloody hands shook, and he was breathing kind of heavily. "I had it handled."

Quickly, I looked away, blinking back tears, and tried to push the sight of blood from my mind before my stomach whirled again. Not that I had anything left to throw up. I pressed the back of my hand to my mouth and closed my eyes. I wanted to explain, to say I was sorry, but I had to put every bit of my focus into calming my stomach. The blood was everywhere. On his shirt, his knuckles, trickling down the side of his face.

When Rick groaned over the sound of clinking brass, I dared a glance in his direction as I tried to avoid Henry's gaze and annoyed expression.

The sight of Rick didn't help my stomach any. There was more blood. I looked away again before I could take in every detail.

"How many others are involved?" Henry asked as he took a step toward Rick. His calm voice raised the hairs on my arms and the back of my neck.

I tried not to look at the guy as he gasped for air and pleaded with Henry to help him. His breathing was labored, and his face was contorted in a severe grimace. I knew he would die if we just left him behind, but I also knew Henry wouldn't take the chance that he would be rescued and survive. He wouldn't give the guy a chance to talk to anyone else. Henry wasn't one for leaving loose ends.

"Do I need to repeat myself?" Henry asked, taking another step.

"You got us all." The words came out in stilted huffs.

"I doubt that."

"Look, man. It was mainly Carl and Hector," the guy said, wheezing. "I don't care about the ammo. Go ahead. Take it. But help me first."

"There's someone else," Henry replied, casting a quick glance at me. Turning back to Rick, he asked, "Who is it?"

"Kent."

"Besides him."

The guy shook his head. "There's no one else."

He was lying; I was sure of it. And I doubted Kent was a threat to us. Why else would he try to help me?

"All right then. Who are you working for?"

"No one. I'm working alone."

"You expect me to buy that?"

I thought I saw Rick shrug his shoulder. "Don't believe me then."

When Henry glanced my way, I met his gaze. I couldn't tell him the answer. I couldn't help him come to conclusions because I didn't know the answer myself. Nothing made sense to me. And except for the rare few, everyone was out for themselves.

"It's just me," the guy said, his voice wheezing.

Why would a person lie? There were so many reasons. And when a person needed medical attention, he would do anything to get it. Wouldn't he? He could be withholding the information in an effort to control the situation. But it was also a natural thing to place blame on someone else. People didn't care what happened to anyone else, so why not share the name?

But yet, he was still claiming to have worked alone.

Maybe he was telling the truth.

"How did Hector know we were in Hopewell?" Henry asked.

Rick sucked in a breath. "He was looking for the ammo. Searching every building for the truck. He must have seen you."

"Who was he working for?"

Rick shook his head. "I don't know."

"All right." He set his hand on the butt of his gun.

"No! Don't shoot me. I told you everything you want to know."

"We don't need you then."

"Just take the truck. Get out of here."

"And let you live?"

"Yes!"

"I can't do that."

"I told you I'm not working with anyone else."

"Yeah, but I don't believe that. I think you're working with someone. Someone on the outside. I can't have you contacting them."

"It was Hector. He was working with someone. I just don't know who."

Henry nodded slightly as he pursed his lips. He was probably trying to figure out how he could find out who this person was. But it was becoming clear that Rick didn't know.

I couldn't help but think if we had just kept Hector alive, we would have been able to find out. But maybe it was for the best. Maybe we didn't actually need to know. Maybe it only had to do with the ammunition and nothing else.

"I told you," Rick pleaded. "It was just me. There's no one else."

"You lying sack of…"

I jerked my head toward the voice that boomed from over my head. Kent and Eric were standing on the road at the edge of the hole.

Kent hopped down and then made his way across the broken pavement as he said, "He double-crossed *both* of you."

CHAPTER 49

MY HEAD WAS SPINNING from all the information. First the ammunition project, then the attack. Now we were finding out Hector and Rick had double-crossed Henry. So much was going on and I was thoroughly confused.

"I swear. I'm not," Rick pleaded, trying to scramble backward as Kent stalked him. His arm gave out and he collapsed to the ground.

Kent turned to Henry. "He's afraid the woman he's working for will kill him when she finds out he's a worthless piece of shit."

"Who's the woman?" Henry asked, turning to Rick.

"I don't know what you're talking about." When Kent pressed the toe of his boot to Rick's chest, Rick squealed. "All right, all right. There's this woman in DC. Said she'd pay me top dollar if I could stash the ammo for a while."

"What does she want with it?"

Rick's eyes rolled back as he gasped for air. "She wouldn't say," he said, his voice wheezing. "She just wanted it out of Scott's hands. At least for now."

"She knows who Scott is?"

"Well, yeah, of course."

Henry gave him a questioning look.

"They work together," Rick said.

"Do you know what work she does?"

"She didn't say."

"What's her name?"

"Jillian."

Henry exchanged a quick look with Kent and then Eric. It didn't appear that any of them knew who Jillian was. And of course I had no clue. I was as clueless in the whole situation as I had been about the attack on Detroit three years ago.

The question was, what were we going to do with Rick? Surely, we wouldn't let him live. Henry wouldn't. There was no way, not after being betrayed.

In the distance, I heard the sounds of vehicles.

Kent turned back to Henry. "Go," he said, his voice low. "Before Hector's guys catch wind that you're back."

"What about Rick?" Henry asked.

"I'll take care of him."

Henry gave me a sideways glance and then with a slight nod, he clapped Kent on the arm. "Thank you. I owe you."

"Just get her out of here."

When Henry held out his hand to me, I stepped closer and let him guide me up the chunks of broken pavement. I could hear Eric's boots clomping and scraping the pavement as he followed us.

At the top, I looked back. Rick lay motionless on the ground, his hand still pressed to his chest. A bullet to the chest and no medical care would mean certain death. And *I* had killed him. To save Henry.

"Go," Kent said, waving us away.

Henry set his hand at my lower back and pulled me from the edge.

I made my feet move along as he guided me down the street, but my mind was elsewhere. What did it all mean? About the woman named Jillian. Who was she? And if Rick hadn't been working for her, would we have been attacked that day? Or was that a separate deal? If Carl and Hector had wanted the ammo so they could get the highest dollar, why had it all happened the way it did? What was the goal? Why hadn't they taken the ammo one night when no one else was around? Why did they have to kill Henry to get it? And if they wanted it so badly, why hadn't they just killed him at the apartment?

Nothing made sense.

But maybe that was because people didn't make sense. Their actions, their thought process...

Everything reeked of amateurs. Guys who didn't know what the hell they were doing. Gang leaders who didn't have a clue how to run a district, let alone the whole city. As much as it pained me to say it, it had been a mistake to kill all of the city officials. They deserved death for their decisions, but they had also been able to keep the city afloat.

When we finally came to a stop at a large white box truck, Henry grabbed me by the waist and forced me into the truck. If he hadn't been recovering from his injury, he would have been hoisting me up and throwing me in.

Reaching up and grasping the overhead support, I scrambled up onto the seat and moved over to the middle to let Henry get in behind the wheel. It was painful watching him get in. He had his hand pressed to his stomach.

With a groan, he sank back against the seat.

"Are you okay?" I asked quietly, casting a quick glance through the windshield at Eric who was now sitting behind the wheel of his own truck that was parked in front of us.

Henry nodded, but he didn't look okay. His jaw was clenched and his nose was wrinkled slightly.

"You want me to—"

"Oh, God, no," he said, cutting me off as he pulled a single key from his pocket.

I watched him as he fumbled with the key getting it into the ignition. I didn't want to think that his pride would lead to me living the rest of my life as someone else's slave. If we got caught again, that's what would happen. They'd kill him, just like he had said, and they would take me. Have fun with me first and then who knew. Maybe I'd be sold to the highest bidder. Was that how it worked?

Finally, the truck roared to life, and then seconds later, we were heading south, back toward Hopewell.

I really wanted to ask him if he was okay to drive, but I couldn't figure out a way to bring it up without questioning him and his abilities. I was pretty sure he wasn't fine. Not if his stomach was hurting him. But there was no way he'd let me drive. Not that I wanted to. And no possible way to get him to admit he needed help. If he crashed the truck, wouldn't it also be my fault? If I knew he wasn't fit to drive, but I let him do it anyway, wasn't I to blame?

But then again, it didn't matter. It's not like law enforcement was going to suddenly appear and haul us off to jail for committing a crime. Nothing bad would happen, other than maybe death or being taken by yet another of the gang members. Law enforcement would be better compared to what could happen if we were caught by the gang.

I wondered what Kent was going to do with Rick. Would he just leave him? "He gave me the knife," I found myself saying.

"He, who?" Henry said, quickly glancing my way.

"Kent. The knife. It was his."

He hummed and glanced at me again as he made a left turn onto the intersecting street. It looked like his brows were furrowed.

"Why would he do that?" I asked.

"He's a better man than Hector was."

I sighed. "What's going to happen to him? Will the gang find out he was helping us?"

"I don't know, Kallis."

"Do they even know Hector is dead?"

He sighed, but didn't reply.

"I thought he was on our side. Hector, I mean."

"He was, until he wasn't."

"He let that girl go after a few days."

"No, he didn't."

"How do you—"

"He killed her."

"Oh."

He didn't bother to explain. And it sounded like he was getting tired of my questions. So, I said, "Rick will die, won't he? I killed him?"

He glanced over at me and gave me a sympathetic look. "I have no doubt."

With a small sigh, I turned my head and looked out the passenger window. I watched as we drove past the rest of the buildings on the outskirts of what had once been Detroit's suburbs. Abandoned houses, commercial buildings, factories, all overgrown with weeds and young trees. Nature reclaiming its land.

That made me wonder if a person could truly reclaim what he had once been. The broken concrete, brick, pavement, all things that would take centuries to turn back into dust, would keep the land from its original form. Just like all the terrible things that had happened to me. I'd never be the innocent girl I had been before. I was tarnished. That kind of thing couldn't be polished out.

When Henry grasped my hand, interlacing his fingers with mine, I bowed my head and closed my eyes. But that just made the tears in my eyes slip out.

Sniffling, I wiped at my face. I was expecting him to say something, to make some comment, but he didn't.

I leaned my head back against the seat and stared at the passenger door. It was better that than seeing all of the buildings and the damage.

Every now and then Henry glanced over, looking worried. But I couldn't bring myself to look back. I wasn't okay, and I really didn't want to explain what was going through my head. It felt too heavy, the thoughts.

"We'll stop soon," Henry said.

I said 'okay,' but I wasn't sure if he had heard me; I could barely hear my own voice.

Finally, maybe fifteen minutes later, he stopped the truck.

I looked up and saw Eric slip through an entry door of an old warehouse building. A moment later, a large roll-up garage door opened, revealing a large storage room. He hurried back to his truck, got behind the wheel, and then drove inside the building.

Henry followed, parking the ammo truck between two tall pillars.

As he opened the driver's door, Eric walked over and asked, "Everything okay?"

"So far, so good," Henry replied, easing himself out of the truck and down to the floor with a mild groan.

When I rolled my eyes at Henry's misplaced optimism about his condition, I caught Eric's gaze. He looked mildly amused.

Pulling the black bag from underneath the seat and then reaching for me, Henry added, "How long do you want to stay?"

"Just for the night," Eric said. "We'll leave in the morning. I'd like to travel at night, but the intermittent road damage could cause problems for us."

After I got out of the truck, we headed across the warehouse and stepped inside a spacious lounge with two leather sofas and three stuffed chairs.

"Wait here," Eric said, heading for a door on the other side of the room. "I'll go get us some food."

While Henry eased himself down onto a sofa, I hugged my arms to my chest as I looked around the room. It looked like a waiting area. A pretty nice one, with a coffee maker and a wide selection of tea packets and coffee flavors still displayed on the counter and collecting a thick layer of dust.

"Come here," Henry said. When I looked at him, he had his arm outstretched toward me.

I swallowed hard and stepped closer as I stared at his hand.

"You look tired," he said softly.

Biting my lip, I nodded. I sat down beside him.

He took my hand again, wrapping his fingers around mine. "He deserved to die."

I nodded again. I knew he was trying to make me feel better, but that wasn't really what was bothering me. At least, it hadn't hit me yet. My dad had always talked about that. Killing someone was a hard thing. And sometimes the true meaning of what you had done took a while to sink in and affect you.

"I'd have done it myself."

That made me wonder why he hadn't. Surely, he hadn't forgotten that Rick had taken his gun. Why hadn't he grabbed it and used it?

But then again, he had been a bit occupied. His bloody hands reminded me of that. And almost made me gag just thinking about them. I wanted to pull my hand away, but his grip was firm.

"How did you know we were going to get ambushed?" I asked, trying to keep my mind from focusing on the dried blood.

"The truck on the road."

"But who?"

He held my gaze and it looked like he was trying to figure out what I meant, but before I could clarify, he said, "Kent put it there to warn us."

I looked away. I had questions I wanted to ask him, but then I heard Eric's footsteps outside the lounge.

"The place appears empty," he said, slipping through the doorway. "There are two bedrooms upstairs if you want to go up there."

"We should stay together," Henry said.

Eric shrugged as he set a cardboard box on the coffee table in front of us. Then he sat down on a stuffed chair in the far corner of the room.

I leaned forward and peered inside the box. There were numerous packaged items. Food, I assumed. I wasn't hungry. Not to mention, I didn't think I had the stomach for food. Not yet.

While Henry lifted his boots to rest on the coffee table, I moved away and curled up on the other side of the couch and rested my head against the stuffed arm. I pulled at the hem of my nightgown, smoothing it over the chilled skin of my bent knee.

I needed real clothes again, but I had worn all the clothes Henry had stuffed in the bag. At least I had had the sense to put on underwear. I was so accustomed not to wear any with the nightgowns that I was surprised that it had occurred to me to wear them when I was with Hector. And thankfully he hadn't seemed to notice in the hallway.

Somehow Henry produced a blanket and draped it over me and tucked it in around my feet. I gave him a small smile. His hand lingered on my ankle and then he pulled away and rested his head back against the cushion.

I couldn't sleep. I was tired, but my mind kept racing. What if we got caught again? What if the gang found us and hauled us back to Detroit once again? And we had killed Hector and Rick. And who knew how many other people Henry and Eric had killed while coming back for me.

"I can hear you every time you sigh," Henry whispered.

I turned my head and caught the shine of his eye in the dark. "Sorry," I whispered back.

He repositioned, stretching out his legs beside me.

"So many people are dead."

"I'm just glad it wasn't me."

Why did he have to mention that? He never wanted to let things go. I hadn't meant to shoot him. And with my hands trembling as bad as they had been, he was lucky I had only grazed his arm.

"It's better that way. Better for you."

"I'm sorry." My voice caught in my throat.

He sat up and then bowed his head as he exhaled a heavy breath through his nose. He set his hand on my forearm. His grip was firm, but not too tight. "Look, it's fine. Just…"

I turned my head and lifted my gaze to his. "What was I supposed to do? You needed help."

He grimaced as he squeezed his eyes shut. Slowly, he exhaled. And then he opened his eyes. "Thank you."

I bit my lip. It looked like he was having a hard time curbing his anger and saying the words. I shifted my gaze to his arm as I sat

Jody Calkins

up, trying to get a better look. There was a thin line of blood across the side of his upper arm. My eyes flooded with tears as I looked up at him again. "Henry."

His expression softened as he lifted his hand and brushed my tear away with his knuckle. "It's fine. Just a scratch."

Swallowing hard, I tried to give him a small smile. "I didn't mean to hurt you."

"Come here," he whispered, wrapping his arm around my shoulders.

When he pulled me into his arms, a sob escaped my lips.

"I'm sorry," he whispered, tightening his arms around me. "For scaring you."

I sniffled.

"For yelling at you."

"I could have killed you," I croaked.

"Yeah, well..." He pulled away and hooked a finger under my chin and tilted my head back.

When I blinked up at him, tears slipped down my face.

"I guess I don't die that easily."

CHAPTER 50

THE NEXT MORNING, we set out again.

"We'll be there in a few more hours," Eric said, patting the doorjamb of the box truck as Henry and I got settled into our seats. "Provided we don't get stopped."

"What's the likelihood of that?" Henry asked.

Eric shrugged. "It's slim."

I closed my eyes. I didn't want to think about that. I didn't want to think about going back to Detroit or Franklin. I just wanted to go somewhere and be left alone for a little while.

When Henry set his hand on my thigh, his warmth seeping through the thin fabric of my gown, I opened my eyes and looked up at him.

He held my gaze for a moment and then he leaned his head back against the head rest and stared into his side mirror as Eric closed the garage door of the warehouse.

A few minutes later, Henry put the truck back into drive and followed Eric.

I stared out the passenger window and watched the green landscape fly past us. We had left everything behind. We were far enough away from Detroit that I felt like I could breathe again, really breathe. And I wondered what the future held now. When the ammo was finally delivered, we'd be able to do whatever we wanted. But I had no idea what I'd want. Did it matter? Did I have to decide?

When the truck slowed to a crawl, I jerked awake, blinking my eyes open and peering through the windshield. We were still following Eric, this time along a narrow dirt road.

"It looks like we're stopping soon," Henry said, glancing over at me.

There wasn't anything around. No houses. No business buildings. No parks with swing sets. Just overgrown land and trees everywhere.

About half a mile down the road, a large building finally appeared. It had a huge door, the kind that lifts up out of the way. And inside the building was a small airplane and two ATVs.

Eric drove inside the building and stopped the truck alongside the far wall, leaving Henry enough room to park the box truck beside the plane.

As I reached over to unbuckle my seat belt, a man walked through a doorway into the large room and headed our way. I looked over at Henry to see if he had noticed.

He had. He was staring in that direction. He eased himself out of the truck and then reached for me. I thought he was going to lift me off the seat, but he just gripped my arm and helped me down. Which was a relief. The doctor had said it would be a while before Henry could lift anything heavy.

"Henry," the man said, closing the gap between us. He outstretched his arms and pulled Henry into a tight embrace. Then he clapped him on the back before stepping away. "It's good to see you again."

When the man turned his attention to me, I stepped closer to Henry and hugged the sweater tighter around my chest.

He wrapped his arm around my waist as he said, "This is Donovan."

The man smiled at me and gave a slight bow.

I tried to smile back. I felt naked wearing the nightgown and a sweater.

With a glance at me, Henry said, "This is Kallis."

"I'm so glad you two made it out of Detroit," Donovan said. "I hear it's been a struggle."

"It has," Henry replied. "I can fill you in later."

Donovan nodded slightly. "All right. Let's get you settled. We'll be leaving the truck here and taking the ATVs the rest of the way. There's a woodland community not far from here."

I was about to ask what a woodland community was when Henry said, "This isn't DC."

"We're stopping here first."

"Why?"

"The DC trip will happen later. After you've had a chance to rest up."

Henry sighed as he ran his hand over his head. He didn't seem happy about the change in plans. I had figured we would go straight to DC and then we'd go our separate ways.

"Trust me. You'll want a short break first. It's not so simple getting inside the prison. Plus we need to time it just right with my team."

I wasn't sure if Henry understood what Donovan meant. But it didn't matter to me and I really didn't care. I needed sleep.

Eric powered up one of the ATVs and then we piled into the four seats, with Henry and me in the backseat.

As Eric drove us along a narrow trail into the tree line, I stared out into the forest. It felt eerie being surrounded by all the trees. I honestly couldn't remember the last time I hadn't been surrounded by concrete and brick. Everything had seemed so dirty and open before, but now here we were out in the middle of who knew where with dirt on the ground and tree branches swaying in the breeze above our heads.

Henry looked over at me and gave me a small smile. He looked tired. Maybe a little worried. Probably still in pain without his medications. But there was a sense of peace about him, like a weight had been lifted. Relief that we were no longer in Detroit.

It took about an hour to reach the woodland community Donovan had mentioned. And when we got there, three men were standing at a tall open gate and holding rifles. They looked just like the gang members in Detroit. Rugged. Muscular. Armed.

When I looked at Henry, he turned his head and met my gaze. He searched my eyes for a brief moment before his frown deepened. Gently, he squeezed my hand.

The guards waved us through, and as we drove past them, I held my breath. If this community was just like Detroit, there was no way I was staying. I didn't want a repeat of the last three years.

"Kallis," Henry whispered, leaning closer. When I looked up at him again, he lifted his free hand and pressed his palm to my cheek.

I covered his hand with my own and let out a small sigh. With him, I would be okay. And I knew he would make sure I was in a safe place before we went our separate ways.

A few minutes later, Eric stopped the ATV in front of a two-story house with a porch and a sidewalk.

Henry helped me down and then the guys led us to the door.

"Please make yourselves at home," Eric said, opening the door.

"Is this community safe?" Henry asked, stepping inside the house and pulling me with him.

"We've avoided the Federal Guard thus far. I'd like to keep it that way. And if any other groups come by and can't be trusted, they are dealt with. We can't afford to take risks. That's how we survive out here."

Henry gave a slight nod.

"There is food and bottled water in the kitchen pantry, and soap and clean towels in the upstairs bathroom. Do you require anything else?"

"Electricity?"

Eric nodded. "This place is solar-powered. As are the rest of the homes."

"All right."

"If you need anything, there'll be a guard nearby. Just ask for me."

Donovan stepped forward. "Get some rest. We'll talk in the morning."

When the men left, Henry secured the door and then headed into the kitchen. As I followed him, he looked over his shoulder at me and asked, "Are you hungry?"

I nodded.

He opened the pantry door and reached his hand inside. Light flooded into the small space.

I peered around his arm and spotted one shelf of food. It wasn't much. Just a few packaged meals and protein bars and six jugs of water.

When I turned back toward the kitchen cabinets and started looking for a cooking pot and utensils, he asked, "Which one do you want?"

"Um," was all I could manage. I wasn't used to making choices based on my own preferences. And most of the time, someone else had decided the meals anyway.

He glanced over his shoulder again as he said, "You don't like fish, so I'm guessing salmon is out."

I cocked my head and frowned, but he had already turned away. How did he know that?

"Beef then?" He studied the packaging as he turned around and headed my way. Looking up, he paused and gave me a questioning look. "What's wrong?"

"How do you know..." Before I had a chance to finish my thought, he raised his eyebrows. "That I don't like fish?"

"I'm not an idiot," he replied. "I can tell when you don't like something."

"Oh," I said, looking away.

He stepped closer. "You really don't think I've paid attention this whole time?"

I bit my trembling lip as I shook my head.

He sighed. "I guess I'm better at pretending than I thought. Or you're..." He let his thought trail off.

Slowly, I looked up at him again. He was turning toward the stove and reaching for one of the kitchen drawers. "I'm, what?"

"It's nothing. Forget it."

"I'm naïve?"

"Well, yes," he said with a small sigh. "But I was going to say you're terrible at reading people."

I narrowed my eyes and bit my lip harder.

He lifted his hand, gesturing toward me. "That's why I didn't want to say it."

Blinking back fresh tears, I shook my head.

"I'm trying to be gentle with you."

"Because you don't think I can handle it?"

"Because I don't think the truth needs to be stated every time."

I felt my jaw drop and my eyes widen. That statement was worse than the other reason.

"I'm really good at digging a hole deeper. Which you should already know."

"Why…" With a sigh, I stopped talking and shook my head. What was the point in arguing with him?

"I'm trying, Kallis." He seemed to know what I was going to ask. "I'm trying not to be an ass."

"But if it's the truth…"

"Knowing it," he said. "Is it going to help you?"

I gave him a questioning look.

"Are you going to learn from it? Do anything with this knowledge?"

"I don't know." I didn't really get what he was asking anyway.

"If your answer is *no*, then all I did by speaking this current truth was hurt you." He set the burner on low and then closed the gap between us as he added, "And I don't want to do that."

My throat tightened as I gazed up at him.

He lifted his hand and set it on my upper arm. "I'm done doing that."

I searched his eyes.

"Your intense stare sometimes…" he said, lifting his hand higher and brushing his thumb over my cheek. "It always makes me wonder what you're thinking."

"Why don't you ever ask?"

"I'm afraid of what you'll say." He bowed his head. "I already know what you think of me; I've been an asshole to you."

I couldn't lie to him and tell him I loved him. I didn't think I did. I wasn't even sure I wanted to. If he could love me, then maybe I could. It was odd, because I felt attached. I didn't want to be with anyone else because I was too afraid my life would be worse. With him, at least I knew where I stood. I knew what to expect. Except for recently. His kindness to me made me feel like things could change. In a good way.

"I know you would condemn me if you had the courage to speak the words out loud."

I shook my head as I turned away and headed into the living room.

"You would," he said, following me. "Tell me to go to hell... Fuck off..."

I huffed at his words as I sat down on the couch.

When he sat down beside me, too close, I bit my lip.

He hummed. Lifting his hand again, he brushed his thumb over my lips.

My body trembled from his touch and my breath hitched.

He sighed. "It's okay. You can say them."

Meeting his gaze again, I shook my head. "I don't want to."

He gave me a weak smile. "You are too kind."

My eyes felt strained, a slight tension behind them. "I don't want to say them out loud. I want to forget all of the bad things I've thought of you."

He bowed his head and closed his eyes. "I'll never deserve you, Kallis."

"Stop," I said, cutting off anything more he was about to say. "Please." I lifted my hand and cupped his cheek with my palm. His facial hair had grown past mere stubble. Normally, he shaved every few days, but he was less motivated now to do the extra work. When I leaned in and pressed my lips to his, he breathed deeply and slid his fingers through my hair as he kissed me back.

His hands glided over my back and then settled at my waist as I repositioned myself to straddle his thighs. When his fingertips slipped underneath the hem of my gown, I sucked in a breath.

He lifted my gown up and over my head and then he pulled me against him with a warm hand at my back. He straightened up and then turned to the side and laid me back on the couch. His fingers shook as he glided them over my sides.

When he glanced up at me, I smiled. I felt a warm, fuzzy feeling inside my chest.

"This isn't right," he said, looking away. "I can't do this with you."

"What?" I failed to keep the disappointment from my tone.

"You don't want to do this either. You don't want this because you love me. You want it for the pleasure."

"I thought that's what sex was."

He cursed under his breath as he hauled himself to his feet and ran his hand through his hair. He bent down and picked up my gown from the coffee table and then handed it to me.

Sitting up, I took the gown and hugged it to my chest. "I don't understand what's happening."

"Of course you don't."

I bit my lip as I stared at the floor at his feet. He wasn't making any sense.

"We can't be together. It's not right."

I bowed my head and closed my eyes. I thought we were a couple. I thought that's what we were. He wasn't sleeping with anyone else. And he wouldn't let me sleep with anyone else either, not that I wanted to.

"You deserve better than me."

I shook my head, my eyes still clamped shut. I couldn't believe this was happening. I couldn't believe he was basically dumping me. After forcing me to be his girl, his sex slave, for over a year, he was breaking it off.

"You're attached to this fantasy of love. I can't be what you want."

With tears streaming down my face, I lifted my head and stared at him. There was so much I wanted to say to him, but I didn't have the courage to speak the words.

Instead, I sniffled and wiped the tears from my face as I looked away. I bit my trembling lip and tried to steady my breathing. The one person who could learn to understand me and give me what I needed was backing away. The one person who understood what I had been through without me having to explain it was claiming he wasn't worthy of me.

"You say you don't want to be with anyone else, but that's only because you're scared. It's not because you've fallen in love with me."

I let out a ragged breath as I picked at a hangnail on my thumb. I couldn't see it through the blur of tears, but it was there, helping me, although not very well, to focus on something other than what was racing through my mind.

He wasn't wrong.

I didn't think I loved him.

I felt warmth in my chest when he touched me with tenderness. I was drawn to him. He was desirable. Strong, assertive, and he seemed to know what he wanted.

Was that love?

I wasn't sure.

We had never been apart. For more than a year, we had been together. It seemed natural for us to be together. But was that love? Or was that just two people who shared common ground?

"You're scared to share the horrible details with someone else. What if he views you differently when he learns the truth? What if no one else can love you?"

"Please stop," I croaked, covering my face with my hand.

"I'm sorry, Kallis, but that's not reason enough for us to be together. All the things I've done."

Sniffling, I wiped at my face again. "Fine," I said. "Just go."

With a sigh, he turned away. He ran his hands through his hair as he walked across the room. I could see him pause in the hallway, look back at me for a second or two, and then disappear around the corner.

When I heard the soft click of the front door latching, I hugged my arms tighter to my chest and leaned over on the couch, resting against the armrest. How could I get him to change his mind? How could I get him to see that we needed each other? That we could be good together?

It was stupid for me to keep trying when all he did was reject me in the end. What kind of self-respecting girl kept throwing herself at a guy who wouldn't accept her? It was pathetic. It didn't matter that he claimed to be unworthy of me. Wasn't that just a lame excuse to get out of a relationship? If he wanted out, I should just let him.

But the truth was, I needed him. And as long as he continued to treat me in a loving way, I wanted him. Could he do that? For me? It seemed like such a simple thing.

He didn't come back for dinner, so I ate by myself. And then I went into one of the rooms and crawled into bed. I lay there for a while unable to sleep. I should have been able to sleep; I was exhausted. But my mind wouldn't stop racing for ideas on how I could change his mind about us.

Sometime later, maybe an hour, maybe two, I heard him come back, closing the front door downstairs. I could even hear the click of the latch and the slide of the deadbolt. I kept waiting for him to find me. To tell me he was sorry again, to crawl into bed and let things play out.

But he never did.

Finally, I crawled out of bed and wandered down the hall. I didn't figure he would sleep on the couch; there were plenty of other bedrooms in the house. Even if he was keeping his distance, he wasn't silly enough to forego his own bed.

I found him in the next bedroom; I could hear his steady breathing. It was almost like he hadn't wanted to be that far away. He still wanted to be close.

I crept into the room, trying to gauge if he was awake. When I got halfway across the room, his voice raised the hairs on my arms.

"What are you doing, Kallis?"

I let out a ragged breath. I was afraid he would reject me still, but I said, "I don't want to sleep alone."

He sighed. "Come here."

He lifted the covers, letting me crawl in beside him. He folded his arm around me, tucking me in firmly against his chest. His chest heaved against my back with each breath. "Better?" he whispered against my ear.

I murmured my response and gripped his arm with my hand in case he thought he'd try to move. If I could trap him against me, could I get him to stay?

CHAPTER 51

I SNUGGLED AGAINST HENRY, moaning softly as his warmth permeated my skin. He raised up on an elbow as he rolled me onto my back.

When my eyes fluttered open and I blinked up at him, he cupped my cheek with his palm and searched my eyes. Then he bowed his head and pressed his lips to mine.

I lifted my hand and brushed my thumb over his stubbled cheek as I returned his kisses. His hand moved over my jaw and then his fingers were circling my neck, his thumb gently caressing my tender skin.

He lifted his head and when I opened my eyes again, he was gazing down at me. His thumb grazed my jaw. He leaned down again, giving me one more gentle kiss, and then he whispered, "Go back to sleep, Kallis."

Closing my heavy eyelids, I curled on my side facing him and pressed my forehead into the crook of his neck.

His warm hand slid over my back as I drifted off to sleep again.

When I awoke, the bed was empty. I groaned as I moved my leg, crossing it into cold territory under the covers. Gazing up at the ceiling, I wondered where Henry was. Was he downstairs making me breakfast? I smiled at the thought.

But when I spotted an envelope with my name written on the front propped against the clock and blocking the digital readout of the time, my heart sank.

I looked toward the door, listening for sounds, and then outstretched my arm to pick up the envelope. My heart sank even more when I saw Liana's deck of Tarot cards sitting behind it.

Blowing out a slow breath, I turned back to the envelope and lifted the flap. With shaking hands, I pulled out a folded slip of paper tucked inside.

Quickly, I sat up on the bed and shoved the bed sheet under my arms. Then I unfolded the paper to find a handwritten note. I turned it over and stared at the signature, Henry's signature.

I was too afraid to read his note. So, I crawled out of bed and pulled on my robe. Grabbing the note and the cards, I hurried across the bedroom to the door.

"Henry," I called out.

I listened for sounds. A rustling in the kitchen. His response. The aroma of coffee. Anything.

But the house was quiet.

Hurrying down the stairs, I called out his name again.

Still nothing.

The kitchen was empty. The living room quiet. And all of the bathroom doors stood wide open.

My heart was racing as I looked down at the note again and finally read what it said.

Kallis,

Words cannot express how sorry I am for how I treated you in Detroit. I know you said you've forgiven me, but I honestly don't see how you can.

You need to move on, Kallis. You deserve better.

I made sure you were safe, like I said I would. Now it's time for me to go. It's the only way to make sure you find someone who is worthy enough to be yours. It's better this way.

We need to let each other go, Kallis. Move on. Do what you've always wanted to do. And fall in love with someone who deserves you.

Tears flooded my eyes as I read the note. I had forgiven him. I had told him everything was okay, but that obviously hadn't been enough. He hadn't forgiven himself.

I sank down onto the step of the staircase and bowed my head as tears slipped down my face. I wasn't ready to let him go. I didn't know if I ever would be.

Quickly, I wiped away the tears and then hurried back to the bedroom to get dressed. I had to talk to Eric.

When I stepped out of the house and headed down the narrow walkway to the road, I heard a man call out my name. I stopped abruptly and looked over my shoulder to see Eric standing on the porch. I must have missed him on my way out the door.

My chin quivered as I held up the note. "Where is he?" My voice cracked.

He stepped down the porch steps and shoved his hands in his pockets. "He's gone."

"I can see that."

He nodded. "He's taking the ammunition to DC Prison."

"By himself?"

He nodded again.

I bit my trembling lip for a second as I stared at the door behind him. "And then where?"

"He agreed to help Scott take out the prisoners."

"For how long?"

"I don't know."

"What if..." I let my thought trail off. I couldn't bring myself to speak the words.

"He's not coming back, Kallis."

Slowly, I shook my head. "That's not true."

"I'm sorry."

I let out a ragged breath. It wasn't true. It couldn't be true.

"He wants you to move on without him. Leaving was the only way he could get you to do that."

My chin quivered. He didn't know. I had told him I had forgiven him, but I had never said the words I was supposed to say.

"You'll stay here," Eric said. "For as long as you like or until we find a safe city. Your choice."

My mind raced for a solution. I knew where he was going; I could go after him. He wouldn't force me to leave when I caught up with him. As long as I could find a vehicle and get there before he did. He had only been gone for a couple hours. Three, at the most.

I closed my eyes. He didn't know. But even if I had told him, he wouldn't have believed me. And he seemed to think he knew what was best for me.

"Let him go, Kallis."

I opened my eyes and stared at Eric. I felt helpless as I gave my shoulder a slight shrug. "I can't."

His gaze shifted away as his lips pursed. He looked deep in thought.

I doubted he was trying to come up with a solution. He was probably trying to figure out how to change my mind.

"It's what he wanted."

I shook my head as I swallowed hard. "What about what I want?"

He looked defeated. "I'm sorry."

With a sigh, I looked away. If Henry had left me behind so I could move on, he wasn't coming back and he wouldn't want me following after him. What kind of helpless individual would I be to follow after someone who purposefully left me behind?

If he didn't want me, fine. I would stay and if he wanted me back, he'd come find me. Maybe he would come to his senses after he dropped off the ammunition.

Maybe he would come back.

Finally, I said, "I don't want to stay in this house alone."

"You're welcome to stay with me."

I studied his face for a moment.

"It's a two-bedroom house," he added. "You'd have your own private room and bathroom. We'd share the kitchen and living room."

He seemed genuine about the offer and I hadn't picked up any bad vibes from him since we met.

"Okay," I said.

"Grab your things. I'll wait here."

I lifted Henry's note and the deck of Tarot cards. "This is all I have."

He nodded slightly and then stepped down the porch. We walked in silence to his house, a few blocks away. I kept debating whether or not I should have changed my mind, but I really didn't want to be alone. I had never been on my own. I was used to someone always being there. And he was the only other person I felt comfortable being around. The only other person I had spoken to.

When we reached his house, he opened the door and held it for me. I glanced his way and then bowed my head as I stepped inside.

He gave me a tour of the house, telling me to help myself to the food in the kitchen and then showing me the extra bedroom. The bed was neatly made with a pale pink comforter with a floral design. He walked in and opened a set of bifold closet doors, revealing a packed closet of old clothing and coats.

"I'll clear out the closet later today. I have a meeting in an hour."

"It's okay. I don't have any of my own clothes."

"There's a town not far from here," he said. "I'll take you there in the morning. You should be able to find clothes there."

"Thank you."

***

Over the next few months, I tried to adjust to life without Henry. For over a year, we had been together. I should have wanted him gone. I should have wanted to move on with my life. But I couldn't seem to refill the hole he had left behind.

And I didn't think I would rest until he was back. If he ever came back.

I wasn't ready to let anyone else in. I kept to myself. Being around others felt awkward and uncomfortable.

Eric protected me, made sure I ate my meals. Made sure I didn't slip away, even when I wanted to. He brought home books for me to read and one day he came back with a sack of flour and asked if I would make my bread rolls.

He made sure to include me in his life. I thought it was only a matter of time before he made a move, tried to kiss me, but he seemed to respect my boundaries.

There had been one awkward moment weeks ago. He had come to my door to ask me a question right as I was walking out. Not expecting him to be blocking my doorway, I plowed right into him. His hands instantly grasped my arms, and I froze. I craned my head back to look up at him, meeting his gaze. When his gaze drifted, I thought he was going to bow his head and kiss me—it looked like he wanted to—but he recovered before I did and apologized. I had been more careful since, making sure to check where I was going before plowing out into the hallway.

Henry had told me to move on. But I couldn't. I didn't know if I ever could. And I felt like letting Eric into my life in an intimate way would be a betrayal.

I shouldn't have wanted Henry.

I should have been able to move on with my life and start seeing someone else, but for some dark, twisted reason, I missed him.

I wanted him to come back.

Maybe I had gotten used to my life with him. Maybe I couldn't imagine what life was supposed to be like without him. Maybe it was because he already knew my dark secrets and in order to let anyone else into my life, I would have to share those details. To live a truthful and honest life with someone, I would have had to share things I would rather have kept hidden.

I didn't need anyone else to know.

Henry had made sure to eliminate the guys who knew. He and Kent were the only ones left.

But to share those details with yet another person...

I wasn't ready for that. I didn't think I'd ever be.

As I was making a third batch of dinner rolls, I heard the sounds of heavy footsteps outside. I looked up just as the front door swung open, banging against the wall, and Eric hurried inside.

"Kallis," he called.

Before I could reply, he spotted me in the kitchen. Frowning, I met his gaze. His eyes were red and his face was flushed.

"Henry said you were a hacker in Detroit," he said, out of breath. "Is that true?"

I nodded. "Years ago, but—"

"I need your help."

ABOUT THE AUTHOR

Jody Calkins grew up in the Minnesotan woods and now lives in rural Virginia with her family. She has a degree in classical studies and literature, loves studying languages, and writes young adult speculative fiction.

She is the author of the edgy and heart-wrenching young adult dystopian thriller series The Hexon Code, including *Shattered*, *Redeemed*, and *Blackout*.

If you would like to follow her for book news and updates on the writing life, you may do so here:

jodycalkins.com